CODE NAME: ZEUS

To: Vince
Gary Andersen.
11/30/15

A Geo-political Saga

CODE NAME: ZEUS

BY

GARY ANDERSEN

Jack Barnett, Sr. 1932

Library of Congress Control Number:		2015917142
ISBN:	Hardcover	978-1-5144-1739-3
	Softcover	978-1-5144-1738-6
	eBook	978-1-5144-1737-9

Print information available on the last page.

Rev. date: 10/26/2015

To order additional copies of this book, contact:
Xlibris
1-888-795-4274
www.Xlibris.com
Orders@Xlibris.com
724739

TABLE OF CONTENTS

JACK, JR. AND DANE

THE TECHIES

GETTING READY

GOSECURE

DEDICATION

This book is dedicated to our nuclear and expanded family; especially to my wife's and my parents and grandparents who worked so hard to prepare us for our lives. It is also dedicated to our immigrant ancestors and those who have native North American lineage who created our personal American history over the past five centuries.

ACKNOWLEDGEMENTS

Anyone who attempts to write his first novel in his late 70s needs a lot of help. I have been fortunate to have people from 4 states read various versions of my manuscript. These people have been friends for from 17 to over 50 years. My thanks to: Bob I., Mary Ann K., Fred H., Roxanna S., and Roger and Milli H. I must give special thanks to Fred who gave me his Texas A&M and attorney's perspectives and Bob who read and edited three different versions. Bob, another techie like me, also contributed to several changes and provided some key content. In addition, Joan N. made important inputs how to organize the story. I also want to thank my sister Sandy and cousin Dwight who searched for the photographs used on the covers.

"Freedom is obedience to self-formulated rules"

—Aristotle

THE MEETING

CHAPTER 1

THE DEATH OF JACK BARNETT, JR.

2007

Chip Faraday drove furiously on back roads for seven hours in an inconspicuous old car, one of several he stored in various cities for this type of situation. He left the Dallas Oilmen's Convention midday through a basement exit and slipped out to a nearby parking lot. He drove rather than use one of the company's planes knowing both the US government and the UNMS (United Nations Monitoring Services) tried to watch every move he made. His years in high technology provided him with the knowledge to detect and avoid most tracking systems. He had been playing a cat and mouse game with governmental agencies for years and did not want to let down his guard one iota.

During the lonely drive his mind reviewed the past 30 years, but it snapped back to the present as he entered the main gate to Jack Barnett, Jr.'s sprawling ranch and oil fields. Len Girard, a longtime friend of Jack's who ran his ranching operations, ushered him through the front door of the old ranch house. The house still seemed to go on forever even after hundreds of visits since he moved to Kursk, TX 30 years earlier. They walked down the long hallway lined with the trophies from decades of hunting throughout the southwest interspersed with expensive artwork. Finally, at the third doorway they took a right down a short hallway to Jack's sickroom.

Jack could be a lovable guy, if you agreed with him, but if not he could be downright mean and cruel. He spent little time with anyone he thought a fool and felt the world rampant with fools. Jack constantly complained how the 'Commiecrats', as he called anyone to the left, totally screwed up the country's education system, the business environment and the average American's drive to succeed. Today Chip faced a failing Jack Barnett, Jr.

His illness began a year earlier. Nobody, except for possibly Doc Benson, knew for sure what happened. Once evident there was something serious wrong with him, a number of specialists were flown in under a cloak of secrecy to the airstrip in the middle of his extensive landholdings. Soon they realized nothing could be done for this once vigorous man. The world did not need to know of Jack Barnett's decline and his impending death. Neither friends nor foes—and he had plenty of both.

"Chip, glad you could make it before the wake," Jack murmured trying to make the best of the dire situation. "You know I'm dying, so none of the sentimental shit."

Chip tried to speak, but Jack wouldn't let him.

"Chip, my boy, you are the closest I have to a son. You won't forget the challenge facing the American way of life and even worldwide civilization. Hell, I don't need to tell you. You are one of a few people who have been as dedicated to the program as I have and I have chosen you to carry the load. I just want you to know I have complete faith in you. Just sorry I have to leave you so soon. You have a big job ahead of you."

With that Jack Barnett drew his last breath and the total weight of 'Project NewLand', Code name: Zeus, fell on Chip Faraday's shoulders and the shoulders of a close network of people.

CHAPTER 2

CHIP MEETS JACK BARNETT, JR.

1987

Chip Faraday ran for his flight to Hong Kong at Narita Airport in Tokyo when he heard a booming voice with a west Texas drawl, "Mr. Charles Faraday, Jr.?"

He came to an abrupt stop and said, "It is Chip."

"I know, I know," said the tall and tanned hickory-stick of a man, probably in his early 50s, who obviously spent most his life outdoors. Chip, on the other hand was 41 and also in good shape from years of running and survival training, but not as tanned.

Immediately Chip thought, "I know who this guy is," but could not come up with a name.

"Jack Barnett. Actually it's Jack Barnett, Jr. so I fully understand your hang up with the junior crap. It always pissed me off too, but I needed to get your attention."

"I'm sorry Mr. Barnett. I have a plane to catch."

"I know that too, but I must meet with you when you get back to the Bay Area. It is extremely important to you, me and the few others who understand. Here's my card. I will call you a week from Tuesday," he barked.

"Do you need my card?" Chip asked almost sheepishly.

"Naw, I know where you live, where you work, what you do, where you hang out and have a pretty good idea of what you think," he responded as he disappeared around the corner towards Customs.

"Strange, how did he know I would be returning to the Bay Area next week?" Chip thought as he hurried towards his gate.

Charles Faraday, Jr. or Chip was well known in the high technology industry for his management skills and hard work. He was always in demand by one growing company or another, spending nearly twenty years as a near outcast in the industry. Not the most brilliant guy on the street, but his uncanny ability to see trends, particularly long-term trends, made him very marketable.

Chip never met a challenge he didn't relish. A factor he often thought to be the primary root of his father's unhappiness. His father, a high school math and science teacher, never got the challenge his Type A personality needed. He felt trapped by the circumstances of getting out of the army broke at the end of WWII with a wife, then a newborn son within a year. The GI bill provided Charles Faraday, Sr. with an education to support his family, but not the challenge he needed. Too late he realized he should have applied himself to other endeavors. As a result he drank too much and died early, leaving his mother and 16 year-old Chip alone. By then, the die had been cast.

The brief encounter with Barnett spooked Chip. Still a fairly young man, he should have been more optimistic about the future, but this gnawing sense the country and the world were not heading in the right direction was always present. It already cost him two jobs and he was on the verge of quitting his current position. To his managers, he was a right-wing renegade with crazy ideas. They could never understand his penchant for taking his family out to the desert or up into the mountains and roughing it for extended periods of time. They thought he must be some kind of survivalist nut. But his ability to verbalize the trends in the market and his persuasive communications skills made him valuable to those who could put up with him. His current boss and board of directors were making life miserable. But he still resisted as they kept trying to force the company into one bad deal after another.

CHAPTER 3

SHENZHEN, CHINA

Chip barely made it to his plane to Hong Kong, where he would spend the weekend and a couple days of business before traveling to Shenzhen, China the next Friday. He traveled to Hong Kong a number of times before. As CEO, he ran the venture capital backed company where he worked. When he travelled, he often assisted his sales crew on major business opportunities. The company's Chairman, Ryan Smith, was the figurehead who represented the lead venture firm, Pacific Primary Capital, which specialized in early stage high-tech startups. After several great successes, they hit a string of 'dry holes', i.e. failures. As a result the venture capital firm became overly involved in day-to-day operations, usually in areas in with no expertise. Ryan Smith, at the board's behest, constantly pushed Chip to do a joint venture with a foreign firm, while Chip disagreed.

Just the previous November, he had a bad experience with a division of a French firm with headquarters in Nice, France. The two companies negotiated back-and-forth for over six months, it was time to 'fish or cut bait'. Chip and the French company's CEO, an arrogant Ph.D. in physics, were having dinner at a restaurant in a 14th Century chalet overlooking the beautiful Mediterranean shoreline. But it was a dark and rainy night, with the mood of the two of them very negative.

Finally, frustrated at not getting his way, the Frenchman said in a condescending voice, “Mr. Faraday, I don’t know how you can be a CEO. You don’t even have a Ph.D.”

Chip responded, “The hell I don’t. I have three Ph.D. s and if I need another one, I’ll hire another one.” That did it. The negotiations broke down so badly Chip thought he would have to walk down the steep hill through the rain to his hotel. The mood during the short ride down the winding streets was colder than the winter breeze off the Mediterranean. The two strong headed men never spoke to each other again.

While in Hong Kong he completed four days of business meetings with major suppliers and customers, and then waited for his quality control manager to fly in from San Francisco. On Friday morning they were on the train to Shenzhen City in the Guangdong Province of southern China to discuss a possible joint venture. Chip, not in a good mood, felt pushed into a potentially disastrous arrangement by his company’s board of directors.

Even though more and more American companies were making agreements with Chinese manufacturing firms, Chip did not believe his company was ready for such a deal. He also believed the company’s technology was not developed enough to transfer manufacturing to a facility where no one in management spoke decent English.

“If we have to have an Asian partner, why not in Hong Kong where English is commonly used or in Taiwan where the business climate is not so hostile?” he pleaded over and over, but the Chairman and the venture firm persisted.

As the train approached the Chinese border, visions of the time he took the train from Seoul, South Korea to the North Korean border came to mind, but it turned out not as imposing. He did not see anything like the barren DMZ with the tanks and big guns visible from across a no man’s land. He vividly remembered visiting his customer’s shiny four story glass building overlooking the DMZ, not more than 600 yards to the north.

He thought, "What do these stupid bastards on the other side think when they look at this edifice? This building would be right at home in Silicon Valley."

The visit to Shenzhen turned bad as soon as they got off the train on the hot steamy day and were met by a cadre of Chinese worker bees in an old English-made van filled with strong body odor. Several times Howie, his quality control guy, looked like he would vomit. In broken English, the lead guy kept talking about what Chip's company's offer to the Chinese firm would be, such as free access to his company's technology and special pricing they could use to compete against his company all over the world. The drone made his pitch over and over, as if he believed if he repeated it enough times, the frustrated Americans would be sold on doing a deal with his company.

Things went from bad to worse by time they reached the 'Commune', as Howie later named it. As they approached the walled compound, its gates magically opened and quickly closed behind them after they entered. It appeared the workers and their families were virtual prisoners of the compound. Chip could only describe it as grim.

As they walked through the hallway towards the office area, Howie ran up to Chip in a panic, "Chip, Chip, this is the first time I have been in a factory with mushrooms growing on the walls! What a dump this place is."

They made a tour of the manufacturing facilities with Chip making a mental note of the equipment being at least two generations behind the state-of-art of the day. They were led to the general manager's office, where they were met by a Chairman Mao look alike, with a round face, yellow teeth and combed back greasy hair. He sat there with a vacuous smile on his face while his henchmen continued their pitch. He periodically waved his arms and ranted in Mandarin. They all kowtowed to this guy.

Chip sat silently, unable to speak due to his frustration. "How the hell are we supposed to work with this pathetic mess," he thought. Finally, he made a feeble attempt to communicate, while all along being convinced he could not work with this abortion of a company. It was just too early and was a complete mismatch.

During the dour ride back to the train station the Chinese mouthpiece kept up with his pathetic pitch. Finally he asked Chip, "How much money is your company going to give us to work with you?"

Chip blew up, "What the hell are you talking about? You are a government controlled firm. You get your money from your government. Don't you realize in America we give money to the government by making a profit which is taxed? There is no way in hell I would give you bastards a single cent."

The remainder of the ride back to the train station turned unbearable. Their hosts were so angry Chip wondered if they would throw him in jail. A couple of the Chinese guys spat on the floor to show their anger and disdain. They quickly got out of the van and on the train and did not relax until they crossed the border into the New Territories north of Kowloon and Hong Kong. Chip knew right then he needed a new job and on the plane ride home wrote his resignation letter.

They landed in San Francisco on Saturday totally exhausted. Howie didn't know what to think and was afraid he would lose his job. Chip, on the other hand, feared he would keep his. Calls were waiting for him when he got home, but he purposely ignored them until he went into his office on Monday morning.

When he arrived at his office, Ryan Smith and the entire board of directors were waiting for him. He could see them seethe as he walked into the conference room. Before they could say anything, he laid several copies of his resignation letter on the table and said, "There is no way in hell I could deal with those 'collective assholes', pun intended, plus there is no way I can any longer work for you assholes collectively!" Chip smiled at the look of shock on the faces of Ryan and the other board members. He immediately walked out the door of the conference room, and then out of the building, never looking back.

Chip did not know what transpired after he left and did not care. He went to the first pay phone he could find and called his wife. This was not the first time Chip quit a job in a huff, so Sue Faraday was not surprised. It was evident for the past six months this job would not last. She still had a good job and they always seemed to land on their feet. Sue continued her complete faith in her husband and so did he.

By this time, the angry Chip forgot the encounter with Jack Barnett in Tokyo just over a week earlier. He called his life-long hometown friend Rick Christiansen to give him the news he had quit his job, not realizing the call automatically re-directed to another location. They spoke for at least an hour discussing different options for Chip to consider. Rick asked, "Do you want to come back to the Midwest?"

"No, I want to stay here or move to someplace like Dallas or Austin. Things are in a lull down there with the oil and real estate busts, but my research tells me it is all temporary. Someone there may give me something new to do," he laughed, not knowing what the future would bring. Little did he know of Rick's involvement with the Barnett people in Texas for the past couple of years or that their old physics Professor Dr. Dane Madsen also joined Jack Barnett and his father in Texas over a dozen years earlier.

The next day he sat at home relaxing, playing with his kids and researching possible job opportunities. It finally occurred to him the word of his resignation would ripple through the Bay Area. It was time to move on, but where would he and his family go?

CHAPTER 4

SAN FRANCISCO MEETING

On a cool summer morning, with the overnight fog beginning to fade away, Chip headed for his meeting with Jack Barnett. Jack picked a small coffee shop just down California Street from the Bank of America building. It seemed odd a man of Jack's wealth and stature would pick such a non-descript location for what appeared to be a meeting which would dramatically change Chip Faraday's life, and what would be the beginning of a long working relationship, as well as an enduring friendship.

He received a call on his private home phone early the previous morning. This surprised Chip. Few people knew the number, but he would soon learn Jack Barnett knew virtually everything about him.

As he walked into the small coffee shop, he saw Jack Barnett sitting in the back corner. "Mr. Faraday, do y'all know who I am?" Jack began, speaking softly so not to draw attention to their meeting.

"Please, sir, it is Chip," he responded somewhat irritated.

Jack's steely eyes locked onto Chip's, "Yes and I am Jack. If you join our effort, we are going to spend considerable time together and we are not always going to agree. Also, we are always going to be informal, unless we are in a meeting where formality is necessary. Understand?"

"Yes, but...," he protested.

"Never pull the 'yes, but' BS on me," Jack said, "What do you know about me?"

"When we met in Tokyo, I knew very little about you, but I have done some research."

"I figured so. Tell me what you learned about me. Then I'll tell you why I am interested in you." Jack offered.

Chip explained to Jack what he learned spending most of the day before reviewing stories in newspapers and magazines on microfiche at the San Jose main library. Before their meeting at Narita he read a number of stories about the reclusive Barnetts, legends in the oil and ranching industries of west Texas. His father, Jack Barnett, Sr., learned the oil business as a young man after arriving in the United States with nothing, leaving his poor beginnings behind in Ireland. Jack Barnett, Sr. never again had any contact with anybody from his family, childhood friends or with anyone from Ireland. Not even his immediate family, his wife and son, knew what or who he left behind. Rumors provided an extensive amount of folklore about Jack Barnett, Sr., but he never admitted nor denied anything said about him. Was he an orphan or a criminal? These questions only added to the mystery surrounding him. The only thing that seemed certain was he probably did not leave a wife and children behind, still being a teenager when he arrived in the Port of Houston in 1918. Even how he gained the cost of passage remained a mystery. Jack became a U.S. citizen as soon as humanly possible.

Over the years he amassed legendary wealth, but no one really knew how much or exactly how he earned it. "He is probably worth more than even those who know him realize," Chip mused.

Chip learned Jack Barnett, Sr. had been befriended by an early oilman by the name of Robert (Роберт in Russian) Barzinsky, known as "Bobwire" (barbed wire for non-Texans), by those who didn't like him, due to his abrasive character and ability to make sharp deals. Most people hated Robert and for good reason, he was not nice to most people. But if you were his friend he would help you any way he could. Nobody knew his personal history either. This may have been the secret element that drew the two extreme misfits together.

Chip learned Barzinsky escaped tsarist Russia late in the 19th Century and had horrendous scars on his back and arms, resulting from brutal torture. Were these from his father or some other sinister source? No one knew.

Chip learned over a period of several years Robert crossed Europe, begging, working and stealing his way, finally catching on as an interpreter on a ship going to the Port of New Orleans, arriving late in 1900 at age 20. Robert had little prior knowledge of the southern part of the United States when he arrived, but that did not hinder this resourceful man. The important thing was to get to the United States. Then he would figure out how to survive.

Chip expanded his research beyond the more commonly known aspects of Barzinsky's and Barnett's business history. They were reclusive and considered anti-social individualists and extremely rich. They hated bureaucracy, in general, and federal government bureaucracy, in particular. Chip told Jack he learned many considered the Barnetts revolutionaries. This brought a hearty laugh from Jack.

Jack realized he had not made a mistake in approaching Chip Faraday for the most important role in what he believed to be critical for long term future of mankind. He thought, "This guy probably has a pretty good idea of where I want to take him and how I need him to help me."

"Chip, everything, and I mean everything, I say to you must not be repeated to anyone except for a few aspects you can discuss with your wife. If you are interested enough to join me, you will be able to tell your wife much more. I must have your word, do I?' Jack started.

"You do and my word is good," Chip replied.

Jack leaned forward in his chair and said, "By time we finish this meeting you will either feel compelled to join us in our efforts or you are going to walk out of here and never want to see me again."

"I head up an effort I call Zeus as a code name for the actual project. In a nutshell, if people knew the charter of our project, most would think we are lost in the twilight zone. Government agencies from local to national to international, especially the United Nations, would do anything they could to incarcerate us. Worse yet they would probably go out of their way to kill anyone involved in our effort." Jack continued.

"We believe civilization as we know it today is on its way to extinction or will be strongly curtailed at some time in the future. No, we are not a religious group going up the mountain to wait for our savior. Instead we are building our own community in preparation for the time when many of the great things man has created will be used to destroy most of humanity as we know it today. Not a pretty picture. Over 50 years ago my father and Robert Barzinsky decided they would create an environment in a remote part of the United States which would be their new base of operations. It would be what some would call 'an earth based spaceship'. A safe environment in which a small number of people would be able to survive for a number of months, years and maybe even decades, until it became safe to venture out into the rest of the world and expand the community.

They did not expect and even today I do not expect life to be totally eliminated like it has several times over the course of earth's 4 plus billion years. They believed, and we continue to believe, it is possible for a small group of people to survive using the advancements made by man, regardless of what happens to the rest of humanity. There may be groups of people around the world who will survive the initial and ongoing catastrophes, but chances are these disparate groups will be separated from us for months or years, if not for decades. We also believe most of these groups will not survive for long without extensive preparation similar to ours.

The problem is how to survive over the period of time required, especially since we do not know what type of disaster or disasters will cause the collapse of civilization as we know it today. This is the eventuality for which we have been preparing all these years. I would like to invite you to join us to be the one to continue the effort after I am gone. I am offering you a unique leadership position.

Robert and my dad are now dead, as well as many of those involved with the operation in the early days. I continue, with the help of my mother Catherine, to lead the effort along with a core group of less than

40 people who have a broad range of education and experience. When disaster strikes, we will have to make some hard choices whether or not we can ask others to join us. Preparations were begun back in the 1930s and we will continue to adapt as technology and political conditions change. We face an increasingly difficult world with more complex technologies continually being developed and we need management help. You have a strong background in management and knowledge of a broad range of technologies. I want you to be the CEO of the entire Zeus operation. Once you are part of Zeus, you will receive a full review of what has been done, as well as what is currently in progress and the plans for the future," Jack stopped and peered into his cup as if as if reading notes from his coffee.

He went on, "You may ask why we haven't given up the effort since nothing like this has happened over the past 50 plus years. You must understand the depth of commitment by our group. You may also wonder about the resources required for this effort. Robert Barzinsky and my father amassed an immense amount of wealth in their successful energy, real estate and ranching businesses and our wealth continues to grow at a steady pace.

In addition, Robert, being a 'gold bug', bought and stored gold from the time he started accumulating wealth during his early days on the streets of New Orleans and in the oil fields of south Texas back around the turn of the century. His harsh childhood in Russia, plus several years of crossing Russia and Western Europe alone left him with the Old World belief of gold being the only real currency. Many thousands of pounds of gold have been purchased over the years, much of it for less than $35 per ounce. As you probably know, gold is around $450 per ounce today. We have never tapped our gold inventory since Robert Barzinsky bought into Wilson Oil back in 1921. At that time he used some of the inventory for collateral to buy 51% of the company, which is now GLO Industries. Today we are still accumulating gold. Just be assured we have considerable resources. We do believe at some point we may need to tap into these resources. This gold will prove invaluable in dealing with any pockets of civilization we may encounter in future generations. Gold will be the basis of our currency at some time in the future."

Jack amazed Chip. He heard rumors about the reclusive and conservative Barnetts. Chip had similar views about the future of civilization. For many years he and his friend Rick Christiansen shared their negative views of the world. Chip had been somewhat at a loss after moving from Minneapolis to the Bay Area a few years earlier. He missed his weekly bull sessions with Rick. They made a pact to never use any form of communications, other than face-to-face meetings, to discuss their views. They were paranoid of showing up on the radar of some organization, especially those of the U.S. government, the United Nations or Non-governmental organizations (NGOs).

Jack continued, "You probably wonder how we know so much about you. In time you will find out. But just the fact we know so much should be a red flag. So do international organizations more sinister than the CIA, FBI, NSA, the Justice Department and the United Nations. Someone will know every step we make unless we are careful. It is imperative we use a completely secure communication system which has been devised for us. At the onset we must have you find a way to 'disappear' for about a week to be oriented into our program. We know you quit your job on Monday, so this should not be a problem. You should find the opportunity we are offering you very interesting. Any questions? Any comments?" Jack asked.

Chip leaned back in his chair, stared at the ceiling and thought, "What the hell am I getting myself into? Do I really want to change my life this completely?"

"Jack, I have a number of questions, but most of them would probably pry into the organization more than you are prepared to reveal at this time, but let me ask some basic logistical questions. First, does this mean I rip up my family and move to some remote location which I have learned is somewhere near Nowheresville, Texas? Do we disappear from society as we know it? What does this mean for my wife and kids?"

"You would not have to move right now, but soon you will have to join us in Texas. I can see you spending at least 3-to-6 months in the

Bay Area, maybe more, doing preparatory work, but then you will need to move. Your role at first will be our interface to the world of high tech commerce by working with some bright people back in Texas, one in particular. I have no children, in time you will be my replacement to run not only Zeus, but also GLO Industries, assuming it survives. If there is a major disruption in civilization, there will probably be little market for petroleum products and GLO Industries.

I know your wife has a Ph.D. in nuclear physics. Although we have built our own hidden oil refinery, we believe someday our project may decide to create a small nuclear power source. Maybe this is a pipe dream, but it is one of our objectives. Your wife could possibly play a major role in such a project when it is needed."

"Next question, what can I tell my wife about the education system for my kids before I have to make my decision? I worry about my son and daughters. They are still young and quite adaptable, but this would be a tectonic shift for my family. My concern for them is they get a good education," Chip added.

"You may not believe this, but one of our basic goals has been to develop and maintain a state-of-art library and data base, as well as educational system. My mother taught school for years and she spearheads our educational efforts. Dad died a year ago leaving her heartbroken and as a result she has thrown herself totally into this project. Both the library and an extensive data base are crucial in case most of civilization is destroyed. We have a small staff of people who are working with my mother on this project. While she has a college education, Robert and my dad were self-educated. I have a petroleum engineering degree from the University of Texas. You will not believe how well read these two men were. Today our town library exceeds many larger libraries in the areas of science and technology and we are committed to go well beyond where we are today. We are in the process of digitizing the entire library, hoping new storage technologies will take us far beyond microfiche and magnetic tape in the years ahead. I think you will be amazed at what has been done to date."

This last comment made Chip think of the comments his former professor Dr. Dane Madsen said about visiting NASA Goddard in Greenbelt, MD back in the early 1960s. Dr. Madsen said he saw hallways lined with cabinets filled with magnetic tape reels of data NASA saved to be digitally compacted sometime in the future using new technologies as they evolved.

Before Jack could ask Chip's interest in the proposition and they discussed compensation, the impulsive Chip said, "I am your man. I need to know how much I can tell my wife. You may not believe this but she is pretty much of the same mind as I am. My family often goes into the mountains or out in the desert to practice our survival skills. We also believe civilization as we know it is in serious jeopardy."

Jack spent the next hour discussing what Chip could say to his wife and talking about his future responsibilities. Then he told Jack his compensation would be considerably more than he previously made. It appeared Robert and Jack set out many years earlier on a program much in line with Chip's philosophy, including his concerns for the future of humanity. Jack then told Chip they chose the name Project NewLand.

The meeting lasted over three hours. Jack gave Chip the algorithmic keys to the sophisticated crypto system they would use to communicate with each other. Chip wondered where they got this. It looked somewhat similar to work Chip and Rick did years earlier, but much more sophisticated.

When the meeting ended, Jack immediately got up and disappeared out the door, barely saying goodbye to Chip, but leaving him with an understanding of Zeus or Project NewLand and his future role. The opportunity both frightened and excited him.

He quickly hoofed it over to the rail station and headed for the south Bay. He took the train and got off at the Mountain View station where he left his car, then drove to his house in Santa Clara. He felt lucky he ran into no one he knew on the train, but was prepared with a story about having to visit a law firm in The City since he just quit his job. Yesterday he had no job. Today he committed himself and his family to a new life with no real understanding of what lay before him.

ROBERT BARZINSKY

CHAPTER 5

RUSSIA TO AMERICA

Russia 1897

Robert Barzinksy's father was a peasant on one of the estates controlled by minor royalty. Vlad Barzinsky drank regularly and often disappeared for extended periods of time, which put him at odds with the estate owners. Vlad got into trouble numerous times and was determined to find a better life. He eventually left his family and joined one of the Socialist groups that protested in the major cities of Russia. He had heard of Vladimir Lenin, born as Vladimir I. Ul'yanov, the major political force of the Russian Revolution, and soon became a follower of the his philosophy.

Robert, his oldest son, did not know what to do. He had a much different view of the world. While his father worked the fields of the estate, Robert worked inside the spacious estate house as a servant. His mother, bound and determined her children would be able to break from their horrible existence, started teaching him how to read at age three. This angered his father who never learned how to read and write. He often berated Robert's mother, sometimes beating her, due to her insistence Robert and his siblings be educated. She then knew teaching needed to be done during their father's absences.

Being bright and observant, Robert always made notes of what he saw in the big house. He told no one of his activity, not even his beloved mother. He knew if his efforts were discovered he would be severely punished and banished to work in the fields or worse. Robert also had a good ear for languages. Not only did he understand the dialects of the many Russian visitors, he learned the words and sentence structure of the languages of visitors from outside Russia. In 1897 he left his home forever.

As they got to know each other during the late 1920s, Robert Barzinsky and Jack Barnett seldom talked about their pasts, both with bitter memories of life in their homelands. Robert first verbalized a small bit of his sad life before America. He opened up to Jack more than to any other person until many years later, but mostly with superficial information about childhood friends and siblings. He only mentioned his mother once, who he said lived a sad life with his alcoholic father. He spoke nothing but disdain for his father whenever he mentioned their relationship. All but the aristocracy and a few chosen elites had difficult lives in Tsarist Russia. While Robert's father's politics leaned far to the left, the son's leaned far to the right.

A steady flow of minor royalty and elites visited the estate. They came mainly from France, but also Germans, Italians, Englishmen and other Russian aristocracy, often visiting the estate for long periods of time. They supposedly discussed various business opportunities, but in reality these people seldom worked. Robert would often hide in the hallways off the dining room and den of the mansion so he could listen to their conversations. The different languages spoken fascinated him and he learned to understand them.

As he did his work as a servant for his master, he often found books in other languages in the rooms occupied by visitors. One day he found a book about America written in English in the room occupied by a visitor from England. He struggled to learn the words and by the time the visitor left, he could read most of the book. Robert slowly learned of this amazing place called America where people freely pursued their dreams.

One day he mentioned what he read to his father, who told him to stop reading those lies. He said he knew this from his reading the works of people like Lenin and Marx. Robert knew his father could not read. He only listened to their philosophies. This created an even larger chasm between Robert and his father.

When he was sixteen a strange new visitor arrived: An American. Robert did all he could do to have contact with this unusual individual who seemed to have a sense of well-being and inner happiness he never saw before. He dressed much more casually and appeared more personable than other visitors to the estate. He seemed so out of place. He had come to Russia to discuss a possible business venture for the shoe manufacturing company his immigrant parents started years earlier in New York City.

The man noticed the inquisitive boy early in his visit. He found Robert to be a bright, eager young man who apparently understood some English. One day while servicing the man's room Robert gained the nerve to say, "Hello, my name is Robert," in distinctive Russian accented English.

Surprised at the young man's forwardness, Douglas Baylor responded in broken Russian, "Do you know English?"

"Only a few words," Robert responded.

"Do you want to learn more?"

"Yes, yes," came the response, "But I must be careful."

Mr. Baylor instinctively knew what Robert meant. The Russian aristocracy did not appreciate anyone, especially an American, talking to the servants. Being a typical brash American, Douglas Baylor knew he must see if he could help this eager young man.

Every day 'accidental' meetings occurred and Robert came with a list of words. Each using his limited knowledge of the other's language and some sign language, Robert soon developed a working knowledge of English, similar to learning French and German over the past few years.

Soon the fascinating friend from America prepared to leave. During the last day he discreetly handed Robert a piece of paper with his address and gave him three books in English. One a brief history of the United States and two novels by an American named Mark Twain. He learned of the wonders of the American adventure and its struggle to be free of England from the history book. From the novels he learned much of the nature of the American people. Fascinated by the fictional name of St. Petersburg Mark Twain chose for his hometown of Hannibal, MO, he often fantasized himself as Tom Sawyer or Huckleberry Finn.

Robert knew he would go to America someday and, better yet, become an American citizen. Making certain no one would ever find the piece of paper he memorized the address and destroyed it. Almost every day he wrote the man's name and address in the dirt or snow, then immediately destroyed the information. He hid each of the three books in a different place to protect from them being found. He did not want his masters or his father to know of the books.

One day his father found one of the Mark Twain novels. He interrogated Robert endlessly and beat him within an inch of his life. His father knew he would be punished for the beating he gave his son and immediately left for Moscow, never to return. Robert knew he would leave too and started stealing small amounts of food and clothing. Several months earlier he stole a map of Europe. With the map and the American history book he learned of places he could go to make passage by ship to the United States. A month later he left the estate on the outskirts of St. Petersburg never saying goodbye to his mother, his three siblings or any of the young people he knew throughout his childhood.

Robert left for Moscow early one April morning. Sadly he had to leave his one remaining Mark Twain book at the estate, but decided to take his American history book with him. The two Twain books would be some of his first purchases once he arrived in the United States.

He watched the distance markers between the little towns as he traveled the over 600Km from St. Petersburg to Moscow, at first having no idea of how far he could go in a day. Soon he found, if he did not have to use too much time to forage for or steal food, he could cover 4-to-6Km in a typical day. He noted if he took the train, he could travel much faster, but Robert heard about people disappearing. Being caught meant one thing, but getting caught on a train could result in a severe beating and possibly being sent off to a concentration camp in Siberia. He made the decision to stay away from the railroads. Sometimes he would be ill for several days, even to the point of not being able to travel. From time-to-time a peasant with a horse drawn wagon would offer him a ride, but he seldom accepted. Even this made him leery. Robert knew if he was caught by the police it could mean being either put in prison or sent back to the estate. He set a goal to reach Moscow in four months and kept a calendar noting his progress on a piece of paper he kept inside one of his ragged shoes.

"I must not get caught!" he resolved repeatedly. He travelled mostly at night, often stealing a small amount of grain or food from the fields and markets along the way. Almost daily he tried to find someone who would trade food for work, but most of the people he encountered were just as poor. Whenever questioned he would fake being deaf, but this did not spare him from beatings. He resolved not to be drawn into any of the protest groups.

Less than a year after leaving his home, Robert crossed the border out of Russia into Ukraine. From then on he continually adapted, realizing the challenges he faced were more dramatic outside his home country, creating entirely new problems. Not being a native of the areas he traveled through, he often did not understand the local customs. The different dialects and languages were difficult for Robert to comprehend. Often discouraged, sometimes to the point of considering suicide, his strong religious upbringing by his doting mother always nagged him away from performing the act. He finally crossed into the Austria-Hungary Empire, almost being killed by Gypsies in Vienna. He then entered Bohemia.

At one point an old man caught Robert stealing a chicken. The angry man soon realized the teenage boy was hungry and afraid. He asked Robert, "Who are you, where are you from?"

Robert developed a detailed story about how he had been traveling with his family when the police arrested his parents. He said he hid deep in the woods until the police left, a good story which often got him sympathy.

"I didn't want to stay near my home. The police would eventually find me." Robert started his well refined lie in his rudimentary command of the local dialect spoken by the old man. "I decided I must leave Russia. I have traveled only at night and continued on until I got here."

"Where are you trying to go and what are you trying to do?" the old man asked, not believing Robert's shaky story.

"I don't know," he lied not wanting the man to know his goal to go to America. He did not want to be ridiculed for such an outrageous objective.

"Will you stay with me, at least for a while?" the man asked. "My wife died three months ago and I am lonely."

Robert looked at the pathetic soul before him and felt sympathy for the first time since leaving his mother and siblings, who probably worried constantly about him. He told the man he would stay but did not know how long. For the next three months he helped with daily chores and tried to cheer up the despondent man. During this time he learned how to read, write and speak the local language and gained enough weight to no longer look like a skin covered skeleton.

One morning, as the dreary cold weather of fall fell upon them, Robert got up to find the house empty. A suicide note lay on the little kitchen table which explained the old man's unbearable depression. He said he could not go on. It went on to tell Robert to take the little money left on the table, as well as anything else he wanted. He cautioned it would be best to leave. People may suspect Robert had something to do with his death.

Robert traveled mostly at night throughout the terrible winter, but at least he had money to buy food along the way. As before, he often looked at the worn map he kept in his shoe. He returned to his original goal to find his way to America. He looked for a port on the Atlantic Ocean and decided to go to Hamburg. A man from Hamburg visited the estate once and Robert thought maybe he could find the man, but he did not know the man's name and had no idea of the size of the city.

He realized the Hamburg Hafen or harbor, to be a major port located at the mouth of the Elbe River in northern Germany, where ships sailed to America.

He continued his trek for over six months before arriving in Hamburg. Once there he tried to find the German businessman, but soon became discouraged when he saw the size of the city. He sat on a pier in the harbor trying to decide what to do next when he heard a ship's captain talking to one of his officers about the difficulty to man his crew due to language difficulties. He complained most of the people fit and willing to join his crew spoke some other language than German or some dialect of German the captain and his officers could barely understand.

Robert jumped to his feet thinking maybe he could help.

"Please don't waste my time young man. What are you trying to say lad?" the gruff old sea captain yelled at him in German.

"Mein Herr, Ich konnen Sie helfen," he responded in his best German.

"So you can speak German and not very well, so what?"

For the next hour Robert approached men who spoke different languages and conversed with them. The awestruck captain watched Robert communicate with men who spoke French, Russian, English and several German dialects. He even made himself understood by several who spoke the various Scandinavian languages.

The captain said, "What do you want to do?"

"I want to work on a ship and practice my language skills," Robert responded somewhat truthfully, but not telling the whole truth. He only wanted to get to America, willing to do anything to get there.

The captain hired him immediately, with the instructions he work anywhere on the ship needing translation help between crew members. Robert's dream had come true, but he did not realize how harsh life on a ship could be and immediately abandoned ship upon reaching New Orleans. As he ran through the French Quarter, looking for a place to hide until the ship disembarked, he finally thought of Douglas Baylor.

"I must write to Mr. Baylor," but could not until he found a way to survive in the strange new world of America.

CHAPTER 6

DOUGLAS BAYLOR

Early 1900s

Robert immediately found a way to survive on the streets of New Orleans. Even with his rudimentary knowledge of English, street vendors found him a useful hard worker. He would do any task as long as he could receive food or a little money. Robert had no problems living on the streets. This is how he survived for three years on his way to Hamburg. Within a few weeks he wrote a letter to his friend Douglas Baylor.

Several months after arriving in New Orleans he realized if he bought fresh vegetables directly from farmers located at the edge of town, he could sell them for a profit in the French Quarter. This meant he had to be at the farms early in the morning. In the dark of the night he worked his way to the farms to be an early customer, and then returned to the center of town as fast as he could to catch the early buyers. Being successful he soon hired other street urchins to help him with his venture. One, a young orphan named Francois Girard, became a lifelong friend. Within a couple of months he bought a hand cart and hired other several helpers bring the food to him at the crack of dawn. In less than a year Robert's business was profitable with several wagons drawn by mules. He used the mules to haul produce from the farms, and then to pull the food wagons through the market. Later he successfully began providing food services, in addition selling vegetables to people on the streets of New Orleans.

Robert kept wondering if he would ever hear from Douglas Baylor. Almost three months after sending his letter, a response arrived. Robert carefully opened the envelop expecting the worst. Much to his surprise, Mr. Baylor not only welcomed him to America, but wondered why it took so long to hear from him. Eighteen months after his first visit to Russia, Doug returned for a follow up visit to the estate where he met Robert. He asked about the bright young man he previously met, but was met with a cold response. They told him Robert ran away and the police were still looking for him. He also wrote he never went back again. The business venture failed to materialize due to the sabotage of businesses by the revolutionaries.

He then wrote, "Robert, I hope you are in America for the right reasons and you have come here not only for adventure, but to thrive in the Capitalist system."

The words were music to Robert's ears realizing he had the right instincts about Douglas Baylor and America. Doug Baylor went on to expand his philosophy and his family's history. He explained his immigrants parents came to America from England in the early 1860s as a young married couple. Their parents gave them £20 and passage as wedding gifts. John Baylor had just finished his apprenticeship as a shoemaker and his new wife Mary was an excellent seamstress. They married early in the spring and immediately left Liverpool on a ship for America. Upon arriving at Castle Garden at the southern tip of Manhattan, they learned of a shoemaker who not only needed an assistant, but had a small living area above the shop for rent in the Bowery district. Mary soon learned many clothing manufacturers existed in the area. She did not like working in the sweatshop environment, but went to work at one of the factories. They were soon financially independent.

They noticed poor immigrants from several European countries settled in the same area, but they did not provide the steady flow of business his employer needed. After a couple of years they found a storefront near Wall Street with a small apartment in back for rent. Much to the chagrin of his employer John quit his job and set up his own shoe repair business, with Mary riding the primitive street car back and forth six days a week to her job as a seamstress at the clothing factory. He found the business slow at first, but soon noticed businessmen came into the area early each morning to work on Wall Street and then left in the afternoon. He put up a sign reading "Same Day Shoe Repair Service" and soon a number of pairs of shoes were dropped off each morning for repair the same day. John always attended to the same day customers first resulting in an ever increasing level of business.

One day one of his regular customers said, "John, do you know where I could get my clothes repaired? It seems like I am always losing a button or getting a tear in one of my shirts or trousers."

"My wife is a seamstress, leave the shirts and any other clothes you need repaired and I will have my wife do the repair in the evening and get them back to you the next day," John responded in his distinctively Liverpool accent.

Within weeks Mary received so much regular business they decided it would pay for her to stay at home and provide fulltime clothing repair services. During this time Douglas and his three sisters were born. The young Baylors' business thrived. Being forever frugal they never suffered financially even during the hardest of times.

One day five years after starting the business a regular customer brought in a pair of shoes for repair. John looked at his customer and said, "These shoes were made in England."

"Why yes," the customer said, "and I wish I could buy more like them."

"I could make shoes like this if I had the equipment and could find the quality of leather for the uppers and the soles," John told his long-time customer.

"If you could, you would have a large clientele just here on Wall Street and I believe they could be sold in many parts of the country.

Give me a list of the materials and equipment you need and I will find you the suppliers. Not only that, I'll bet I can get a couple of friends to help me finance your shoe manufacturing business. Are you game to try?"

By the time Douglas finished high school, the Baylor brand was sold throughout New York City. But Douglas thought more could be done. When his parents urged him to go to college, he said he would like to get his education in the business and expand the sales of their shoes. This disappointed John and Mary. They saw Douglas as potentially being not only the first high school graduate, but also the first college graduate in their family. They agreed to let him try for a year. He proved to be an outstanding salesman.

Douglas regularly rode on the railroads, first in New York and New Jersey, then up and down the east coast from Virginia to Boston. Baylor Shoes became a household name under Douglas's sales leadership in the homes of men from the financial community and throughout the business world. When the company went public in 1888 and it was immediately a Wall Street darling. In 1892, John and Mary decided they could and should retire after 30 years of hard work.

Doug Baylor found considerable demand for the quality products the company produced. He established factories in several large American cities, and then decided to expand into Europe. He first established a factory and sales organization in Liverpool working through relatives of his father, and then built a factory in Germany. This is what got him to Russia in the 1890s when he met the young Robert Barzinsky. The potential venture never developed into a Russian partnership, but established the friendship with Robert. Although they only saw each other three times in America, they kept in contact through regular mail correspondence.

As Baylor Shoe Manufacturing blossomed, Douglas involved himself with various trade organizations. He saw a need for involvement in politics, vehemently opposed to the trade union movement due to his strong bent towards capitalism. He closely watched the various left-wing movements throughout the United States and Europe. They frightened and concerned him about the future of America which he saw as the one bright light on the world stage.

In his next letter he first outlined, then expanded on, his political and economic views. Robert immediately wrote back to Douglas stating how much they agreed. They became 'Comrades in Capitalism', a strange but accurate description of their views of the world. They were two warriors in the front line of the battle for the survival of capitalism.

Happy to reconnect with his friend, New Orleans proved to be an ideal incubator for Bazinsky's fertile mind. With his penchant for learning languages in the cultural melting pot of the southern Louisiana port and his work ethic, he succeeded beyond his fondest dreams. While hawking food in the French Quarter, he became fascinated with the rich men coming from the newly discovered oil fields in east Texas. Robert Barzinsky amazed many with his business acumen and work ethic and thought he may be Jewish. If he were, no one ever knew, not even his closest associate for forty years, Jack Barnett, Sr. He actually was raised by a devout Eastern Orthodox mother, married to an amoral man who drank too much.

Two of the oilmen, the Wilson brothers from Beaumont, TX, often bought food from his mule drawn wagons while visiting New Orleans. They liked his spunk and hardworking nature and soon were his first real friends, other than Douglas Baylor, in America. A raucous hardworking and hard partying pair, they often came to New Orleans. Not until years later would others become friends of this strange little man.

They invited him to come to the Texas oilfields with his fledgling food services business and went on for hours on how a man with his talent could flourish in the rough and tumble environment. They told him about the thousands of men who came to work in the oil fields needing food and shelter. Robert saw the opportunity and bingo, he bit. After several weeks of setting up a network of food suppliers and delivery services he moved to Beaumont, the home of the Spindletop, just two years after the discovery of oil and was a respected, but seldom liked businessman by the end of the first decade of the 20th Century. His food services business spread across the oil fields like wildfire bringing the daily food needed to feed the thousands of workers flooding the area.

Few hotel and rooming houses existed in and around Beaumont so he started building rows of bunkhouses to house the weary workers as they came off long hard shifts in the oil fields. Working for Robert proved much less dangerous than working in the oil fields, thus he always had an easy time of hiring workers at wages less than the going rate. With this new business, Robert, literally drowning in cash, learned the meaning of 'positive cash flow'.

He learned from his early years in Europe he wanted as little to do as possible with paper money, which he called 'shit scrip'. He demanded silver or gold coins rather than paper money for rent, even though the hard currency created a storage problem for him. In his food services business, he gave a 10% discount for gold and silver coins. Because of his distrust of banks and the government, Robert found more and more creative ways to hide his gold and silver around his property.

In one discussion years later, Jack Barnett, Sr. said Robert told him of his anger with the passing of the income tax amendment in 1913 and was inherently suspicious of the new thing called the Federal Reserve. Although never proved, many considered Robert an early practitioner of tax evasion. The twists and turns in the oil industry and the U.S. economy made him nervous. He despised the progressive President Woodrow Wilson, but did not know someday he would be the owner of Wilson Oil Exploration. He was quite sure the snobbish North Carolinian was not related to the rough and tumble Wilson brothers he knew so well.

People considered Teddy Roosevelt the father of Progressivism. Robert, totally aware of this, said Teddy truly wanted to help the poorer people in the U.S. Whereas, the leftist Wilson, being an elitist, pounced on it as a way to get more control of the populace, as his segregation policies demonstrated. To him Socialism, Communism or any other big government philosophy only wanted more control. His hatred of Woodrow Wilson almost got him in serious trouble with the government during Wilson's presidency. He called Progressivism "Regressivism" which angered the backers of Woodrow Wilson.

Relieved to see Warren G. Harding as the new president in 1921, Robert openly discussed his feelings with others. The first couple of years with Harding as president pleased him, but he kept hearing stories of corruption. The death of Harding in San Francisco in 1923 shocked the nation, but Robert liked what he saw in the no-nonsense man from New England and soon Calvin Coolidge proved to be his favorite president. He had a reputation as being as reserved and taciturn as Robert. He thought of Silent Cal as his kind of man.

Robert continued selling food to the workers in the ever growing oilfields, first from an old wagon drawn by a team of mules, then several wagons and teams of mules. He learned in New Orleans that mules, rather than horses, were much better suited to the hot, humid weather of the gulf coast of the United States. Within a few of years, he purchased a small fleet of used trucks to supplement his teams of mules.

He read about a man named Frederic Tudor from Boston. A man obsessed with shipping blocks of ice from the north to distant places around the world. Always on the search for improving his business, Robert learned of how years earlier the Argentines successfully shipped beef to Europe using ice blocks for refrigeration.

"Why Argentina and not the U.S.?" Robert asked himself, but never understood why. He soon realized ice made it possible to ship and store seafood from the Gulf of Mexico the ever more affluent oilmen relished. He also made sure the staples and fresh foods needed to feed the constantly growing force of oil field hands could be preserved and eventually he was the largest buyer of blocks of ice in the south.

Robert constantly innovated and learned new ways to make money. Although an honest man, many questioned how he could become so wealthy in such a short period of time. His secret: He never wasted anything; a vestige of his poor childhood and struggle to make it to America. He had none of the typical vices of the men in his surrounding environment and he carefully invested his money in building more rental properties and expanding his food services business. Also, Robert did not waste money on alcohol or gambling.

From time to time, an oilfield worker and sometimes an oil well wildcatter ran short of money. Robert began providing loans. His customers never complained about high interest rates due to his always being always fair and honest. By taking some form of collateral, e.g. an expensive watch from a wildcatter or an oilfield worker's keepsake, he prospered. Loaning money seemed a natural companion to selling food and providing housing for the rowdy workers.

He continued a frugal man and within a few years his loan business proved as profitable as his food vending and rental housing businesses. Few of the increasingly wealthy oilmen, in their arrogance, considered Robert a man to be reckoned with in future decades. But Robert wanted more. He wanted to participate in the oil exploration and production business. Being an astute observer, he soon knew the financial side of their businesses better than many of the oilmen did, often helping them with their accounting and tax preparation problems. One day the Wilson brothers came to him in a panic. They got drunk while playing poker during a week of carousing in Dallas and ended up with a large IOU to a Dallas land developer. They needed a $500,000 loan to save their oil business. A lot of money in 1914!

Joe Wilson, the older brother, wailed in total despair, while his brother George raged around the room. What could they do? Did Robert know anyone from whom they could discreetly borrow such a large sum? Robert listened to their story, with his mind racing as he realized the opportunity before him. He completely shocked them when he said he knew someone who could help them, Robert Barzinsky. After several days of negotiating, Robert came up with a $500,000 loan from a Houston bank, using his gold and silver holdings as collateral. As the 51% owner of Wilson Oil Exploration, he finally forged his reputation as a hardnosed businessman. Competitors of the Wilson brothers never understood what happened.

Being great oilmen, but lousy businessmen, the deal turned out to be just what the brothers needed, especially in the area of money management. Robert proved himself to be just the opposite and for the next seven years the company flourished. Then one day in 1921 a huge explosion occurred at a drilling site killing both of the Wilson brothers. No one knew where the brothers came from and whether or not there were any heirs. Robert had the unusual sense to realize he could be faced with lawsuits from heirs discovered in future years, so he sought the best legal advice he could. After months of negotiating with the courts, he put the Wilson brothers' share of the thriving oil exploration and production business in escrow for that possibility. Year after year he managed the business as if he owned the entire company, always aware sometime in the future people claiming to be heirs of the brothers could demand their share. No heirs ever appeared. Seven years later Robert Barzinsky became the 100% owner of Wilson Oil Exploration. Robert changed the company's name to GLO Industries, Inc., with "G" for gold, "L" for land and "O" for oil.

Douglas Baylor made his first visit to Texas several years after Robert made his move to Beaumont. Robert immediately saw Doug had some serious physical problems which made travel difficult for him due to having to use crutches. He learned Douglas had been in a serious train accident in Connecticut a couple of years earlier, but he never let Robert know of the accident or complained. Even after the accident, Douglas Baylor continued to travel around the country giving speeches opposing the works of Marx, Engels and Lenin, as well American left-wingers. This often resulted in violent attacks against him in the press and he often received death threats, even being considered a pariah by those who should have been strong supporters. This was not the case with Robert who admired his friend, realizing the true nature of the press. They understood 'yellow journalism' first hand.

Doug constantly mentored Robert with long letters sent almost every week over the years as their collective philosophy evolved. They believed both the world's economy and basic civilization were at risk. Robert constantly amazed Douglas with his command of the English language, as he remembered Robert learning some of his first English words back in Russia. By the end of the Great War in 1918, they published their collective writings in a document titled *The Danger Ahead!* anonymously under the name of John Walborn and distributed the book out of a warehouse in lower Manhattan. In time, a loosely organized group of followers, tabbed the 'Walbornists' evolved.

The organization died when Douglas Baylor suddenly died in the spring of 1921. Robert often thought about reviving the group, but decided dissolution as the best way to create an aura of mysticism. No one ever found out how it started and by whom, but the memory of John Walborn and 'Walbornism' never died and the philosophy developed by Doug and Robert over the years played a major role in the creation of Project NewLand.

Robert was depressed at hearing about Doug's death, but additional concerns arose, being faced just six weeks later with the deaths of the Wilson brothers. Still his memory of Douglas remained with him for the rest of his life. During these busy times the concept of NewLand began to develop in Robert's subconscious. He continued to write long documents, the basis for his beliefs, and he created a plan for long-term survival of at least a few members of the human race in case of a world-wide catastrophe. He told no one. People would consider him mentally ill and a dangerous radical. Not until a few years later did he verbalized these thoughts to anyone.

As always, Robert went on toiling in his various businesses, soon to be one of the richest men in not only southeast Texas but all of Texas. Yet people knew so little about the man. His harsh childhood in Russia made him reclusive and cautious. He spent little and his wealth grew and grew, as did his problem of storing his gold and silver assets, mostly hidden around his house and buried on his property. Nobody realized the magnitude of his wealth.

By time he assumed full ownership of Wilson Oil in 1928, he had been worrying about the country's economy for several years. Years earlier the country briefly entered and survived The Great War at a terrible cost of life and treasure. The fiscal policies of the teens and the cost of the war put an extreme strain on the country's financial stability.

Although the company continued to grow and generate tremendous profits, not having the oil industry experience of the Wilson brothers made him more and more paranoid about protecting his resources. Remembering gold as the refuge of the old world economies of Europe and Asia, Robert converted more and more of his assets into gold. Storage became an ever mounting problem. His interest in the ownership of more land with oil potential grew. Robert heard many places in Texas could potentially prove to have petroleum waiting to be discovered and believed the American economy would eventually need many times the amount of oil being drilled and refined at the time. But he had no idea of where to look or how to do it. Robert realized he needed help. He needed someone paranoid and committed to amassing wealth like him. Someone he could completely trust and would complement his abilities.

CHAPTER 7

FINDING A PARTNER

Robert searched for a junior partner for several months before finding the man he wanted. He never married and was without encumbrances or heirs, but he longed to share the load of the business with someone who thought like he did. He also began to develop some health problems, resulting from the harshness of his early life and continued hard work. In his late-40s, he found himself tiring more easily than in the past. He started watching a gawky young man with a thick accent who joined the company as a roustabout a couple of years earlier. Robert soon realized maybe the young Jack Barnett could be just the man he needed.

Jack, a tall lanky Irishman and a strong physical specimen, towered over the short and overweight Robert. Robert observed the young Jack Barnett giving him increasingly more difficult tasks. Nothing seemed to faze Jack. He not only worked longer than anyone else, he usually found more efficient and effective ways to attack the job at hand. In his spare time he studied every business or technology oriented book he could get his hands on, particularly anything to do with the petroleum industry.

Finally one day in late 1928 he called Jack into the little shanty he called an office. "Jack, what do you know about me?" he quizzed the younger man, but did not expect what Jack said.

"You are a loner like me," he responded to challenge his interrogator in his heavy Irish accent. "You do not like nor trust most people. That is okay with me. I don't either."

When he heard what Jack had to say he knew he finally met someone who thought like he did. Robert knew where to go with the next question. "How much do you want success?" he asked Jack.

"What do you mean by success, money or control of one's destiny?" The beady eyed young Irishman barked back at Robert.

"You are an interesting young man, Jack. Let me see, both are important, but control of my destiny has always come first with me. It is the only way I can assure satisfaction with my life. We need to talk more, but I have much to do this evening. Think about what you can do to help me as well as yourself. Then we will talk again."

Weeks later Robert asked Jack to have dinner with him, a totally uncharacteristic act for the reserved little man. Jack ate from a china plate, something not done since his childhood in Ireland. He fondly remembered the fried fish served with garden greens and the ever present potato so common in the Irish diet, with a cup of strong bitter coffee. For a moment he thought of his home and family back in Ireland, something he seldom did.

"Do you want a drink of whiskey, Jack?" a complete surprise. Robert did not drink alcohol and Prohibition began several years earlier.

Jack said, "Of course. I would love a drink." Giving no thought to whether or not it would be taboo and knowing Robert would have bought illegal alcohol. Robert knew Jack drank, almost all of the oil field workers and a number of successful bootleggers flooded the area. He just wanted to see if Jack would admit he drank liquor and whether he could manage his alcohol use.

"Jack. That is another thing I like about you. Everybody knows I never touch alcohol, but I don't judge other people negatively if they drink just as long as it is not too much! You are honest enough not to act as if you didn't drink."

They ate in complete silence, so typical of both of their personalities. Finally Robert said to Jack, "Have you thought about what I said?"

Jack stiffened and said, "Yes and I believe I can do a lot for you." For the next 45 minutes Jack outlined a number of tasks he felt he could do. "The way I look at it, if I can take some of your load you will be able to accomplish much more and if you accomplish more, I can do more for you."

He went on to tell how he watched the moves Robert made, often going into detail how he could be of assistance. He did not hesitate to criticize somethings Robert did even to the point of making sensible suggestions on how he could be more efficient. As his steady talk continued he made more and more references of how he could fit into the organization and made specific comments on what he would want from their association. Nobody ever talked to Robert in this manner before. He had a number of assistants among his workforce through the years, but most lacked the drive, total self-assuredness or the complete honesty Robert needed. His other assistants played important roles in his various businesses but none with the intellectual capacity or drive of this young man.

Jack's comments stunned Robert. He thought, "Who is this kid? How did he grow into such a strong, knowledgeable young man without any apparent guidance?" He had not felt such kinship to anyone since his childhood.

At the end of Jack's long narrative, they sat in silence for a long time. Finally Robert said, "I guess now is time for me to do some thinking. You obviously have done your homework."

For the next week they seldom spoke, other than for Robert to direct Jack to what needed to be done or Jack asking what he could do next. Soon their relationship grew.

Robert always seemed to be a man with a cause. Most of those who knew him believed he cared only about amassing wealth, but did not know of his passion to create wealth for his self-appointed destiny of planning for a future world-wide disaster. He always believed at some point man would destroy most, if not all, humanity. Even though he was a man who struck out early in life to travel far from Tsarist Russia at the end of the 19th Century with a well-defined world view, he did not know to how to create this new world he long visualized. With the partnership with Jack Barnett, it all changed.

Robert and Jack finally made their pact to be partners, with Jack a minor partner. They developed a strategy to increase and preserve the wealth of Wilson Oil Exploration, the basis to build much larger operations, with ever expanding investments.

They had many things in common. Both, having escaped poverty in Europe, strongly believed someday gold would be much more valuable than paper money in case of an economic upheaval. They did not they realize how prescient they were, a belief further strengthened a few years later when FDR staged his bank holiday in 1933 and also prohibited most gold holdings by Americans pegging the price of gold at no more than $35 per ounce. This remained the price, later part of the Bretton Woods agreement in 1944, until the early 1970s. The partners were so secretive about their gold buying program not even the federal government could find any of their gold or determine the size of their holdings, a real accomplishment in a world of more and more government snooping. Robert strongly believed a problem was developing with country's economy in the late 1920s. Protecting his assets became of utmost importance to him.

Jack accepted Robert's path to future ownership with gusto. They often discussed economic issues. In many respects, Robert became an early venture capitalist. Beside his investments in providing food services and loans, the oil industry and housing for oil field workers, he invested in Jack Barnett. Jack flourished in the role of junior partner. Jack came from nothing and his strange man, who he admired, provided the pathway to future wealth beyond belief.

Robert continued to regularly invest in gold. He first accumulated many thousands of dollars of gold and silver coins from his food vending and rooming house businesses, but then bought additional gold, usually in the form of ingots, whenever he could take the time to travel to make purchases as his businesses prospered. At first he traveled by train to buy gold, sometimes even riding the rails as a hobo.

Buying his first automobile reliable enough to venture on long road trips made acquiring gold easier. Before the outlawing the ownership of private gold, he would drive to New Orleans, Houston, and Dallas in his reinforced vehicles to make buys. He went to gold mines in Mexico and around the U.S. to buy more gold directly from those who mined and smelted gold ore. Safe and secure storage of the gold became a bigger and bigger problem as his inventory grew. He and Jack discussed the gold storage problem on a regular basis, but had a difficult time coming up with a satisfactory solution.

While pondering the storage problem one evening, Jack screamed, "Land!"

"What the hell are you talking about," Robert yelled back in his still thick Russian accent.

"Land! You always say you are interested in investing in land. You have been buying land for years for oil exploration and to build housing units here in Beaumont. I think we should store gold on land we purchase, only not here in Beaumont. We buy land in some remote area," he yelled back at the puzzled Russian, but Robert soon understood the brilliance of Jack's exclamation.

Robert and Jack talked for hours about what land should be purchased and how best to hide gold. They determined buying land with little appeal to the average investor in some remote area in Texas to be the best approach...and to buy a considerable amount of land. Next they needed to learn as much as possible about central and west Texas, a vast wasteland with little investor interest at the time. They did not realize how much their first land acquisition would shape the future of their businesses and fit into their long-term plan for survival.

But where and how do go about finding and buying the right land? At the time they gave little thought to the possibility the new land investments would lead to more oil. Most nights after a full day of work, they worked on developing their plans, with the objective to find a safe place to set up ranching operations and store their gold inventory. In the early 1930s, much of Texas offered great opportunity for Robert and Jack. No need to go beyond the state's borders they decided. They learned all they could about the state.

With the Great Depression already under way, the horrible Dust Bowl years would soon begin. The summer heat would soon burn like Hell's cauldron followed by bitterly cold winters, especially when the strong winds blew from the north. Both the farmers and the ranchers suffered from the weather and the worsening economy. Soon crops would not grow and cattle started dying, providing the partners the opportunity to buy extensive pieces of land at low prices. They knew then they were going to be large land owners leading to other business opportunities.

Their paranoia about the future of the country and the world grew. Robert would again take on the full load of the day-to-day business of GLO Industries. He sold the food services business to a Dallas-based company which had been pursuing him and secretly acquired more gold. By this time his buys ran into hundreds of pounds per acquisition on a single trip. He also had agents in several cities around the country buying and shipping gold to him. He developed a secure courier system to transport the gold in large wooden crates labeled 'Used Oil Field Equipment'. Each box contained some old and virtually unusable oil field equipment, thus thieves showed little interest, regardless of whether shipped by train or truck. Fortunately he established this method before FDR made the ownership of gold by the public illegal. They developed a sophisticated system for buying gold in foreign markets and brought it across the Rio Grande. Robert continued to have no confidence in paper money and banks.

Jack, in turn, became an early 'land man' searching around the state for land for GLO Industries, an excellent role for his reclusive life style. He spent many long days of visiting court houses for records of repossessed land, followed by hours of driving across the endless terrain south and west of towns like Abilene, Lubbock and Odessa, TX. Jack relished the solitude, often living out of his car and tent. He would read by kerosene lantern about the local area long into the night, then wake early anxious to further his search.

Along the way since coming to America, Robert accumulated assets of over $20,000,000, a lot of money for someone who came to this country penniless just 30 years earlier. They soon found they could buy an extensive amount of land without making a dent in Robert's net worth. Each month he made a transfer to an account he kept for young Jack, which only motivated Jack more. They thought the next job would be to hide the purchased gold on the land soon to be acquired by Jack in the selected area of west Texas.

JACK BARNETT

CHAPTER 8

BUYING LAND

Early 1930s

Dressed in his only suit, which he seldom wore, Jack just closed the sale of the first piece of property he purchased, an irregular shaped parcel south of a small village with a fast moving stream running through it. His fertile mind thought of possible uses. The land was first homesteaded early in 20th Century by Germans pushed out of their lands during the century after the death of Catherine the Great of Russia. Unfortunately for them, the harsh farming methods of the day and the dry years resulted in a broken land. The millennia of native trees, grasses and cacti torn up by plows allowed the naked land to be worn bare by the vicious winds. Followed by a horrible drought, it resulted in the dust storms of the 1930s, which turned out to be the hottest decade of the 20th Century.

Germans began immigrating to Russia as far back as the early 16th Century and the rush to the Ukraine and Russia greatly increased during the 18th Century. During the latter part of the 19th Century political and economic pressures reversed the flow of these people. As the Bolshevik Revolution brewed, the pace of departures increased. Many could not return to Germany for a number of reasons and, as time passed, more and more made the ultimate choice and immigrated to North America. German Russians spread across the Great Plains of America, plus the Canadian provinces of Manitoba and Saskatchewan.

Many settled in the future Dust Bowl lands of the south central plains of the states of Kansas, Oklahoma, eastern Colorado and down into Texas. Some went far into the bowels of southwest Texas. As the dreary years of the drought of the 1930s evolved, many settlers known as Okies moved on to the west coast. A few brave and determined souls stayed and fought the elements. Many broken souls faced a life of sadness and poverty. Most of the older settlers wished they had never left Europe. But some, especially the young, persevered for they knew no other life and with no memory of any other place, determined to not only survive but eventually flourish.

Less than two hundred German Russians established and settled in and around the small village of Kursk deep into the open lands of southwest Texas. They were from the Kursk Oblast, located at the confluence of the Kur, Tuskar, and Seym Rivers in Russia. Several towns of farmers mixed in with ranching towns, such as Valley Center about 20 miles to the northwest.

Each town settled in this part of Texas looked eerily like the next, regardless if it were a ranching or farming village, with a downtown consisting of a block or two of a few small buildings along a narrow dusty street. County seats, such as Valley Center, had a courthouse square the center of downtown. A single room school building, offering basic education for grades 1 – 8, sat on the edge of each village. To go to high school a young person lived in a town with a high school located at least 30 to 40 miles away. It meant while in high school they lived with a family far from home, where they helped with chores to pay for their room and board since their families were too poor to pay. A few, mostly young girls, went to teachers' college and often came back to teach in a rural or small town school.

Kursk was located at the southern tip of the Dust Bowl which prevailed from 1931 through 1939. The combined impact of the drought and the Depression overwhelmed the residents of the area. Over those years all parts of the United States witnessed some aspect of the Dust Bowl. The red soil of Oklahoma spread east as far as Boston during one particularly bad series of dust storms during the mid-30s. Stories of oddities were rampant, such as the man whose horse developed a large belly. After the horse died, the farmer cut open its abdomen to find a large ball of dirt accumulated by the animal's foraging for bits of grass. Farmers also told of surviving only because their teams of horses knew the way home during the 'black storms' which totally obliterated light, even in the midday sun.

A tight knit group of mostly Evangelical Lutherans made a pact to stay and fight as long as possible, along with a small group of Catholics with their own church a block down the street. Little did they realize the appearance of the strange lanky Irishman would be their long-term salvation! Others now owned the land they worked for so many years and they became poor laborers. Each month several farmers lost their farms to a bank due to not being able to pay the mortgage. The banks took their property, leaving the families in a lurch with nowhere to go. Most families were given a deadline by the banks of how long they could stay, but sometimes the banks allowed the farmers to remain on the land, with no buyers for the properties. Local businesses were beginning to fail. Everybody worried about their futures. Some families, especially close relatives, lived together to get by through a dreadful time with little or no hope.

On a Wednesday morning, Jack left the small county courthouse with the deed to the 960 acres he just bought 10 miles to the southwest of the small village of Kursk. He already walked the periphery of the land twice and crossed it several times. The dry years and dust storms caused much damage to the land which had be tilled and farmed vigorously for the past 20 to 30 years. The possibilities fascinated him, but the land needed to be repaired.

"Can the land be recovered by the planting of grasses to allow cattle grazing in the future?" he pondered as he walked to his car.

A railroad had been built through Kursk years earlier making it easy to ship herds of young cattle into the area for grazing and out again for slaughter when ready for the market. Jack believed the harsh years of drought and the damning Depression would someday abate. Could cattle grazing provide a cover for their real intent of finding a place to hide their ever growing gold assets? Who knew, maybe oil or some useful mineral deposits existed on the land they accumulated. If so, Jack knew they would be in the catbird seat. Nobody else could afford to buy the re-possessed land.

Even though he appeared to be a man who cared for no one, Jack had much compassion for others. He remembered the hardships of his childhood in Ireland and how his family suffered through poverty, illness and death. He would never forget the day he watched the city of Cork fade away into the horizon as the small freighter headed for his new land. Once it disappeared, he never looked back, figuratively or literally. Now an American, he pursued the American dream no matter how much time or effort it took to achieve.

Jack being an Irishman and the settlers German concerned him, but they were both raised in Christian lands, even though the traditions of the Lutherans appeared to be much different than his Irish Catholic upbringing. He already told the Grauman family, one of the families who lost their farm, he wanted them to stay and farm a portion of the land he purchased. The other family, named Schmidt, left the area for California as soon as the bankruptcy occurred. Jack buying their former farm and allowing them to stay was the first ray of positive news for the Grauman family, but it took them several years for them to realize how fortunate they were. Little did they realize they would have a large cattle ranching operation and be the owners of oil producing land in a few years. They would achieve the American Dream and become well-to-do.

"But how will we pay the rent?" Franz Grauman asked in his broken English. He bought the land with a partner twelve years earlier after being a farmhand for other Germans as he worked his way across Kansas, Oklahoma, to the Panhandle of Texas and down into west central Texas. The family, which consisted of Franz, his wife Hilda and identical twin sons Kurt and Kristian, eked out a hardscrabble life on their farm, which became much more difficult as the Dust Bowl years evolved.

"Don't worry, we'll work out something," Jack reassured the worried man in his late forties. "Our plans are long range. We have plenty of time. Just get to work and take care of your family." And work they did because hard work had always been their life.

Although the best news Franz received since he and his partner lost their farm to the two banks, it provided little comfort to the hard working farmer and his family. He went home to tell his wife of 18 years and their two teenage boys they could remain on their farm. Little did they know what it meant in the long term and in the years to come they would end up wealthier than most of the 'Okies' who gave up and went west!

What did Jack have in mind? Not much at the time, but he and Robert had been developing their survival plan for over a year. He did not consider caring for this family's welfare to be much of a problem. They had vast resources and a long-range plan to make a major presence in the small community. The grand plan required a number of families to continue working the lands they would purchase over the next couple of years. Jack believed their success depended on a number of the families staying.

For the next several days after the closing, he traipsed over other parcels of land repossessed by the banks in Kursk and Valley Center located about 20 miles to the northwest. The banks were run by two groups of investors who not only hated each other, but were also scared of what the future held for them. Both parties realized, although they owned thousands of acres, they had no idea of an exit strategy. No potential buyers existed until Jack Barnett showed up.

Both banks were the epitome of 'land poor' ventures, completely aware of the strong possibility they could soon be facing the same fate many of the poor farmers faced, as the combined impact of the continuing dust storms and the Great Depression worsened. Contrary to many banks which stayed solvent during the Depression years, the two banks seemed to be racing towards bankruptcy. They knew it. Jack

Barnett knew it, but little did they know how he would resolve many of their problems.

Robert and Jack established their goal: Be the major land owners in the area. With the company's vast resources, they believed they could prevail no matter what happened. The previous month they budgeted an initial $250,000 for land investments. The first 960 acres cost them $25 per acre, including expenses they had a little over $25,000 invested.

The out-of-place Irishman, soon the chess master, was playing two boards at once. On one board he faced the owners of the Prairie River Bank of Kursk, on the other the owners of the slightly larger Bank of Valley Center.

The Valley Center bank owned a 1250 acre piece of land known of as parcel 14. Jack believed it to as fertile as the first land he purchased. That proved not to be true, but its strategic location would be crucial to their long term success. Located just to the southwest of the range of hills from which the stream emanated, a considerable amount of oil would eventually be discovered on this land. The previous owners built a bridge across the stream flowing through the original land Jack purchased, providing a road to the south side. Jack decided he could limit the bankers' access to lands they owned on the south side of the bridge making these properties less valuable. He strategically bought more property over time making access to others almost impossible.

A strange geological formation provided the source of the stream which ran from southwest to northeast in an area where the rivers and streams predominately flowed to the south. Jack focused on the area where the stream flowed out of the range of hills. The first parcel purchased cupped the nose of the valley. It made sense to expand their holdings in both directions from the original purchase.

The valley between the hills spread about a mile wide at the northeast end, but the hills ran for a number of miles to the southwest. It appeared the range of hills widened as the valley narrowed when he looked to the southwest. The state of Texas owned the land, but Jack wondered if the state even realized it.

He then made the long trip back to Beaumont to discuss his findings with Robert. After a hearty dinner of fresh fish, potatoes and fresh vegetables, Robert sat back and listened to the details of Jack's trip.

Robert excitedly listened as Jack told about the first parcel of land he bought and the other 1250 acres he wanted to buy. The strange hilly property fascinated Robert even more than the other parcels. "Jack, do you know what is in that area?"

"No, I have been concentrating on whether or not the land we just bought has future farming or cattle grazing possibilities. That land is too hilly and rocky for either of these uses." Jack responded, as he related to Robert the close proximity of the railroad which made ranching on the land feasible.

"Has anybody but the Indians ever investigated those hills? I am sure they knew the area well, but they are gone now. You know me Jack I am always interested in the unknown. The stream must start somewhere in those hills and there may be some minerals. Better yet, it may provide a wonderful place to hide some of our gold," Robert, almost breathless, pondered aloud. Jack often saw this side of Robert: He wanted to be the one to learn the unknown.

Jack thought, "What the hell. Robert may have something. What use did the state of Texas ever have for the land anyway? They already owned much larger properties, such as Palo Duro Canyon south of Amarillo, Big Bend and much of the Davis Mountains. What possible value could this property be to the state? Hell, the state is struggling as much as most of the people are. What do they want with a bunch of hills? Maybe we can buy a chunk of it or at least get a long-term lease?"

He then quit worrying about taking any immediate action.

CHAPTER 9

OFF TO THE HILLS

Little did he realize what he found! As Jack traveled back to the area the following week, his mind raced from one subject to another. Upon arriving in Kursk he immediately set about to buy the 1250 acres of land he discussed with Robert. During his meeting with the Valley Center Bank, which owned the property, he reminded them he overpaid for the parcel jointly owned by the two banks. Both bank owners knew they made a good deal on the sale of the parcel of land to Jack.

Within a day, he made an offer for $5 an acre less than he paid on the previous purchase just a few weeks earlier. They did not like the offer, but were well aware this parcel did not have the value of the previously sold land. After six hours of discussion, he realized he needed to throw them a bone, so the price ended up at $25,000 an extra $500 as a $100 'sweetener' for each of the five board members. Jack then got up to leave. Kenneth Peek, chairman of the board of Valley Center Bank, asked, "How do we contact you?"

"I'll contact you," ignoring further questions as he went out the door of the bank. He went back to Kursk and purchased a week's supply of food from the general goods store along Main Street and then stopped for coffee and a sandwich at the local cafe. He really would have liked a beer, but Prohibition prevented that. Many of the German immigrants brewed their own beer, but no other source existed.

With the end of Prohibition the next year a local brewery appeared, when a former farmer would be provided startup funds by Robert and Jack. The beer would be excellent, brewed in the old German style of using only natural ingredients: Barley, malt, hops and the pure water from the local stream.

He headed his 1928 Chevrolet sedan to the south reaching the hilly area just before dusk. He hid his car behind some large bushes and headed toward the valley separating the range of hills. A few minutes later he found a clearing giving him a clear view of his car. He set up his tent near a large cottonwood tree, making sure no snakes or other critters would bother him. It was late May and the warm evenings would soon evolve into hot days.

Being the dark of the moon, millions of stars provided a comforting glow across the skies. He could hear the various sounds of nature, including coyotes in the distance. Just to be safe, he kept his revolver loaded and at his side. After taking a long drink of the cool water from the stream and eating a peanut butter sandwich, he prepared to bed down for the night. Once he pulled the screened flap of small his tent closed he fell into a deep sleep on his bedroll.

Just as dawn broke he awoke rested, hungry and ready to explore, remembering he ate little the night before. He started a small campfire and filled his coffee pot from the stream. After eating a can of beans, fried eggs and bread, he placed his tent and equipment in his car. Taking only a canteen of water and some beef jerky, Jack headed up into the valley between the two sets of hills, wondering what lay ahead.

Jack decided he would only walk for three or four hours, make some observations along the way, then return to his camp. That night he would establish a plan of action for the next three or four days. He did not want to be seen anywhere in Kursk or Valley Center for a while knowing full well the two sets of bankers and local residents wondered what this stranger intended to do next.

Two hours into his trek, the incline of the slope increased and the stream dropped slightly with respect to the bank. The terrain became rockier and the trees fewer and smaller as the width of the valley narrowed considerably. Stones along his path ranged from little balls the size of a baseball up to six or eight inches in diameter. He did not realize these were geodes as he worked his way towards an ancient volcano. The hills rose gently on each side of the river as the incline continued to increase. Short of breath, Jack took a break, lunching on his beef jerky and drinking some of the stream's cold water.

After sitting for an hour enjoying the solitude provided by the hills rising about 1000 feet above his head on both sides of the stream, Jack proceeded for another two hours and then decided to come back the next day with his full backpack. He followed another bend in the stream to the west as the terrain became much more rocky and rugged. The round stones increased in size and the stream seemed to gradually narrow, deepen and flow more rapidly.

Another third of a mile up the slope, the stream made a gradual bend to the south. As he continued to climb, the hilltops seemed to reduce in height with respect to his elevation. Most of the rocks along the stream now were more than a foot in diameter. At this point Jack decided he had gone far enough. He found a relatively flat topped stone outcropping then pulled out a piece of folded paper and spread it on the surface of the rock and for the next hour drew a map of the path he followed, noting points of interest.

He started his return to his base camp, stopping periodically to add details to his map indicating distances and changes in elevation. What he experienced excited him. Mentally he was already planning the next several days. "Too bad Robert isn't here," his imagination piqued as he thought of what he would find as he trekked along the stream.

"Why is the water so cold? Where is the source of this water? How far will I have to go to reach it? Maybe I should have driven around the set of hills first?" Jack pondered as he worked his way back down the path, but this time on the other side of the stream which he crossed using a series of randomly spaced rocks.

Returning to his car famished he immediately started a fire to heat water for coffee and a can of stew, which he ate dipping in pieces of bread. Jack planned for the next several days, wanting to be back in Kursk in four days, but felt it important to plan for at least a fifth day. Realizing he would be walking a considerable distance into an ever increasing elevation, he planned carefully.

Laying in the relative safety of his small tent, he wondered, "What if there are poisonous snakes, bears, wolves and coyotes? What if there are banditos hiding along the way?" Soon, feeling the weariness of the long day, he fell into a deep sleep.

In the morning he woke early and got up just as dawn began to break in the east, eating some dried beef from his backpack along with bread and several cups of hot coffee. He then made sandwiches with the balance of the meat. From there on he would depend on canned beans and stew, beef jerky and some ever-hardening bread for the remainder of his tour. He packed his tent in his car, pulled his backpack and bedroll over his shoulders and began his trek.

He made his way back into the valley, quickly getting to the point he reached the day before. Realizing he carried a much heavier load than the previous day, he found it necessary to rest for quite a spell. After an hour nap, he ate a sandwich washed down with fresh water from the stream. Jack longed for a cup of coffee, but considered a coffee pot and frying pan to be luxuries, although he did include a package of ground coffee in his backpack.

As he continued, the terrain became more difficult, making it necessary for him to fashion a walking stick from one of the small trees along the stream. He continued on for the next four hours, taking notes and adding to his map periodically. The terrain became flat for the last two hours of the day. With the steep hills on each side of the stream, it soon darkened even though it was not yet 5PM; a strange experience for one who lived on the flat lands of southern Texas for more than a decade.

Jack chose a flat area near the bank of the stream for his campsite, intending to use it again on his return trip. Being concerned for his safety from snakes and wild animals, he built three fairly large campfires surrounded with ring of rocks to keep the fire under control. A large amount of dry firewood lay nearby. Once the fires were under way, he heated his stew over the fire and then realized he could use the empty can to make fresh coffee.

After dinner he laid out his bedroll, found a comfortable rock to work on his map and added to his notes continuing to detail features he saw along the way. Unfortunately, Jack found no potential location for storing their gold inventory other than digging a hole and burying it. Fatigued, he laid down on his bedroll with his revolver close to his hand and fell asleep.

When morning came, Jack woke to find himself still tired and aching from head to toe. The activity of the previous day had been more strenuous than he realized and it took some time to face the day. He ate an uneventful can of beans and dry bread for breakfast and brewed coffee in the empty tin can. With no assurance as to whether he might venture beyond the source of the stream, he filled his canteen with cold water from the stream.

Again the pathway steepened and the hills turned into solid rock, with the foliage sparse. Entering a different geological formation about two hours into his trek, he stopped to rest and added notes to his map. Whereas the day before he saw numerous rodents, snakes and a lonesome coyote, he saw no animal life. Why? Nothing explained this phenomenon.

At noon Jack stopped for beef jerky, bread and fresh cool water from the stream. As he sat down, he noticed something different. Before he only heard the sound of the stream, but now in the background he heard a definite sound of falling water. He again updated his map and notes estimating he walked about 12-to-15 miles along the rock filled winding path since his starting out the day before. Passing around the next bend in the narrow valley, the sound of falling water became much more prevalent and he saw the peak of a hill from which the stream emanated. His heart pounded with excitement. Could this be the source of the stream he followed for the past two days? Jack ran as traversed he the last half mile, stumbling and falling down as his sense of anticipation built.

Nearing the roaring waterfall, he saw the water sprung from a hole about 500 feet below the top of what appeared to be a massive solid rock peak. It looked as if placed on top of the hill at the end of the valley by a giant. His interest piqued by the way the water flowed out of the side of the rocky structure and he was sorry he had neither the time or supplies to pass around the rocky peak. Laying his backpack and bedroll on the ground and putting on a pair of leather gloves, he began to work his way up the steep rocky structure. After an arduous hour of pawing and crawling, he approached the opening from where the stream emanated and a narrow ledge appeared.

Finding it pitch dark inside what appeared to be a large cave and wishing he had brought a lantern along, Jack cut off his shirt tail with his knife and wrapped it around the end of his walking stick. After closing his eyes for five minutes after moving slowly into the cave he then used a match to ignite the fabric. He knew he had only a couple of minutes of light, but wanted to see as much as possible. As the small torch flared, Jack realized the immense size of the cave and to his surprise a large pond of water lay before him. A raging artesian well supplied the pond inside the cave.

Jack let out a roar, "What have I found?"

He moved his torch around to learn as much as possible, making mental notes along the way. The cavern appeared almost circular and close to 1000 feet across, but he realized he did not have sufficient light to determine the height of the large cavern. Soon the torch flickered and died. Jack stood transfixed in wonder. He stood with his eyes tightly closed frozen for at least ten minutes. He opened his eyes he receiving another shock. Off in the distance across to his left he saw a glint of light, which both excited and disappointed Jack. He did not have the time or resources to explore the large cavern any further on this trip. He then carefully worked back to the opening where he entered, making a mental note to bring a lantern on his next visit to the area. Exhausted from the climb, he sat with his back against a large rock and fell into a deep sleep for several hours.

The sun already sunk below the horizon when Jack woke up wondering, "Where am I, what have I done? I have to get back to my gear before it gets too dark." He then scrambled down the rocks to his backpack and bedroll and set up a camp with three campfires for the night, just like the previous night.

With the surprisingly cool air, he welcomed the heat from the fires. His mind wandered as he thought about the events of the day. He wondered what he had found and what the native Indians and settlers thought when they explored the area. He found no sign of any recent human activity in the valley. No doubt Indians used the stream as a source of water and as a protected area to camp. They must have explored the cavern and the pond with the artesian well, but there was no obvious indication of their ever having been there. Totally exhausted he quickly ate some beef jerky and bread before falling into a deep sleep.

When he woke in the morning he needed to decide whether the trip back to his car should be done in two days or should he try to make the entire distance in one day. After consideration, Jack decided to take his time and explore the area in more detail on the way down and to explore the possibility of caves or potential hiding places to stash gold.

Hourly he stopped to add notes to the map, such as the types of trees, shrubs, birds and animals, plus any unusual aspects of the soil and stones. He rued he did not bring along binoculars to study the hillsides more thoroughly. By mid-afternoon he passed his previous camp, about half way back to the car. He decided he did not want to arrive back at the bank too soon, so he went on for only another two hours before stopping. He noticed fish in the stream and decided to see if he could catch a few for dinner. After 30 minutes, using what remained of his shirt as a net, he caught two fish. After setting up a camp with three campfires, he cleaned the fish and cooked them on heated rocks. It was a feast after three days of nothing but canned food, beef jerky and dry bread. He again used an empty tin can for hot coffee.

Being satisfied with the past three days of exploration, sleep came quickly even though there were few answers and many more questions. Robert would be anxious to hear about the trek.

The next morning he ate some beef jerky and bread, not even making a cup of coffee, anxious to return to town for a decent midday meal. Afterwards he checked into the local hotel and ordered hot water for a bath. He wanted to be ready to visit the Bank of Valley Center the next morning. After his bath and donning clean clothes, he decided to make himself visible and walked up and down the street and was not surprised a message from the Chairman of the Board of the Valley Center Bank awaited his return to the hotel. Apparently their spy network alerted them of his return to town.

The next morning, after breakfast and checking out of the hotel, his day started with a trip to the local gas station. The owner asked him where he had been for the past four days, to which he responded, "Just driving around."

By 9AM he started the 20 mile trip to Valley Center and found the entire board of directors waiting as he parked his car in front of the bank a bit before 10AM.

"Time to close the deal" he thought.

The five men had been cooling their heels for some time. "Where the hell you been?" the Chairman asked.

"Around," Jack responded, "What do you guys want to do?"

"We want to negotiate."

Jack got up and headed for the door without saying a word, but before he got there one of the directors stopped him saying, "We want to discuss the deal."

"Nothing to discuss" he said as he pushed the man away.

The Chairman protested his leaving, "Okay we have a deal. $25,500 if we can close quickly."

"How about I get my bank to send a cashier's check? Just like the last time you can call my bank in Beaumont to check the funds exist. Here are the phone number and the name of the bank president," Jack responded. The account remained only in his name since they were not ready to let anybody know the involvement of the infamous Robert Barzinsky.

He drove back to Kursk so as not be subjected to more inquiries from the bankers or the people of Valley Center.

A couple of days later, the check delivered and with deed in hand, Jack entered the county courthouse in Valley Center to register the deed, and then started the long drive back to Beaumont. Realizing Robert wanted to know what happened and not wanting to take a chance with a phone call, he sent a short telegram of three words: "Eureka. Thomas Edison." Eureka meant the deal closed, while Thomas Edison meant the mysterious valley produced an exciting discovery.

CHAPTER 10

BACK TO BEAUMONT

Typical of past trips Jack drove for several hours and then found a remote place with trees where the car could be hidden. After a quick meal, he went to sleep sitting in the driver's seat. This seemed an uncomfortable way to rest but it was something he trained himself to do over the years of working in the oil fields. Even Robert could not understand how a human being could sleep in such a position, just another indication of Jack's self-discipline.

At 2:45AM Jack woke in a start with an eerie sensation. He opened the door of the Chevy to stretch his legs and faced a cool wind from the northwest. The air crackled with a strange electricity and a monstrous black wall cloud could be seen as the bolts of lightning spiked to the ground in the distance.

"Is this a dust storm?" he questioned. Even though he made three previous trips to this part of Texas over the past eight months, for the first time he was experiencing the evil plaguing the plains. Sure he had seen the drifts of dirt that streaked across the lands and the huge piles of tumbleweeds while crisscrossing the plains, but Jack never witnessed the ferocity of this phenomenon before.

He faced a completely new situation. Fortunately, the storm approached from the northwest and he decided to outrun it. To stay ahead of it, he estimated he needed to travel at least 90-to-100 miles to the southeast to escape the danger. With almost a full tank of gas, he headed for San Angelo wondering if fate would allow him to get there safely.

He coped as best he could with the dust raised by the wheels of other cars as he drove through the drifts of sand and piles of tumbleweeds on the road. Luckily most of the traffic headed to the southeast, but he kept proper distance from the few vehicles on the road to maintain visibility. Three hours later, while still dark, an exhausted Jack rolled into San Angelo. The small café on the main drag soon opened and, after a large breakfast of bacon, eggs and coffee, Jack filled up with gas and headed towards Houston, which he hoped to reach before the end of the day. It would mean driving another 350 miles.

Thirty miles outside of San Angelo, the left back tire blew. Fortunately, Jack always carried at least three spare tires. Another hundred miles down the road another tire blew and only one spare tire remained, but the rest of the day went well. Due to fatigue, he stopped about two hours short of Houston. Again Jack found a quiet sheltered area off the road where he rested until about 4AM the next morning. Eating the last bits of food he bought in San Angelo, he rolled into Beaumont by late morning without making another stop.

As the car rolled into the driveway of the small house, Robert, excited and full of questions, came running out of the front door like a 10 year-old welcoming his traveling salesman father home from an extended trip. Exhausted and almost catatonic, Jack entered the house where a large bowl of soup and a pot of hot black coffee awaited the weary traveler.

Once rejuvenated, the questions from Robert went on for hours. As expected, he wanted to know the minute details of the trip. First to be covered were the details of the financial transaction. Often Robert would let go with an uncharacteristic whoop of approval. Jack described the two parcels of land in detail and why he felt they could start their ranching operations. Jack liked the larger of the two parcels. It allowed them to maintain a higher level of secrecy for their future operations and provided further access to the southern side of the bank of hills. He also told Robert he believed former owners would remain on one of the properties they purchased, if presented with the right deal. This not only protected their land, but provided a source of future labor as they initiated their ranching operations. He said he liked the Grauman twins, strapping youths of 16 with a strong work ethic similar to theirs. As he learned from his brief experience with them, their tough old man made sure his sons knew how to work. Most of the other families he met so far only had little children, thus would not be as good of a source of workers for several years.

Jack remembered how the young woman at one of the farms he visited glared at him when he informed them he intended to buy the property her uncle and aunt lost through bankruptcy. She thought of him as just another enemy of the family, but Jack could not get her out of his mind. Later he found her to be the beautiful Catherine Gruenberg with whom he would eventually fall madly in love.

Finally, ready to talk about the strange valley he took out six crumbled pages of the maps and notes and spread were out on the tabletop. Robert again became animated. They meticulously discussed each bend in the stream and the details of the surrounding hills, so typical of Jack's attention to detail. Robert was most fascinated hearing about the mysterious source of the stream.

After a break to eat some more soup and drink several cups of coffee, they went back to discussing the strategy for their west Texas project, with Robert all ears. Jack presented a well thought out plan for starting their cattle ranching, with the strategy of running a small operation until the rains returned. The land needed rain to heal from the ravages of years of plowing and grain farming. He told Robert he would do his best to make his newly acquired tenants understand the wisdom of this strategy. He needed to spend time with these families and additional tenants as he acquired more land from the near bankrupt banks. Dealing with their paranoia and fear was a major challenge he met with his full commitment. This trait made Robert happy with the decision he made a couple of years earlier to make Jack his partner.

Jack told Robert how the location and makeup of the town could provide the support needed, from the local businesses to the road system to the railroad which passed through the lonely little village. He said they may need to help local residents until the drought ended and the economy recovered. Should they start their own bank? No! They believed too many government regulators were sticking their noses into their business already to make creating a chartered bank of any interest to them, particularly with the meddling crew in Washington. They decided instead they would provide loans directly to a select group of farmers and businessmen, as needed. Both Robert and Jack continued to have a strong dislike for most government involvement, especially anything smelling like federal government, enough reason alone for Project NewLand to be created. They continued to believe civilization would eventually either end or go through a major transformation at some time in the future, but did not know when the time would come.

Robert then raised the subject of what they should do about the valley and hills. Jack begged off due to obvious fatigue. Five minutes later he was asleep in his attic bedroom while Robert mused about the prospects with great anticipation.

Early the next morning Robert left early to check the progress of the various new oil wells being drilled, as well as the production of the previous day. He still missed the Wilson brothers' knowledge of the operations end of the business. Fortunately, over the years Robert hired and developed a cadre of capable field managers. Some were natural at learning the business, while others took a lot of training and support. They had a steady turnover rate and at times dismissals were necessary. Some of the dismissals created lifetime enemies of the company, as to be expected.

Two of the terminated employees were real problems. They vandalized their wells and challenged Jack to fight. He refused. One night when they were drunk, Sid and LeRoi ambushed the Jack who grew up in a brawling Irish family. He easily handled the two drunks. Fortunately, several witnesses saw the fight and testified at a makeshift trial at the local Justice of the Peace office who told the ruffians they could get out of town or go to jail. The next morning the local constable released them from jail with the promise they would never return. Apparently Jack beat them severely enough for them to keep the promise and they were never heard from again.

Neither Robert nor Jack ever mentioned the event, but their employees sensed if they screwed up they were finished, but on the other hand if they worked hard, this unlikely pair would treat them fairly and provide them with opportunities to advance.

Three key managers for the oil exploration and production business evolved over time: Ward Roskin, manager of drilling, Tim Harbaugh manager of production and Francois Girard, or best known as Frank, manager of transportation. Ward, tough and hardworking wildcatter could handle any situation rising in the grimy world of oil drilling. Tim methodically managed pumping operations with the precision and coolness of a machine. Frank, the Cajun Robert pulled off the streets of New Orleans as one of the ragged waifs he hired years earlier, worked tirelessly keeping the company's trucks operating and on schedule. Next to Jack, Robert considered Frank his next closest confidant. Not as smart as the other two managers, but he outmatched others in the ability to work long hours and never complained. He proved to be a faithful helper to Robert and Jack until he died in an oil tanker accident at the age of 45. His son Len Girard stepped into his father's shoes and remained as faithful long after the two of them passed away. Len made sure he took care of his widowed mother and went on to provide the same loyal support to Jack's son Jack, Jr. as well. Later in life, wanting a change, he became the manager of the company's ranching operations.

Ward and Tim preferred to play background roles in the growing oil company. They each seemed to dance to a different drummer. Ward a life-long bachelor, much like Robert, would play poker whenever possible, well-known for the ability to nurse a single drink for an entire night. Often outlasting the others until they became tired, drunk or careless to the point where Ward would inevitably win. He would play poker with anybody and as a result often ended up in some nasty fights.

Conversely, Tim was a family man married to his childhood sweetheart from their early years in Arkansas. Quiet, organized and religious, he seemed out of place in the rough and tumble world of the oil fields. Always being fair and honest with his men, they not only liked him, they also respected him. Sometimes after a review of the week's oil production at a local café he and Jack would talk politics and religion. Tim, a born again evangelical, and Jack, a wayward Roman Catholic, spent hours discussing a wide range of subjects. They always respected each other's views. In some ways their personalities were alike. Both were strong physical specimens but also quite cerebral in their approach to their work and their thoughts about the woes of the world. They would discuss books they read, often one referring the other to an exciting new entry at the local library, which seemed to grow much faster than one would expect. Little did Tim know, Robert and Jack, both avid readers, were the major benefactors to the town's library.

Tim often asked Jack if he wanted to get married.

"Not really, I saw so much sadness in my parents' marriage I don't think I want to chance it," he would respond in a rare reference to his early life in Ireland.

And Tim would always have the same comeback, "Someday a woman will steal your heart and you will change your mind. There is nothing like a good woman in your life." Then they would go back to their previous subject.

Robert returned from his early rounds in his seven year-old Dodge pickup truck. People always wondered why, with all his money, didn't he dress decently and drive a newer car? Little did they know he also owned two other beat up old cars used for his secret gold buying adventures. No fancy new vehicles were in his garage.

Jack heard the car come into the driveway and poured a cup of coffee for his partner. When Robert entered the house, "How is it going Robert? Is production holding up?"

"Yes, but I am concerned the market is getting soft. Something is wrong with the economy. You remember the big flood of the Mississippi back in 1928, a real pain in the ass? First the farmers from Cape

Girardeau, MO south to the delta were flooded out for a year. Then the next year they were ready to go and the field hands had gone to Chicago and other northern cities. It seemed nobody knew what to do. Now we have been saddled by the Hoover/Roosevelt Depression. Sure they want to blame Hoover, typical of these 'Commicrats'. Maybe he may have been partially responsible, but look at what is happening now. Now these damn Dems want to break the country with their spending programs. Just wait, someday out of control spending will bring down this country," Robert said in another of his moods.

Exasperated by his emotions he barked, "Jack, you got to get back to working on Zeus," using the code name rather the project name. "You know we need it for our future, maybe sooner than we expect. I want to be in a safe place when the world goes to hell."

"If it is ok with you, I am ready to leave tomorrow. I want explore the set of hills more completely from the southwest side to see how far they extend, to see if there are any more streams available and where the light in the cavern comes from. Also, is there access to the cavern from the southwest where the artesian well is located? But the first thing needing to be done is to get started on trying to buy parcels 7, 8 and 12."

Obviously Jack had been obsessing on what needed to be done and they identified a dozen additional parcels of land forced into foreclosure. If he purchased half of this property, they would own over 17,000 acres, not including any of the mysterious hills. But 7, 8 and 12, the keys to building a contiguous property around the foot of the valley were the ultimate goal. Once acquired, they could then move on to Phase 2. They needed to expand the ranching operations well to the southwest to increase their level of secrecy. The hills could end up being critical to the entire project.

CHAPTER 11

RETURN TO KURSK

At six the next morning, after one of Robert's fantastic Eggs Benedict breakfasts, Jack headed his car back towards Kursk to purchase three parcels of land. He drove until late afternoon, and then found a small area to hide his car settle to down for the night. Once well secreted, he ate some of his sandwiches rather than chance someone seeing a campfire. He thought of the danger of being robbed by a lone gunman or one of the gangs roaming the area.

Jack spent the hour before dark reviewing his strategy with the two banks. The bank in Kursk owned Parcels 7 and 8, located adjacent to the original 960 acres purchased, known of as Parcel 6. The two parcels consisted of a total of well over 1000 acres of fairly fertile land which ran directly to the northwest of the hill for a bit over a mile. Parcel 12 being much less desirable in terms of arable farm land, ran to the southwest along the edge of the southern hills. It consisted of 1650 acres, worthless for farming and with little promise as range land. He had to be careful not to make the banks too suspicious of his plans with these properties being critical to their eventually attaining complete control the south side of the range of hills as far as the ancient volcano. Whether they needed to pursue buying land further along the northwest side of the hills back as far as the artesian well was the subject of many future discussions.

He decided to pursue Parcel 12 first. The next afternoon he drove directly to the Valley Center Bank being careful to make sure no one recognized him as he passed through Kursk. He went into the bank and asked the sole teller to see the chairman. A few minutes later he sat across from Kenneth Peek.

"Mr. Peek, am I correct your bank owns Parcel 12 which is directly to the southwest from Parcel 11 I recently purchased?" Jack said looking directly into the man's eyes.

"Yes, why do you ask" he responded almost speechless from the directness of the lanky Irishman.

"I want to buy it, but it is not worth what Parcel 11 is worth, which is not worth what I paid for it," as Jack played his hand.

He wanted the clueless Mr. Peek to think they had taken advantage of him. The purchase of the 1250 acres of the fairly well isolated Parcel 12 gave him a path to control much of the southwest side of the hills. Parcel 6 to the north and Parcel 11 to the south gave him virtual control of the stream. He could then make his case to the state of Texas for the purchase of the entire valley and set of hills at a future date. He wanted ownership at least to the source of the stream, a tricky proposition, but now he could wait until the right time. He did not want to raise too many suspicions.

"I'll write a check for $19 an acre for that worthless piece of property. $31,350 and there will be no special deals for you and your cronies! And with my history, you should be totally acceptable to taking a personal check on my bank. Furthermore, I won't have access to the deed until the bank clears my check for payment," Jack spit back at Mr. Peek. "Take it or leave it. You have 24 hours and if you don't like it, I'll make sure I deal only with the guys over in Kursk."

Peek clenched his fist and was speechless as his normally pink face turned a bright red in anger. He knew Jack had no sympathy for him. The piece of land, without the easy access through Parcel 11 and 12 had little value and he knew Jack would limit access through the properties he already purchased.

Jack rose and stretched his lanky body then headed for the door. "How do I get in contact with you?" Peek pleaded.

"I'll be at the hotel in Kursk," he responded as he left for his car, wanting to be in a position of leverage. The Valley Center Bank had no more property of immediate interest to him, but he knew the bank needed him as a customer. He would continue with his plan to buy the other two parcels from the Kursk bank, and then determine where their land purchasing program should go next. "Like shooting fish in a barrel," he chuckled to himself.

He spent the afternoon being visible around Valley Center visiting businesses and meeting the owners and their staffs. Lunch at the local café gave him the opportunity to meet other several residents of the town and surrounding area. He remained friendly, but aloof. Finally, near the end of the afternoon, he walked down the dusty street, dodging slowly rolling tumbleweeds, to the local school. There he met Hiram Hammer, the schoolmaster, dressed in a crumpled old black suit accompanied by a nasty gray tie covered with coffee stains and speckled with burn holes from his briar pipe.

After introducing himself as a land investor from the Beaumont area, he asked Mr. Hammer a number of questions, such as "How many students do you have? How many are boys and how many are girls? How many of these children will be able to go on to high school?"

Hiram Hammer stared at the much taller man and asked, "Who are you and why do you ask?" being suspicious of a man obviously not from the area or even a native of America.

"My name is Jack Barnett. I am from the Beaumont area, here buying property and intend to move to the area. I will need to hire some people in the future and am interested in the young people who are growing up in the area and want to stay here."

After twenty minutes of conversation, Hiram Hammer loosened up a bit remaining protective of his students and dedicated to find a better life for them. Jack told the older man of his sincere interest in the future of the area. Hammer, who had taught in the town school for over a decade, remained aloof. He heard stories of the Irishman who seemed to spend more time in Kursk than Valley Center.

Mr. Hammer worried he could not educate his students in a way they would be able to compete in the dire days of the Depression. How could they find jobs if their parents are unable to find a way to support their growing families? Jack spent the next hour explaining how he felt the area could be isolated from the problems of many of the large cities in the nation.

At the end of their two hour meeting, Hiram Hammer began to believe the lanky man with the strange Irish accent may be a positive for the local community. Yet his skepticism remained in the back of his mind.

Jack closed the discussion with, "Mr. Hammer, let me know if I can help your school in any way." He then wrote a check for $1000 to be used for books and materials for the Valley Center School. Hiram Hammer stood in complete shock and thought, "Is this guy for real or is he the biggest conman we have ever seen?"

Upon his return to the hotel in Kursk, Jack went to the local café for a quiet dinner. People in the streets would stare into the café and wonder about this outsider's intentions. It would take years before his plan would totally unfold. As it did, there were those who would be his acolytes and those who would always be doubters.

The next morning Jack again toured the countryside to determine which parcels of land he would pursue next. He purposely ignored any property owned by the Valley Center group. They had three experiences with him and he knew they wondered if there were any other properties they could unload on him. The man from Beaumont tried to ignore them in the foreseeable future, but he did identify one more parcel in addition to the two already under consideration, which totaled another 1800 acres he wanted to purchase from the Kursk bank. These properties provided an additional stretch of land to the northeast of the artesian fed stream.

With the offers made for the properties he recently identified, Jack again 'disappeared'; glad to be able to leave the scene for several days. The offers caused much heated debate among Chairman Wilhelm Steiner and the other four directors of the Prairie Creek Bank of Kursk. They soon realized Jack Barnett controlled more and more of the stream flowing down from the hills through Kursk. Although several other streams merged with it before it reached the town, the purest water came from the hills. Chairman Steiner grew alarmed this man now controlled the source of the river running through their town they took for granted for so long.

"What if he dams up the stream at the edge of his property? It supplies a major portion of the water flowing into Prairie Creek. We will be left high and dry if he used all of the water. I realize this is not a big river, but it is a key to our survival as a town. I say we file suit against this sneaky bastard. He is going to cause of death of Kursk," Wilhelm Steiner barked, obviously upset.

Peter Krueger disagreed "On what basis are you going to sue Barnett? I think it is time to join forces with this guy. He has some sort of long range plan. We are stuck with having our destiny controlled by Washington, Austin and the weather. What the hell does Washington or Austin care about our little part of the world? What control do we have over the weather? This guy may know something we don't know and may help us keep the federal government out of our hair."

Two of the board members agreed with Pete. Unfortunately, Steiner and Rolf Haugen owned almost 60% of the stock of the bank, but they were faced with another offer from Jack and decided not to sue at the time. This time prices were a bit higher than the previous sales consummated, but again they faced an all-or-nothing proposition.

Once this was completed, Jack knew a real battle faced him on any future deals and he believed it would be a good time to further investigate the set of hills he previously explored. Only this time he would work his way around the entire range starting out along the southwest side of the hills. He estimated this would take approximately a week. No towns and farms and few ranches existed in this area. He spent the next day stocking his old Chevrolet for the trip with his curiosity almost as intense as Robert's. He needed to get away from the daily grind of negotiating for property. Before leaving town he sent a telegram to Robert: "Doing the circle!" Robert completely understood the message.

That afternoon, fully prepared for his trip, he walked to the northeast end of Main Street as school let out for the day. At 4PM the students streamed out of the one room school. He waited until the teacher came out of the building and locked the door. His mouth fell open in shock as he recognized her as the young woman he saw several months earlier at one of the first properties he purchased. He thought her to be about 16 years old at the time.

"The cat got your tongue?" Catherine laughed at him. "Are you surprised? Yes I am the teacher. I may look like I am in my teens but I am older than you think."

"I am Jack Barnett" he said "and I am pleased to meet you. Your name is Catherine, isn't it?"

"Wow you are a bright one" she said sarcastically. "People are leery of you. So am I. We don't like outsiders around here and you seem to be a different person than us. We are mostly of German descent. Many of us were born in Europe, either in Russia or Germany. You may be a European but your accent makes you a stranger. Our people are wary of strangers. What do you want?"

"I immigrated to the United States from Ireland through Houston a number of years ago. I love this country. I love the challenge and am a hard worker. I want to help others," He offered.

"Why here? This is the end of the world. Why here?" she quizzed.

"Fortunately I began working for a successful man in Beaumont several years ago. He has been gracious enough to reward my hard work by making me his junior partner. We are disturbed by the Depression and by the politics in Washington, as well as with what is happening in the Europe and Asia. Most people consider us radicals, but we are not left wing radicals like the Communists and the trade unionists. We don't like what is happening. We are pessimistic about the direction of the country, so we have been searching for a remote place for our new home base. If the world keeps getting more unstable, we will move our entire operations to this area," so struck by the beauty and the poise of this young woman he lost his normal composure. Jack knew he said too much.

"Why are you telling me this?" she asked.

"I don't know you just seem like such a special person," he stammered.

She laughed, "When I first saw you several months ago, I thought of you were a real jerk now I don't know. You seem to be such an outsider, but then I heard the kind things you have done for some of our people, including my aunt and uncle. Maybe you are an ok guy." Catherine's parents emigrated from Russia shortly after the turn of the century with her father's younger brother and his wife. Her parents contracted the Spanish flu and died in 1918. As an only child, her aunt and uncle brought her into their family and she grew up with two younger girl cousins.

"Don't you live on the farm with your aunt and uncle?" he asked.

"I used to, but now I just spend weekends there, if someone can pick me up on Friday and bring me back on Sunday night. Our church made it possible for me to go to Odessa for high school. Then the congregation chipped in so I could attend teachers' college for two years on the condition I would come back to Kursk and teach school. I am finishing my third year of teaching and each summer I attend summer school. Next week I leave for the summer."

Jack feeling dejected and tongue tied blurted out, "I will miss seeing you around." He felt like a fool. No woman he ever affected him like Catherine did. Although about 6 - 8 years older than her, he felt like a teenage boy caught with his hand in the cookie jar.

Catherine looked shocked. "What do you mean? Aren't you a bit brash? We barely know each other."

Embarrassed Jack handed her a $1000 check for the school which surprised Catherine even more. "Please don't feel like I am trying to impress you with the money. I gave a $1000 check to Hiram Hammer for the Valley Center School yesterday. It is my intent to help the area survive the hard years and I am a strong believer schools are the key. I did not receive much formal education, but I read whatever I can get my hands on, especially American and European history and anything to do with economics, business and the energy industry."

"Mr. Barnett, you are an unusual person. I don't know if I like what I see or not, but I know the school can make great use of these funds. I just hope they are from the heart and not the act of a devious man," she responded. "I know the people of the area are suspicious of you. For your sake we hope you are not a conman."

"That hurts, but I understand. I am sure Hiram Hammer has the same impression. Except for my business partner and several of our business associates and their families, I have never had any real friends since my childhood in Ireland. I sincerely hope the people of Kursk and Valley Center will eventually welcome me as part of the community. I know my land buying is highly suspicious, but look at the state of the local and national economy. Maybe my business partner and I can make a positive contribution to this area and the people who live here.

He said goodbye and walked back toward the little hotel. The interchange both disturbed and excited Catherine. Something about this man fascinated her. Being away for the summer would be good for her to sort things out.

The next morning, still quite excited by the conversation of the previous evening, Jack realized it was time to get away for a few days before coming back to close the recent land buys. He knew she would be gone when he returned. He wondered how much of a fool he appeared to be the day before and she remained constantly on his mind. Jack packed his car and headed for the property by the stream. The local people did not know of his plans to further explore the strange hills!

CHAPTER 12

ROUND TRIP

Jack spent most of the day cleaning up paperwork. He left Kursk around 4PM and drove to the area where he camped during his initial exploration several months earlier. Taking a lead from Robert, he packed fresh food packed in ice, fully aware it would not last for his entire trip. He set up his tent and cooked one of the steaks he brought along. He had no idea of how long it would take to drive completely around the set of hills, allowing for numerous stops, but planned for a full week. Earlier in the week he traced a copy of the map of the area he found at the county seat in Valley Center, but none of the existing roads in the area passed close enough to the hills to help.

To prepare for the drive in rough territory, he packed four spare tires and tire patching materials, plus an air pump. He threw in a pick ax, sand shovel and winch just in case a sandstorm blocked his car or it got mired down. He also included a kerosene lantern, binoculars, and ten gallons of drinking water. He purposely did not include a camera, not wanting any pictures to be accidentally found.

The next morning he cooked bacon and eggs, packed his tent and started his trek, driving as close to the base of the range of hills as possible. He slowly dodged rocks and prairie dog holes as he drove along the hills, often stopping to look for cave entrances and other interesting features. As usual he made notes and sketches in a notebook purchased during the last trip to Beaumont.

After two uneventful stops he found a small cave, probably created by falling rocks. He showed little interest and went on. Mid-afternoon he drove around a corner and saw an unusual rock structure jutting out from the main rocky hill. It stood at least 1000 feet above the base of the hill and looked like the stern of a ship. He could see a sparse stand of fairly tall evergreen trees across the top of the structure reminding him of the masts of a sailing ship. Jack immediately named the formation "The Hull".

Parking his car, he took his pick, leather gloves, a canteen full of water, plus the lantern in case he found a cave to investigate. About 100 yards from the base of rocky structure, he encountered a large boulder standing at least 30 feet tall. Once past the boulder, piles of large rectangular rocks came into view.

Jack took a long drink of water from his canteen and thought, "They look like a giant's building blocks." After lighting his kerosene lantern he passed through the opening into a cavern so large his lantern did not produce enough light to see the opposing wall or ceiling.

"Wow," Jack exclaimed loudly as to tell the world, "What the hell have I come across? Is this one of a kind or are there others?"

He sat on a rock making notes and sketches, and then proceeded towards an opening between a pair of large boulders. A bit later an opening into what appeared to be another fairly large cave appeared. At first he did not comprehend the size of the cave.

He cautiously entered, wondering what dangers and mysteries lay ahead. The cave interior had a fairly level floor, much like the area where he parked his car. "Hmm, were these rocks thrown here by a large volcanic explosion? What else am I going to find?" he pondered.

For the next half hour he slowly edged himself around the periphery of the cave, came across a passage to much smaller cave, and then made a note it may be a good place to store some gold. He continued around the irregularly shaped cavern, and returned to the opening to the outside.

Fatigued, Jack thought it best not to get too carried away with this discovery. He wondered how many other caves he would find, "I always thought caverns like this would be below the surface of the surrounding area, not inside a set of hills at ground level."

Returning to his car, he sat for a long while making sketches and writing notes, amazed by what he found. Late afternoon he decided to call it a day and took a long nap before preparing dinner. As it got dark, the wind increased creating weird noises as it passed through and around the strange structure rising above him. He started his usual three campfires and set up his tent in the middle of the triangle created by the three fires. After a hearty meal he cooked over one of the fires, he retired for a sound night of sleep looking forward to what he would find the next day.

Shortly after dawn he packed his tent in the car and ate a large serving of scrambled eggs and ham when he realized he drove only about five miles the day before. "Good grief," he thought, "At this rate it will take me several weeks. I don't have that much time and certainly not enough supplies."

The second day went much more quickly, as he saw little of interest for most of the day. He had to change one tire after accidently driving over a sharp rock. Several more short stops were made, but saw nothing of interest. Then late in the afternoon, after traveling another 6 miles, he approached an area with the tallest peak to his right.

"Is this the hill where the artesian well is located?" he asked himself. At this point he decided to stop for the day and do some preliminary exploration of the area. First he set up his tent and prepared his usual campfires without starting them. He then headed towards the base of the large hill, seeing some piles of large boulders similar to the day before. When a storm blew in from the northwest, he decided to return to camp, take down his tent and sleep in the car. Wary of the weather he lit only one campfire to cook dinner.

This turned out to be a good decision. The wind increased greatly about 8PM as Jack hunkered down in the car for the night. The wind rocked the car back and forth. It concerned him he might tip over. He was happy to be parked near the hills and not subjected to the worst of the wind. The skies were not as dark as his previous experience with a dust storm, but the winds continued to rage for over eight hours, allowing him little sleep.

Jack woke about 5:30AM amazed by the large piles of tumbleweeds and sand dunes deposited around his car by the wind during the storm. The sand was dusty yellow rather than black as with the previous dust storm he experienced. His car was partly covered by sand, with several tumbleweeds jammed against the northwest side. After 30 minutes of shoveling sand, he decided it would be best to use the winch to pull the car free. Once done, he ate cold cereal rather than take the time to cook eggs for breakfast. He was eager to see what mysteries he would find.

By mid-morning Jack started his adventure toward the hills along a wide winding pathway towards the base of the large hill. Nothing seemed to pop out like two previous days and he started to get a bit disappointed.

Minutes later, rounding a bend in the pathway, another opening into to the base of the hill appeared. Not as rocky or as big as the previous opening, but definitely an opening. As he entered, he lit his lantern and found another large cave even larger than any of the previous ones.

Edging around the internal periphery he was surprised several times. He found an entrance to yet another cave, wide enough to drive a large truck through, and then another cave larger than could be viewed across with the kerosene lantern.

Jack came to the conclusion there may a whole series of possibly interconnected caves that ran through the range of hills. By late afternoon he decided to go back to camp realizing he forgot to eat lunch.

Being very hungry he immediately started a camp fire to fry the largest steak he brought with him along with boiled potatoes. While his steak and potatoes cooked, he opened one of the few bottles of beer he bought from a local German farmer and sat back mulling over what he experienced the last few days. Still he found no clue to the source of the light he saw while in the cave of the artesian well he found a few months earlier.

After dinner he documented what he had seen. He drew a map of the path he had followed, making numerous notes thinking, "What I have found? Just think how excited Robert will be when I tell him."

After a good night's sleep, he started the 4th day wondering what else lay ahead of him.

Driving another six or seven miles, the terrain became much less difficult. Several stops later he realized he had definitely passed around the far end of the set of hills and was driving across actively ranched properties. He spent the night in a quiet grove of what looked like stunted oak trees. Jack surmised these trees to be much older than they appeared, roots probably growing farther below ground than the branches reached above ground. He later learned the trees were Harvard Oaks. As usual he spent time making notes and sketches. His mind raced as he reviewed the past few days, not wanting to forget anything. He knew it could be a long time before he would have the opportunity to fully explore the areas he had just seen.

The next morning he made a large breakfast, eating as much of his remaining food as possible and headed for the main road to Valley Center. Along the way he found a pond of water where he washed his car hoping not to make the people of either Valley Center or Kursk suspicious of his activities for past the five days.

He ate a late lunch in Valley Center and ran into several people he knew, who were curious as to what he had been doing. "Just out looking at some land," he responded, not telling them what kind of land. Anxious to tell Robert of his discoveries he sent Robert a telegram from the local rail station: "Ring around the rosy. Found a bunch of posies." Robert understood. After lunch he proceeded back to Kursk where he filled his car with gas and bought some food, before heading out to what he named the "RJ Ranch".

CHAPTER 13

TIME TO START RANCHING

It was time to start planning for their ranching operations. A parcel on the south side of the stream seemed to be the best place to start. As he surveyed the area, Jack decided where to build a bunkhouse with a kitchen for the future cowhands he would hire and a barn for caring for sick and injured cattle, as well as for storing supplies and tools. Impressed with the work ethics of the Grauman family he approached Mr. Grauman, "Franz, how would you and your boys like to work with me on my ranch?"

At first Franz took the proposition as an insult. He did not risk his life leaving Russia and traveling to America to this desolate place to be a slave. He answered in his heavy German accent, "Mr. Barnett, are you trying to insult me and my boys?"

"No, my friend, I want to hire the three of you on the following basis. Each week, Monday through Friday, two of you will work for me. You decide who will work for me each day, leaving one of you to farm the land where you live. You will have Saturdays and Sundays free. In addition to decent pay, after the ranch is operating you will receive a steady supply of beef for your family once I can build a refrigerated storage place. What I need to do is to fence several sections of land for my ranching operations. I don't want the problem of having to search for stray cattle. I also need a barn and bunkhouse. At first, we will build a fence around each of four sections of land, feeding stations and a building to store supplies and animals needing care. If all goes well and the economy warrants it, I will have you help me fence additional parcels of land, possibly as many as twelve."

After another hour of discussing his plans and how the Grauman family could fit into the future of the RJ Ranch, Franz began to see the advantage of joining with Jack in his ranching operation.

Jack pressed on, "Better yet, after one year, I will deed your family 80 acres of tillable land which you will totally own in five years. There is no reason to deal with the banks, in particular those guys in Valley Center. I want my business to flourish which is not possible without access to dedicated workers who also flourish. You are overcome by the Depression, drought and dust storms. You came here to build your life and raise your family, but these are difficult times. My partner and I own thousands of acres of land, some of which we want turn into ranching operations and some to remain as farms. I am not a farmer, but there is a continued need for farmers…farmers who will have a way to own their own land again. In time, additional workers will be needed. I will offer a similar deal to them, but your family will definitely be taken care of if our business relationship works out, plus hopefully we can also be friends. You are living the misery of being immigrants living in difficult times. Let me end your misery."

Within an hour Franz, his wife Hilda and their two sons were huddling in their little kitchen to discuss the proposition, with Hilda the most skeptical. The years of struggling with the dust storms and the economic hardships made her leery of anything her husband suggested, but the two sons, anxious to find steady work, convinced their parents they wanted to work for Jack Barnett. They would work for Mr. Barnett for six months, and then decide whether or not to continue. The family never regretted the decision. Over the next 30 years they would become very wealthy and well respected members of the community with interests in farming and ranching. In time they would also own valuable oil and gas property.

Jack finished his breakfast the next morning as the entire family arrived where he pitched his tent. Anticipating their visit, a full pot of coffee awaited them. As the family and sat on empty nail kegs around a makeshift table, they discussed and then accepted Jack's proposal.

Two mornings later a truckload of rolls of barbed wire and posts rolled onto the ranching property. Jack had already purchased the tools and materials required for a three man team of fence builders. The entire Grauman family arrived to initiate the fence building project, with Kurt and Kris ready to work under the direction of Jack, but he surprised them when he joined in the hard work. Jack noticed a smile on the parents faces as they walked back across the bridge. They knew Jack may be an Irishman but he was like them in many respects.

Anyone who ever built fences knew the difficulty, especially working in the heat of a late August day in Texas. The task of fencing the first section of land took about a month. Sometimes Jack left to buy supplies or tend to other business at hand. The Graumans continued to work hard during his absences. Usually Kurt and Kristian worked, but sometimes Franz would fill in for a day or two. The older Franz worked side-by-side and kept up with the others.

Once they completely fenced around the first section of land, primitive buildings, including a bunkhouse with a refrigerated room for storing slaughtered beef, were built. Next the first trucks filled with cattle started arriving. Soon they added a wind charger with a series of backup batteries to provide enough electrical power to keep a refrigerated room cold, supplemented with blocks of ice. The people of Kursk watched in amazement at how quickly everything happened. The Grauman twins were particularly interested in the cattle and dreamed one day they could have their own ranches. Little did they know in a few years Jack and Robert would make sure they would.

Next they started fencing another section of land adjacent to the first. This made sense to Kurt and Kristian, but they could not understand what would be done next. Most of the other land Jack owned did not lie along the stream. They wondered how the cattle would be supplied the water they needed, but soon answer came as they watched the partners' head of exploration and drilling, Ward Roskin, drove a drilling rig onto the property. They did not know of Jack's involvement in the oil business, but they soon understood their new neighbor and Ward Roskin knew how to drill holes in the ground. Within two weeks several water wells were drilled and the piping installed. A truck then delivered a load of steel for building wind mills for drawing water from the wells. Next windmill vane assemblies arrived and were assembled. Soon the wells were pumping fresh water into a series of tanks for the cattle. Watching the rapid flow of events and the efficiency of the team of workers was a new experience for the Grauman family.

It pleased Jack to find a good supply of well water less than 200 feet below the surface. He then knew his plan for large ranching operations made sense. He wondered, "Is this supply of water in any way connected to the phenomenon of the artesian well? Who knows? Someday we may be able irrigate farm land around here."

It got to the point the Graumans expected some new excitement on a regular basis. Soon they were fencing the fourth section of land. Jack told them they had eight more to go for a total of twelve sections, resulting in over 7500 acres of fenced cattle grazing land. At first Jack tended to the needs of the cattle, but then brought the Grauman family and others to help with the ranching operations. Before long they were overwhelmed with the amount of work, making it necessary for Jack to recruit members of additional farming families, such as the Jacob Gruenberg family, on a similar basis as he did with the Graumans.

Initially, they did not realize they created a new form of 'sharecropping' with a unique twist. As they hired each new family into the ranching operations, the family received a similar deal to own a piece of land to farm based on their contribution of labor. Robert and Jack came up with this scheme during the planning of their ranching operations when they realized they would need a number of dedicated workers. They did not want to be involved in dirt farming, but it would be a necessary to the success of Project NewLand to provide food for the animals, plus self-sufficiency for the families of the area which was always the goal.

Less than a year into operations, five families were involved and well over 1000 young cattle had been brought onto the ranch. Trucks brought young calves to one section of ranchland each month to be ready for market 12 months later. Thus, a new shipment of young steers was brought in each month while a shipment of grown steers a year older shipped out each month by truck to the loading chutes they built at the local train station in Kursk. Jack decided it was better to buy young stock rather than try to breed cattle in the harsh environment. Fully grown steers were shipped to meat processing and packing facilities across the south and to the north. Jack could see from the outset some of the parcels of land would support more cattle than other parcels. He supplemented the poorer land areas with hay he would buy from the farmers. Right from the start each farmer had a customer for any hay they could produce. It took several years before they achieved sufficient production and at times additional hay needed to be purchased and shipped to Kursk by rail, and then trucked out to the ranch. Later, the farmers grew enough hay to reverse the trend and sell and ship to other parts of Texas, as well as Oklahoma and New Mexico.

CATHERINE AND JACK

CHAPTER 14

A RIDE IN THE COUNTRY

On a brutally hot day, Jack Barnett returned to Kursk to complete the purchase of another large parcel of land. This land appeared to be worthless and ran for several miles along the southwestern side of the hills beyond the source of the artesian well, but was of great interest to Jack as a result of his recent discoveries in the hills. Due to his and Robert's experience in the energy business they believed oil might be discovered sometime in the future on the properties they purchased. Jack liked the fact it gave them ownership of the entire southern side of the hills. The drought continued and the third dust storm of the summer just ended. Life for the people of Kursk remained grim.

Jack intended not to do any more deals with the Valley Center bank for a while, but they sought him out with a desirable proposition. He first spent three days in Kursk finishing the purchase of several more parcels of land to the north of the range of hills before heading to Valley Center. After these purchases, Jack and Robert decided not to make any more purchases...at least for the next six months to a year. Jack approached the state of Texas at a later date, open to either a purchase or a 99 year lease for the range of hills. They opted for an all-out purchase four years later when the state of Texas saw no value in continuing to own the land.

Famished, Jack went into the local café for lunch which seemed cooler as a gentle breeze flowed from the open entrance to the open back door of the building. Sitting with his back to the door, he did not notice when Catherine Gruenberg entered and surprised him when she walked up and said, "Well, hello Mr. Barnett when did you get back in town?"

Jack jumped his feet, momentarily unable to find the right words, sheepishly saying, "Just a few days ago. Will you please join me? And please call me Jack."

"Sure as long as you are able to speak and you call me Catherine. May I join you?" gently mocking his stammering.

Stunned Jack thought, "My God, she is even more beautiful than I remember." He asked her about her summer as they ate a pleasant lunch with each more comfortable speaking to the other than during their previous meeting. Catherine described her summer classes and said she needed only two summer school sessions the next year to complete her four year degree in teaching. Jack never spoke to a college educated woman before meeting her and seemed ill at ease. Sensing this Catherine turned the conversation to Jack's life experiences. She seemed to be sincerely interested in his story. After a bit more conversation, he relaxed and told how he got to America and of his work since arriving. He offered nothing about his childhood in Ireland and why he left and she did not ask. At the end of an almost two hour lunch, they definitely were interested in seeing each other again and she gave him a piece of paper with her address and phone number.

The only times before meeting Catherine he had talked to a woman since coming to America were in group situations when the women present were the wives or girlfriends of the men also involved in the conversation. Jack always assumed his life would always be so difficult he would live it alone. His perspective on life dramatically changed that day.

A week after his encounter with Catherine, Jack called to see if she could go to lunch with him. Catherine, preparing for the new school year, could not join him that day, but said she could on the coming Saturday as she planned to remain in town for the weekend to be ready for the start of school the next Monday. Friday night he came into town and stayed at the hotel and bought new clothes for the date. Before this he never thought about his clothes or how he looked. Sometimes he did not shave or bathe for an entire week. He even washed and shined his car hoping she would join him in a ride into the country to show her his project, still mostly a dream.

In the morning Jack went to the country and picked a bouquet of wild flowers. When Catherine arrived at the café just before noon on Saturday, Jack stood just inside the door with the bouquet and blushed like a little boy. Even more at ease than during their last meeting, they had a pleasant lunch. As before they talked about their pasts, but now they talked about their futures. They discussed their long-term plans to remain part of the Kursk community. After lunch Jack asked her if she would like to take a drive into the country.

"Why Jack I would love to do that but I only have a couple of hours. What will I do with my flowers?"

Jack replied, "Let's take them back to your rooming house, then we can take our drive. I would like to show you some of the land my partner and I have bought. As you know, I have already hired the Graumans to help set up our ranching operations. I am also helping them be land owners again and intend to do the same for your aunt and uncle. I grew up poor and my sympathies are with those who have been struggling to eke out an existence in this part of Texas."

Catherine said she already knew about his actions, particularly involving the Graumans and the plans for her uncle and aunt.

They started their drive into the country with the car windows wide open allowing the dry breeze to cool them. At first they remained quiet as they drove away from Kursk, to the south of town. Catherine had a quizzical look on her face, "Jack, as I have asked you before, why are you here? What I mean is why did you pick this place? Texas is large and there are much nicer areas. Why here?"

"Good question. My partner and I have done nothing but work since coming to the states, me about 15 years ago, mostly working for and with Robert. He has done the same for well over 30 years since he first arrived from Russia. It took him almost a year to find his way out of Russia, hiding from the authorities, and another two years to get to a port where he got passage as a member of a cargo ship's crew providing translation services. He came from a peasant family on the estate of minor royalty who had a many foreign visitors. He is different, but a smart and caring person. Most people do not like Robert, but they never take the time to get to know him.

He seldom mentions his family, but he has told me about an American, named Douglas Baylor, who visited the estate in the 1890s. Mr. Baylor's parents started Baylor Shoe Company. I am sure you have heard of the company. They remained close friends until Mr. Baylor's death in 1921, several years before I met Robert. Robert learns languages with ease and by the time he got to the United States he could speak not only Russian, but also German, French and English. I can only speak is English with a horrible Irish accent." Jack answered sheepishly.

"I think your accent is cute." she said as she smiled a wide grin only embarrassing Jack even more. "You don't give yourself enough credit. I am impressed with what you have accomplished. I like you Jack, especially your spirit and your ability of always knowing where you want to go and your willingness to help others. You are a welcome addition to our community which has suffered so much over the past several years. Not only is the economy depressed but so are the people. We need a lift."

As they drove past her aunt and uncle's tiny house where she grew up and spent most weekends, they discussed their opinions of each other the first time they met. He told her he thought her to be pretty, but possibly younger than her real age and she looked like she had a snooty attitude. At first being leery of the lanky stranger, she told him she thought of him as just another mean banker or some other outsider taking advantage of the local people. They both laughed.

They went around the last bend on the old dirt road as they passed through his and Robert's ever growing land holdings. As the car drove across the farming area and by the house where the Graumans lived towards the bridge across the stream, Jack pointed at the valley leading to the hills to their right.

"I spent several days exploring that valley. It is a fascinating place," Jack told her in an almost mystical way, but did not tell her more about what he found or that he had driven around the entire set of hills.

He then outlined their ranching plans, but did not mention their goal to build a self-reliant community. They could not tell anyone of their plans. They would most likely be targeted as 'end of the world' nuts. During the Depression years there were many stories of groups, some cults, who went off to the wilderness to wait for the end of the world to come. Jack did not tell her they believed someday civilization as they knew it would change in a negative way.

Before heading back into town, he drove to the mouth of the valley and they took a short stroll along the stream. They stood marveling at the serenity and beauty of the strange hills cropping out from an otherwise flat area of land. He reached for her hand and looked into her pleasant face, then gently kissed her. His act surprised both of them.

She blushed and said, "Jack, I did not expect you to kiss me."

"I didn't expect to either, but I liked the experience very much," he said quietly. Jack never kissed anyone other than his mother before.

Then hand-in-hand they walked back to the car and drove back into Kursk in complete silence, with an obvious change in their relationship. As he walked her to the door of her rooming house he said, "I have to go back to Beaumont tomorrow and won't be back for a week."

"That is ok. School starts on Monday and the first couple of weeks are extremely busy. I have seven new children this year, four are first graders and the others have recently moved to the area. Some of these children have been forced, along with their families, to move in with relatives." She then said quietly, almost in a whisper, "Please come and see me when you return."

He looked into her eyes and said, "I will. I most definitely will."

During the drive back to the ranch, Jack had a hard time concentrating on the many things he had to do the next week. On Sunday afternoon, after the Graumans returned from church he reviewed the work to be done while on his trip back to Beaumont. He gave them a list of action items and the freedom to work the plan the way they saw best, an amazing incentive for the hard working Germans. Each night the family would discuss what they accomplished during the day, both on the ranch and on their farming effort. Life became a joy to them again, as it did for Jack.

CHAPTER 15

ROBERT GOES TO KURSK

Two weeks after Jack's return to Beaumont, Robert made his first trip to the area. Jack orchestrated the entire visit for major impact by talking to the two banks, then to the various business owners and farmers. He made a special effort to make sure Catherine knew the details of the visit in advance so she could help with the preparations.

He wrote an article for each of the towns' newspapers telling a brief history of their strange path to success, emphasizing their belief in the American Dream and their intent in moving their operations to the Kursk and Valley Center area. The articles quoted Robert about how he came to New Orleans with a thirst for success and the belief all Americans should have an opportunity for success. Jack followed with a short narrative of Robert's difficult early life in Russia and how he made it to the shores of the New World. He underplayed his own role. Jack scheduled the articles for issues printed two days before Robert's arrival.

Many old timers in the area, primarily those around Valley Center, remained skeptical about another foreign stranger moving to their area, but the German Russian immigrants were interested in meeting someone from Russia.

Jack rented the largest halls in both Kursk and Valley Center for Robert's visit, with the first meeting held in Kursk. They set up a large buffet luncheon on tables borrowed from the churches and the local restaurant in each town. He worked with the local restaurants and the ladies groups from the local churches to prepare a wide range of foods purchased from Robert's former suppliers. He also brought in trucks filled with ice blocks for preservation of the food. Ice tea, coffee and soft drinks flowed freely on request. Each person who helped received payment for the hours they worked preparing, serving and cleaning up after the events.

There was a tremendous turnout for the Kursk luncheon. Jack made an opening statement, first introducing Robert and then discussing their plans to help the community businesses, farmers and ranchers by heavily investing in the area.

With the food served on long tables, people enjoyed the meal as Robert and Jack went from table to table to greet each guest. By the end of the day a definite sense of acceptance by the town's people occurred, even by the members of the board of directors of the local bank.

The next day they repeated the process in Valley Center, with people less welcoming of these 'outlanders', as they called Robert and Jack. Their jealously showed since they were chosen to be second. Robert explained their intent to build their homes on the land at the foot of the hills just a few miles to the southwest of Kursk. The bank directors thought they were playing 'second fiddle' to the people from Kursk and complained Jack took advantage of them several times.

"I realize you are skeptical, but let us demonstrate our commitment. We are the antithesis of the government," Robert said trying to mollify the skeptics. After he finished, Jack noted a number in the audience did not know what 'antithesis' meant, so he went on to explain the meaning of the word.

At the end of the two days, Robert and Jack moved from the hotel in Kursk to the recently completed bunkhouse by the barn, built with the help of the Grauman men. During the next couple of days they discussed what kind of houses should be built, how large and where the houses should be located. They learned two impoverished German farmers who lost their farms were carpenters back in Russia. Robert hired them to build the houses. They selected a site near the stream. Little did Jack realize Robert's grandiose plans until later, with both houses ending up much larger than Jack expected. The carpenters went on to become successful builders as the area later recovered from the terrible Depression years.

With the Depression still raging, Jack and Robert thought the time had come to review all of their operations. As so often in their history, they knew they had different perspectives, but still had complete faith in each other. Jack went back to Beaumont for the next two months to review and make some changes in their operations. Robert stayed in Kursk and had their houses built.

Jack first capped several wells not yet in production, having his crew be careful in capping the wells and documenting what would be needed to quickly re-establish production at a future date, not realizing how prescient he was, since the problems developing in Europe and Asia were not yet critical to the United States.

After a complete review of the exploration and drilling situation with Ward Roskin, he next spent time with Tim Harbaugh, where he reduced production for recently drilled wells to better meet the level of demand.

He then met with his transportation manager, Frank Girard, to make certain their operations matched the changes in production. In reality, Tim only reduced production by about 20%. Transportation costs were cut by over 30% due to increased efficiencies.

But rather than terminate personnel, he reduced their hours by 10% while promising continued employment and made agreements with local businesses to get discounts for goods and services bought by his workforce. As he and Robert expected, most workers understood, but several employees grumbled. Some quit, which helped the situation, while others threatened unionization. Jack made it crystal clear to their workforce they would resist such efforts.

Meeting with the manager of his boarding house operations was his next priority. In this case, not much change in operations resulted.

Instead of closing any units, he made sure all employees still had a place to stay. As usual, here again a few tried to cause problems.

Last, he picked a crew to do a number of cleanup operations to prepare for the sale of their energy and real estate operations in the Beaumont area. That would be Robert's job. With Robert's strong suit in selling and Jack as a superior buyer, this partnership succeeded.

At the end of the two month period, Jack drove back to the ranch to find the houses almost completed. Much to his surprise Robert built two almost identical structures side by side, only separated by about 30 feet, with one of the two structures quite a bit longer than the other. This puzzled Jack and he asked, "Why?"

"Jack, the smaller structure is yours while the longer one is for me and for our offices. I can see some day you will have a family and may want to keep our business operations separate from your residence. I don't see me ever marrying, but I have met your girlfriend Catherine and you two are destined to be married." He went on, "We can easily add on to either structure, but also, someday we may want to connect the two structures across the front to house our headquarters offices. These are just my thoughts."

At first this puzzled Jack, but as he considered Robert's logic he liked the flexibility it offered. A few days later Robert made the trip back to Beaumont. Satisfied with what he saw of their west Texas operations, he again focused on their business operations in Beaumont.

While in Kursk, Robert used his spare time thinking about the future. The news from both Europe and Asia bothered him immensely. This prompted him to believe the need for the development of NewLand should be intensified and its implementation needed to be expedited. They decided they needed to sell their oil properties and move their headquarters to Kursk. Robert believed another war would increase the demand for oil. He and Jack believed the land they owned still had extensive oil deposits and decided a sale would be the best route for them to take.

Robert negotiated the sale of the oil properties to a single company at a fairly low sales price, but with significant royalties being paid for the next twenty years. This turned out to be a stroke of genius as the economy turned around and WWII loomed. Production dramatically increased over the next five years. Their management staff stayed on with the new owners, but the three senior managers let Robert and Jack know they would move to Kursk at the drop of a hat if the opportunity arose. He then sold the rental properties to a property management company wanting to expand into the area.

CHAPTER 16

THE WEDDING

Catherine and Jack continued to be busy with their work, but spent as much time as possible together, often at the ranch having a quiet dinner discussing a book or some aspect of nature. They were destined and anxious to get married. Picking a date with Jack's frenetic work ethic and Catherine's school schedule proved difficult. The normally brash Jack Barnett amazed Robert how gentle he could be when around Catherine as the romance grew.

Their wedding took place on a beautiful day in late spring. Catherine Gruenberg completed the school year just the day before. The cool weather usually ended in early June and they expected rest the summer to be very hot. Contrary to common belief years later, the 1930s proved to be the hottest decade in recorded history in the U.S.

Catherine wanted to marry Jack as soon as possible. Many wondered why. The gossips of the town were a buzz she may be pregnant. Since the age of eleven when her parents died of influenza, she never had a home of her own. Over the past two years, she and Jack Barnett became very close. They wanted to be together as much as possible...and she wanted to live on the ranch with Jack. Sure, it took a while to get used to the unusual Robert Barzinsky, but she accepted him as part of the package. Soon she also realized Robert adored her and considered her his own daughter more than he ever considered Jack as a son. Jack was always his partner and friend.

They held the wedding on the patio area between the two houses, with the local Lutheran minister performing the nuptials. Catherine's two cousins were her bridesmaids, with Robert in a brand new suit as the best man. A strange sight since no one, not even Jack, ever saw Robert in a suit before. The only solemn moments of the event were the saying of the vows.

Students and former students of Catherine's decorated the entire area and the ladies from the local Lutheran church prepared the food and beverages Jack purchased for the event. After the ceremony the people mingled and congratulated Catherine and Jack. It was the biggest social event in Kursk since Jack Barnett first appeared on the scene early in the Depression and Dust Bowl years.

They wanted a honeymoon, but felt it should not be too ostentatious due to the hardships of the Depression. They drove to Dallas in one of the older Model A Fords owned by the company. Robert and Jack were beginning to be noticed by the media and trade unionists and they did not want any undue publicity. While Jack had been to Dallas a number of times, Catherine never had been there.

They stayed without any fanfare at the beautiful Adolphus Hotel August Busch built in downtown Dallas in 1912. She could not believe the opulence and beauty of the famous hotel nor the extensive menus of the restaurant. When they arrived in Dallas, a city of over 300,000 residents, the area was recovering from a major flash flood with crop losses of over $100,000 locally. This seemed so strange since the city experienced another dust storm a few months earlier.

With the Depression still in full force they walked the streets of the downtown area and drove around city. She heard the stories of how Bonnie and Clyde lived on and off in West Dallas until their deaths in Louisiana just a couple of years earlier. Their brazen bank robbery in nearby McKinney still rattled local residents.

The poverty on the streets and in the neighborhoods bothered Catherine and made her happy not to be living in the big city. She said to Jack, "I am beginning to understand what you and Robert have accomplished and what you have done for our community. Kursk is a gem in a pasture of waste."

Jack smiled at her and said, "Thanks to my venture with Robert bringing me to Kursk."

The next day, before driving back to the ranch, they drove to Ft. Worth and ate at the recently opened Joe T. Garcia Mexican restaurant. They had never eaten Mexican food before and they both loved it. They vowed Mexican food would always be part of their diet. It took many years to convert Robert who had a hard time tolerating the jalapeno pepper. Being a teetotaler, he often joked he would have to take up drinking large amounts of vodka if he ate jalapenos.

The thought of moving to the ranch excited Catherine. Some of the house's rooms were larger than the entire house she lived in years earlier with her parents. While living with her aunt and uncle, she shared a room with two younger girl cousins. She could not believe a man like Robert could do such a good job in designing and building the house they would share, but knew two accomplished German carpenters the designed and built the structures. The kitchen was almost the size of her little schoolhouse where she taught for the past several years. She was further amazed when she realized their wedding present from Robert allowed her to buy all the furniture, dishes and utensils they would ever need.

She immediately took on the chore of setting up their household. Jack lived alone in the house for several years and not lived in the same house as a woman since he left Ireland. Catherine proved up to the task and within a few weeks Jack understood she ran the house. Robert on the other hand still remembered his days as a domestic servant back in Russia, understanding what it took to run a household. Catherine soon realized Robert had more couth than Jack. Over the years he told Catherine more about his early life and his close friendship with Douglas Baylor than anyone else.

The return to the ranch drew Jack back to running their small oil exploration business. The previous year Robert completed selling off the Beaumont energy properties with ongoing royalties and they ended up with more cash than they knew how to invest.

"Robert, what are we going to do with all of this cash? The stock market still looks shaky and I cannot see how we can buy much gold more with the Roosevelt government monitoring our actions. What do you think we should do?" Jack asked.

Robert, as usual, had an answer, "You know I am a student of history. Look at what is happening in Europe and Asia. This Mussolini clown in Italy is saber rattling and the German creep with the moustache is going to put Europe back into a big war and drag Italy with him. Also, Stalin is increasingly dangerous killing and enslaving more and more people. Then, what the hell is going on with Japan and China? Damn, someone is going to invade someone. The world could blow up again, only this time it may end up being worse than the Great War and the world is going to need much more oil and beef to fight the bastards."

Robert sank into one of his moods. Jack made sure Catherine did not see Robert when this happened. She would no doubt be upset to see him in such a frightful state.

But as usual, Robert came out of his dark world with a brilliant insight of what to do, "You know we are almost out of the oil production business since we sold out down in Beaumont, but if war comes we are going to receive a lot more royalties than we are getting now. All we got here are a few wells we are pumping just to keep a few people busy. We need to bring Ward, Tim and Frank to Kursk, but if we don't keep them busy they won't stay. They have been loyal and they tell me they want to re-join our organization, but they have to think about their futures, too. I think it is time to ramp up our exploration, drilling and production. Damn, I don't want to be sitting on the sidelines when demand shoots up."

This was music to Jack's ears. It meant they could move their key people to Kursk. They had the land, the resources and access to the railroad in Kursk. Now they would have the people they needed. He knew they would have to build up a fleet of trucks for transporting the oil to the refineries until the railroads developed the specialized tanker cars required.

CHAPTER 17

WAR CLOUDS RISING

Late 1930s

As the 1930s wound down, the dust clouds began to subside, while the war clouds began to rise. Many countries, including several European nations along with Russia and the U.S., had imperialistic interest in China. But natural resource poor Japan acted first by attacking China in 1937. Japan gained strength on a regular basis in Asia ever since the Great War in the teens and by the early 1930s it controlled Manchuria and Korea.

Being the pawn of China and Japan, Korea was the chess board of Asia for centuries. Sometimes hordes of Chinese would attack by land from the north, only to be followed by hordes of Japanese attacking by sea from the south. Those who have ventured to Korea over the decades found themselves confused over the genealogy of the Korean populace. While many had definite Korean characteristics, others appeared to be Japanese or Chinese. Most were not surprised, when Japan finally attacked China.

At the same time Europe descended into its own unique form of chaos. It started with the ongoing atrocities of the Bolshevik Revolution, then the millions of Ukrainians dying at the hands of Josef Stalin, the sawed-off monster from the country of Georgia. The Great War raged and ended poorly in 1918, only to set the foundation for WWII. Stalin and his cronies exiled millions to the horrible gulags of Siberia. Benito Mussolini had been active in the Italian Socialist Party from a young age, but was expelled during the Great War. He returned and by 1922 he returned as and remained Prime Minister until 1943 when King Victor Emmanuel imprisoned Mussolini. The Germans freed him from prison a few months later to the head the Italian Socialist Republic, basically a German client state. Captured and executed in 1945 near Lake Como in northern Italy by Italian citizens, his body was then taken to Milan and ignominiously hung upside down at a service station to confirm his death.

But Adolf Hitler (birth surname Schicklgruber) was the despot most associated with the worst atrocities of World War II. An unsuccessful artist born in Austria, he left after being rejected by Austrian art circles and went to Germany. A decorated German soldier in the Great War, he joined the German Workers Party in 1919. A riveting orator and political idealist, by 1921 he took over its leadership, but ended up in prison after a failed coup in Berlin in 1923. While in prison he wrote *Mein Kampf*, i.e. *My Struggle*. His NAZI Party, i.e. National Socialist Party, gained a majority position in 1933 and soon became Chancellor. During the next six years Germany rose to be an economic power. But his social and political bent worried Robert and Jack, even though the isolationist Joseph Kennedy, aviator Charles Lindbergh and many others strongly supported the appeasement of Hitler. To Robert a NAZI was just another kind of Socialist with the biggest difference being how large corporations were managed. To Robert a "Socialist" government owned everything. A "NAZI" or Fascist government allowed private ownership of businesses just as long as the government had ultimate control. Most Americans did not realize that Nazism meant National Socialism. The September 1938 appeasement of Hitler by Neville Chamberlain drove Robert into another of his dark moods.

At the same time many in the United States Democrat Party and media strongly supported Joseph Stalin and other Communists around the world. The New York Times correspondent in Moscow during this time, Walter Duranty, constantly wrote of the wonders of the Russian Revolution. Many of the gullible American populace swallowed it hook, hammer and sickle.

This was almost too much for the little Russian who went into a period of serious depression. He saw many atrocities during his childhood and three year trek from Russia to Hamburg before sailing for America in 1900. Not only had he seen the early Russian revolutionary movements in action, this self-educated scholar studied the evils of despots throughout history. Jack strongly concurred, even though his experiences were less harsh. Robert often visualized the threat of another "Vlad" in the future meaning another villain as vicious as V. I. Lenin.

As the rumors of war turned into the reality in both Europe and Asia, the two men became more and more dedicated to moving to the next stage of Project NewLand. They redoubled their efforts by making sure to be part of the economic recovery that brought the United States out of the dreaded Great Depression.

Hitler's attack on Poland on September 1, 1939 further disturbed Robert. With the Japanese attack on Pearl Harbor on December 7, 1941 he was so depressed Jack worried the little man would commit suicide, but this only made Robert angrier and soon he was operating in full attack mode. They let key industrialists, such as Henry Kaiser, and important politicians know they would do everything possible to support the war effort…and support the war effort they did in spades.

It also made it possible for them to invest some of their own wealth to provide the extra human and material resources to build the war effort infrastructure. They believed these could also be used for their survival plan after the war ended. For example, they secretly developed the caves to support the company's storage and production capabilities. The fact these facilities remained undiscovered by the government or spies from the Axis countries during the war years proved the competence of the organization's planning and implementation.

After the war President Harry S Truman commended their effort, but never did he or anyone else from the federal government realize all that transpired near the little town of Kursk, TX. The few who knew were sworn to secrecy. People like the Grauman twins, Klaus and Kris, were keys in recruiting those who would be part of the future survival plans of Robert and Jack. Even with their German Russian heritage, they remained committed to the cause of the Allies and never thought about being supporters of Hitler.

JACK, JR. AND DANE

CHAPTER 18

JACK BARNETT, JR.

1940s and 1950s

Jack Barnett, Jr. remembers when he first realized his family and its close circle of associates were different than other people he knew. He listened as his father and Robert Barzinsky reminisced their early days in Beaumont and how they made the decision to move to west Texas.

His first memories were of the ranch house where he lived and that Robert Barzinsky was always part of his life. His mother Catherine was the daughter of German immigrants whose ancestors settled in Russia over one hundred years earlier at the behest of Tsarina Catherine, who was a German by birth. Many thought of her as "Aunt Catherine". But that changed with Tsar Alexander II, who wanted the Germans to leave Russia. Tsar Alexander was assassinated in 1881 near the start of the revolutionary period, which ended tsarist rule with the Bolsheviks gaining control of Russia over 35 years later. Tens of thousands of these Germans left Russia and settled in the central part of the United States, later the heart of the dreaded Dust Bowl. Many others settled in central Canada. Those who remained in Russia were faced with the Bolshevik Revolution. When the statutes of Tsarina Catherine and other Russian royalty were torn down, Russians knew their lives had changed dramatically forever.

Catherine's family and others settled throughout Kansas, Oklahoma, Texas and adjacent states the last half of the 19th Century and the first two decades of the 20th. Jack, Jr.'s father first saw his mother as a young woman who lived with her aunt and uncle on one of the many parcels of land lost to the banks during those terrible years. She initially viewed him with the same hatred for the vicious bankers who, in her mind, stole her relatives' property

Born in December 1937, Jack Barnett, Jr. grew up prematurely during the war years. By the end of the war with Japan in August 1945, he knew the evils of war. He was also fully aware of what his father and Robert were preparing for in the future. Catherine often worried the lad did not have a normal childhood. Little Jack never saw it that way. He dearly loved his parents and adored his Great Uncle Bob or 'GUB'.

What he did away from the local grade school and recently opened high school made him different from the other children. His parents and Robert regularly read to him from the time of his birth. At age four they realized he could read and soon he was reading to them. His personality grew into a combination of his parents and Robert. He had the easy control of his emotions like his school teacher mother along with the amazing ability to implement plans and control his destiny like his father. He also learned much through osmosis from Robert who he studied constantly.

Due to the need for more security at the beginning of the war, the two houses were joined to form a "J", with the much larger Barzinsky wing since it contained most of the company's headquarters. Living in the great double house with a library of thousands of books, he often curled up in a corner in the house or sitting on a rock somewhere on the vast properties GLO Industries reading a book, totally oblivious of his surroundings. Many times only his mother's strong voice with her unique tone calling "Jack, time for dinner!" could break his concentration.

By his 13th birthday in late 1950 he was immersed in the planning and implementation of Project NewLand and he already knew he would be the person to carry on when Robert and his partners could no longer continue.

Jack, Jr. had a typical formal education. He went through grades 1 through 12 like any boy who grew up in a typical post WWII town in west Texas. He studied the same subjects as his classmates. He played football and basketball and ran track for the Kursk Vulcans, whose most hated opponents were the Valley Center Cowboys. He played end on the town's six man football team and center in basketball. But he excelled in track over the other sports, particularly in distance running. This resulted from his spending so much time running on the ranch and in the oilfields, often leaving his beloved mount Blanco to romp through the ranchland on foot with the family dog Sheba at his side.

As expected, he graduated at the top of his class and received a number of scholarships, which were transferred to other students in his class. In addition, Robert and Jack, Sr. made sure any graduate of the local high school who wanted to further their education at a college or trade school received aid.

The painful shyness of his high school years seemed to melt away when he entered the University of Texas in 1956. Why did he finally come out of his cocoon? Being away from the towering personalities of his father and Robert probably allowed Jack to relax and be his own man. His parents thought he would fold into the anonymity of the university campus, but that did not happen. Jack, Jr. believed his destiny required him to be a serious student who excelled at whatever he did, having the same tremendous thirst for learning as his mentors. He studied primarily science and technology. From a young age he knew his college education would be in petroleum engineering, but also wanted to be prepared for any challenge that came his way.

He enjoyed his college years. He was active in college organizations and played intramural sports, always feeling too committed to the future of NewLand ever to consider being a serious college jock. Jack had casual girlfriends, but once he met Maria Santiago during his senior year he immediately fell in love. He wanted to be with her for the rest of his life, so when she died so tragically a few years later, Jack, Jr.'s life took a dramatic turn. He would never experience the joy of a woman's love again.

After graduating with honors in petroleum engineering, his professors urged him to enter graduate school and pursue a Ph.D. Jack, Jr. had other plans. He knew his life plan would take him back to Kursk and GLO Industries where he soon became the key man in expanding oil exploration and production for the firm. By 1965 production grew at a rate of more than 25% per year. Business writers and bankers pursued GLO Industries to issue an IPO.

Jack, Sr.'s normally taciturn persona, as the main interface to the business world, rapidly evolved into sarcasm as he discounted the possibility of it happening by saying, "I don't do New York."

Robert the planner, now in his 80s, concentrated on converting the vast cave system of the mysterious hills into a sanctuary for the future. After the war, his cadre of dedicated workers began the conversion of each cave from its war mode as needed for the long-term survival of NewLand. His planning methodology provided for continuous iterations as demands required, with a commitment to thorough planning evident, but they all realized that at some point they needed help following the rapidly evolving technology.

Two caves were dedicated for living units complete with their own kitchens, bedrooms, bathrooms and living rooms. They dedicated an area in each of the residential caves to education, initially traditional schools, but years later they would incorporate the most advanced electronic technologies as they evolved. Their educational system became the epitome of computer driven homeschooling around the turn of the 21st Century.

Two other caves were dedicated to food production, including livestock like beef, chickens and swine, plus extensive hydroponic fruit and vegetable growing capacity with another cave dedicated to food storage. This included large supplies of meats and vegetables, which were preserved either by refrigeration or freeze drying, but cycled on a continuous basis to assure foods were as fresh and vital as possible. Foods with long shelf life were used as much as possible, but even these were rotated to assure survival during the longest period of isolation that could result. As expected, cave ventilation and climate control were important factors in everything they did.

The largest caves were dedicated for the oil refinery and equipment storage, including airplanes, trucks, farming equipment, spare parts and materials for resuming oil exploration and production when again feasible.

Two smaller caves were reserved as a library for the information they found essential for the future. Little did they realize the importance of the future 'harvesting' of the vast data on the Internet some 40 years later. A basic library existed in one cave for educational and pleasure reading and the other library cave for the history of various fields from economics to medicine to electronics to energy development and resulting products. Lastly, they dedicated several smaller caves for future uses, such as stores, restaurants, etc. so a normal social order could be maintained. Unfortunately, Robert's death in the early 1970s in his 90s put the entire project on hold until Dr. Dane Madsen contacted the Barnetts as a result of reading Robert's obituary.

As Catherine later related to Dr. Madsen, a Ph.D. in physics who joined the effort after Robert's death, the 'boys' became despondent from losing such a dear friend and close associate. They were also overwhelmed by the tremendous loss to the progress of building the infrastructure of NewLand. Dane proved to be the real brains behind the development of the technology infrastructure of the cave system, essential to long term survival. They also realized at some point in the future other experienced personnel, including a true generalist to be recruited to manage Project NewLand.

Dane implemented the data storage system after the initial efforts by Robert. When he came on the scene only rudimentary computational and data storage capability existed. Before that they had no idea of how to keep up with the rapid evolution of technology. They did know they needed to reserve space for a wide range of technical equipment, including and ever evolving state-of-the-art computational and data storage capability.

Accommodation for spare parts or the means of creating spare parts proved to be a critical part of the planning process. Ironically, by the end of the first decade of the 21st Century some 35 to 40 years in the future, the development and popularization of 3D printers made this much simpler. Dane's people spent considerable money assembling the equipment and materials required for them to manufacture replacement parts for almost 90% of their needs by the early 2000s, and then made sure the remaining parts were stocked. In retrospect, until Dane Madsen arrived on the scene, much of this preparation remained haphazard by comparison.

CHAPTER 19

UNIVERSITY LIFE

1960s

Chip Faraday actively participated in campus engineering organizations from the beginning of his freshman year. One day a quiet professor by the name of Dr. Dane Madsen, who taught him and Rick Christiansen freshman physics, approached him knowing Chip and Rick were conservatives. Dane, nicknamed 'The Little Dane' as a complete towhead as a small child, and later called 'The Dane' as a teenager. In time his nickname became just 'Dane'. Few people knew his real name, Hans Christian Madsen, having been named after one of his Danish grandfathers. One of his prized possessions was a Danish New Testament, with his grandfather's signature inside the front cover. The Physics Department directory listed him as Dr. H. C. "Dane" Madsen.

Although technically oriented, he also studied history, particularly 19th and 20th Century American and European history, as a hobby. His grandparents immigrated to the United States late in the 19th Century penniless but with the will to make a new life. His grandfather told him of the hardships of growing up on an island in Denmark and why at age 19 he left his family, which consisted of his mother, stepfather and a gaggle of half-brothers and half-sisters.

Like so many immigrants, who were the only members of their family to leave the old country, his grandfather seldom talked about his family back in the old country. He regaled Dane with many tales of growing up in a different world working on fishing boats in the summer and going to trade school the rest of the year. A carpenter, he worked in and around various towns in South Dakota and Minnesota. Although Dane's grandfather seemed to be in 'lock-step' with the socialistic views of his homeland, he never lived them. An entrepreneur at heart, he had difficulty adapting to American ways, due to having to learn English as he struggled to survive.

His son, Dane's father, grew up with little opportunity for education and moved to Detroit to work in the automobile factories. He did factory jobs like stacking motor blocks due to his being a large man with abnormal strength. Neither Dane's father nor mother went beyond 8th grade. The stock market crashed in the fall of 1929 and the Great Depression began soon after their marriage. This left his father without a job in Detroit, so he and his new wife went home. They lived a hard scrabble life. Dane was born in the middle of the Depression, a factor shaping much of his life. Never a farmer at heart, Dane always yearned to be somewhere else. Seeing his first B-36 fly overhead on maneuvers between two upper Midwest airbases sparked his interest in physics and engineering. Over several years he established himself as a competent lecturer in the Physics Department. He initially taught pre-engineering students physics, but eventually achieved tenure teaching junior and senior level courses.

Being a life-long student of the history of governmental economic systems, he evolved into a strong capitalist, totally against the trend of academia towards the left-leaning philosophies of socialism and communism. This left him at odds with many of his professorial cohorts, but led him to his friendship with Chip Faraday and Rick Christiansen.

Charles Faraday, Jr. or Chip, had a dark side at a young age and when his father died, he felt the weight of the world on his shoulders. His mother struggled for them to get by as he approached high school graduation. With a SAT above 1400 and good grades, scholarships were never a problem. Chip always worked at least one part time job in high school, as well as in college, to help pay his way. Adjusting to the Twin Cities or to the large University of Minnesota campus were not problems.

Chip never forgot the day he met his first avowed Communist, Mort Murphy, at the University of Minnesota. Chip despised the downright hateful, nasty little man, who attacked anyone who did not agree with him. The son of a pair of uber-left-wing New Yorkers of the 1930s and 1940s, Murphy pissed off Chip from the first moment they met. Mort constantly proselytized for the far left. How he ended up at a major Midwest university puzzled Chip. Even the heavily DFL (Democrat-Farmer-Labor) oriented state of Minnesota could not tolerate his politics.

"Why didn't he stay back east where he belonged?" Chip always wondered. He thought maybe the perpetual Communist Party presidential candidate Gus Hall, being a native of Minnesota, played role in his decision to come to this mid-west university.

Chip was raised in a liberal home, but his high school coach, Mr. Johnson, had a good grasp of American history. Chip's grandparents emigrated from England shortly after the beginning of the 20th Century. He also found Coach Johnson grew up under similar conditions, only with parents who emigrated from Norway. Coach Johnson and Chip's father remained great friends and usually agreed except for one area: Politics.

Both served in the military during World War II, but each came out with a much different perspective on politics. Charles Faraday, Sr. was a committed Democrat, with the coach just as adamantly a Republican. As Chip studied the history of the first half of the 20th Century, he began to question the politics of both of his immediate and extended family. His mother, a Minnesota liberal and a true believer of the politics of the likes of Hubert H. Humphrey kept the family together. As he read his mother's family history, first written by a great aunt back in the 1920s and then expanded by later generations, he wondered why everyone so quickly accepted the politics of Woodrow Wilson, Franklin Roosevelt and Lyndon Baines Johnson. He could understand supporting JFK, a much more conservative President than FDR or LBJ, but not the others.

His grandparents left England with nothing and landed in Boston with nothing, struggling for a future in their strange newly adopted homeland. His grandfather eked out a living as a blacksmith while his grandmother took in laundry for a number of 'blue-blood' New Englanders. Rugged individualists, they never complained.

Chip could not understand what happened to his father, Charles Faraday, Sr., until the family spent hours talking as his father prepared for his death after years of hard drinking and depression. As a youth, his father always seemed to get into trouble. Shortly after graduating from high school he started drinking heavily and one night got into a fight with a young man from the next town. They ended up in court and were given the choice of joining the military or spending time in jail. He joined the army and spent the next 3 ½ years in the infantry seeing considerable action in the war. Surprisingly, the two became good friends during their army years.

Although born and raised in New England he did most of his military training in the Midwest where he met Chip's mother while based at Camp Ripley near Little Falls, MN, a frontier fort named in honor of Brigadier General Eleazer Wheelock Ripley, a hero in the War of 1812. The government closed the original fort in 1877, but in 1929 they built a new Camp Ripley incorporating the original site. At first it was a training camp used only during summers since tents were the only facilities available, later a year-round base where soldiers prepared for fighting winter battles in Europe.

When Charles Faraday, Sr. entered the army in 1942, he could not understand why he would be sent to such a god forsaken part of the country as northern Minnesota in the winter, but during his first pass he met Miriam Baxter at the drugstore in downtown Little Falls. They immediately fell in love and married.

Charles found a home in the army, but at the same time was a tragedy of the Second World War. Spending two years in one battle after another in Europe took its toll. Charles ended up fighting in the Battle of the Bulge in the Ardennes, which left serious physical and mental scars greatly affecting his life. He came home from Europe a beaten man with what would years later be defined as 'post-traumatic stress disorder'. He managed to struggle through college with the help of his devoted wife. The heavy drinking he did in the army continued and affected the welfare of the family. Over the years he kept it together enough to be a good and well-liked math and science teacher.

Chip became fascinated with the grim aspects of history at a young age partly because of his friendship with Rick Christiansen, who was fascinated with disasters and tragedies. Instead Chip became obsessed with how the world seemed to go from one war to another. He seemed to be more worried about the future of civilization rather than with specific disasters and tragedies. Maybe it was because his dad would often go into periods of depression and raged about his misery while fighting in WWII in Europe. Chip promised himself he would not face the same fate. Charles, Sr. would read an article in the paper or hear a piece on the radio about someone's recollection of the war and his rage would again return making it difficult for Chip and his mother to be in the same room with his dad.

Chip, born just a year after the war ended, felt as if he experienced the horror himself. Charles, Sr. responded differently than the fathers of his friends who also served in the war. Most WWII veterans never wanted to speak about the war. Charles, Sr. constantly talked about it.

As a kid he voraciously read books, magazines and newspapers. By fifth grade in school, he read everything of any consequence in the local library. He started going to the Carnegie Library in a town 6 miles away, riding his bike or hitch hiking. He loved the library. The librarian, aware of the constant visitor, made sure a wide variety of books were available to him. He read all of the history related books in the library, including the Greek tragedies as if they were comic books.

Chip had only Rick Christiansen, who studied disasters and tragedies, as a close friend. Why did Rick obsess on disasters and tragedies? No one knew. Rick kept notebooks cataloging diseases like the Black Death and Cholera, major earthquakes and floods, shipwrecks and on and on. Chip, by contrast, created his own track of the history of wars by building what he learned years later in college were flowcharts.

Chip's passion was an intense interest in things going wrong, but he approached them as problems needing to be solved rather than something to wring his hands and worry about. His world view began to develop. Early in life he felt civilization seemed to recycle its problems over and over. Later in life, he made the observation as technology evolved civilization seemed to go backwards, often referring to the Greek scholars. Rick agreed, but lessened his obsession with his hobby later in high school as he became an active hunter and fisherman. The outdoors seemed to temper his dark side.

Most people in the area considered Chip weird, much more so than his good friend Rick. Hunting and fishing seemed natural in rural Minnesota. Chip spending his time alone with a book out in the woods or in a corner of a library did not seem normal. He seemed to be way out on a limb by many of his peers and elders. His views were different than his school mates in his home town of less than 1,000 people. Some of the adults in town made fun of him. His mother could not understand him and his father raged whenever he went into his world view. Was he destined to become an outlaw or an anarchist? What they did not understand was his maturity and genuine concern about the future of civilization from a very young age.

At age 13, at his father's insistence, they sent Chip to a psychologist in Minneapolis, who referred him to a professor at the University of Minnesota, who gave him a bank of psychological tests, including the MMPI (Minnesota Multi-Phasic Inventory), a widely used personality test. The prognosis he was just a different kid than his peers made him angry. This experience only created a greater chasm between Chip and his father.

As much as his experience at the University left a sour taste in his mouth, he decided to go to college there after receiving a sizable scholarship. He majored in electrical engineering.

Meeting Mort Murphy agitated Chip again and his advisor at the engineering school asked him to visit a campus psychiatrist. Chip refused. He told his advisor the rest of the world did not understand him. He decided to keep his feelings to himself about his disgust with the despicable Murphy and dove into his freshman engineering courses. He definitely had the intellectual capacity for engineering school and he decided to only show that side of himself.

Chip found it necessary to always to have a part time job in order to remain in college, including everything from janitorial work to being a draftsman at a local engineering company. In order to get a handle on his homework for the next week, he developed a practice of studying Friday nights after he finished his after class job. He sequestered himself in his room and studied most of the night so he could have the rest of the weekend free. Sometimes he studied through the entire night. This practice and his self-discipline proved to be the key to his getting good grades throughout his college years.

In his senior year he met Sue Hedenstrom, a couple of years older than Chip, who was working on her Ph.D. in nuclear physics. They soon became a couple with many common interests. Rather than following Sue with an advanced degree, he went to work with a local electronics company and supported his wife as she finished graduate school. He had no interest in graduate school. His friends and associates considered this an odd thing to do, but Chip wanted a job instead of more years of college life.

After college Chip and Rick continued their close relationship, but did not work together. They decided it might affect their friendship.

CHAPTER 20

ROBERT BARZINSKY DIES

1970s

Dane Madsen often asked himself, "Why are successful Americans viewed so negatively by the media and those from the political left?"

In the spring of 1974, he heard about the death of Russian immigrant Robert Barzinsky at age 94. He read stories detailing this man's amazing trek from a poor immigrant to a rich man. No one knew how rich he and his partner Jack Barnett were and why they were so reclusive. The two men were vocal regarding their conservative political and fiscal views, resulting in much negative media coverage over the years. The government, starting with FDR, who almost constantly investigated the two men and their businesses, in spite of the significant contributions they made to winning WWII.

This morbid interest in their business activities stopped for several years when FDR died and Harry Truman became president. As a senator, Harry Truman played a pivotal role in working with industry to assure supplies to the military, including oil and food supplies, were sufficient. He also effectively monitored major government contractors for fraud. Few knew the magnitude of Barzinsky's and Barnett's contribution to the war but Harry Truman did. By comparison, the media's attention obsessed on the production of the tanks, airplanes and ships needed. Fortunately media did not pay as much attention to companies supplying the energy and meat necessary for the successful war effort.

These stories fascinated Dane and shortly after Robert Barzinsky's death he wrote a letter to Jack Barnett explaining his admiration for the accomplishments of the two men. Instead of hearing from Jack Barnett, Sr., he received a long letter of appreciation from Jack Barnett, Jr. He thanked Dane for his kind letter. Dane immediately wrote back and expanded on his interest in the Barnetts and explained his philosophy. Another response came from Jack, Jr. who invited the professor to visit his ranch near Kursk, TX. Jack sent him a first class round trip ticket to Dallas and specified they continue to communicate only by mail. This began a long friendship and is how Jack, Jr. learned of Chip Faraday, who one day would be Jack's protégé charged with the future of NewLand and GLO Industries.

The mid-June visit took place shortly after the end of the spring session at the university. He took the 6AM Braniff Airlines flight from Minneapolis arriving in Dallas a bit after 8AM. Dane never forgot being met by a tall lanky, deeply tanned man at the recently opened DFW Airport. Little did he expect he would be met by Jack, Jr., which deeply moved him and he took an immediate liking for the rough-hewn man from west Texas. The timing could not have been better with the father and son in a state of deep depression having just lost their dear friend and mentor. Dane offered a new dimension to their lives.

A skycap in a cart drove them to a remote area of the airport, where they immediately boarded a Lear Jet and flew to the Barnett ranch. Jack piloted the plane for the 90 minute flight as he gave Dane an overview of their history.

Jack said the left-wingers in the U.S. and around the world deeply hated them, but only saw the tip of the iceberg of the significant achievements of this powerful partnership. Few people knew the commitment they made many years earlier to create a structure which would allow the re-birth of civilization after its possible destruction.

The house consisted of more than 20,000 square feet, in the shape of a large "J", and built in the style of a 'bunkhouse on the plains'. Barnett residence was on the left and Robert's on the right, with the headquarters for their wide array of businesses in Robert's wing of the building. The center section consisted of a common area with several rooms, including three rooms for the exclusive use of Jack, Jr.'s mother, Catherine. Exquisite furnishings and numerous souvenirs of the wide range of experiences of its residents filled the house.

When he met Jack, Sr., in his early 70s and Catherine just turned 65, he found them to be active people who fully enjoyed life and each other. Dane immediately understood why Jack, Sr. loved the gracious Catherine so much. Only later would Dane learn the sad story of why Jack, Jr. never married.

Catherine served coffee and rolls to the three men. Then Jack, Jr. took Dane on a two hour tour of through thousands of acres of ranch land spotted with numerous oil wells connected by a sophisticated pipeline collection system. He did not tell Dane anything about the secure facilities located at the heart of Project NewLand, including a fully camouflaged refinery, built during the 1960s, ready for use when needed at some future date.

Back at the house they ate a late lunch of BBQ beef, home grown vegetables and strong coffee. Afterward the father and son motioned Dane to come back to their den, an expansive room with many hunting trophies, a pool table, a wet bar and a conference table. He soon got to know them as 'SR' and 'JR', which made things easier. Everybody referred to them in this way except for Catherine who would say Jack in a way everyone knew who she meant.

As they enjoyed a cold draught beer, the grilling started. "How did you hear about us? What do you know about our family and Robert Barzinsky? What do you know about our political views? What are your political views? What do you think of Richard Nixon?"

They went on and on. Dane's head spun as they peppered him with one question after another. They obviously planned for his visit. It turned out they researched Dane Madsen like no one had before.

Dane wondered, "Do they represent a government agency, and if so, from which country? Had he misjudged these people?"

The interrogation puzzled Dane, but then JR explained, "Dane we are sorry to put you through the 3rd degree, but it is because we like you. Our family and Robert have been concerned for decades about the state of the world. We have learned you have similar views. Most people consider us nutcases, but we believe it is our duty to be prepared for a time when civilization as we know it will collapse. When? We don't have any idea of when. We just believe it will happen someday."

He continued, "Why should we play this role? We have more wealth than anybody could ever need. We have resources accumulated through many years of hard work plus a lot of good luck. We like our little town and neighbors. Our research of you and our correspondence shows you share many of our ideas. They are going to label you a kook, too, if they haven't already. We want you to consider being part of our organization, not here at first, at least until sometime in the future when you get tired of the idiocy on the outside. You would be our first outside management recruit. We are looking for a tight cadre of like thinking people. We are interested in you with your depth of your knowledge of the trends in technology development and the people you know."

In a state of shock, Dane pondered how the Barnetts knew so much about him and how he thought. Dane looked both confused and exhausted. JR said, "Let's call it a night. Think about what we talked about overnight and we'll pick up our conversation again in the morning. If you don't want to go any further, no problem. All we ask you give us your word none of our conversation is discussed with anyone...ever unless you join our effort."

"I understand. It has been a long day," he replied and he went to his room in the Barzinsky Wing. The room was nice and outfitted with a new 27" color TV, quite a device for the time. He was amazed to see the ranch with access to satellite TV, just introduced a few years earlier with a significant number of channels available, some foreign. Exhausted, none of this interested him.

He went to bed and noticed the complete silence of being out in the country and thought to himself, "What have I gotten myself into? Is this for real? These guys think like I do."

He thought of his wife back in Minneapolis. "If I get involved with the Barnetts, will I ever be able to tell her anything? What about my friends and relatives? Could I be getting myself into something sinister?" His mind raced on and on till he fell into a deep sleep sometime after midnight.

He woke in the morning with dawn breaking through the windows to the east. He felt remarkably refreshed and clear headed. A new pathway opened allowing him to think about his worldview. As he entered the front area of the house he found the three Barnetts deep in conversation about one of Catherine's charities.

"Excuse me, I didn't mean to interrupt," he said sheepishly.

"No problem. We are just finishing our plan for funding our Vietnam Vets program for the remainder of the year. Someone has to make up for those horrible protestors. Someone has to help these poor guys who are coming home to the likes of Jane Fonda and these other creeps," Catherine offered. "Ready for some breakfast? Bacon, eggs, toast and coffee ok? These two lugs are always up early and have already eaten, but you can join me. They have a couple of things they need to take care of this morning. They'll be back in about an hour."

"That would be great. Can I have my eggs over easy?" he said looking famished.

Within 15 minutes the Barnetts' cook brought him a pot of hot coffee and his freshly cooked breakfast. As he ate, Catherine told him about the area around the house and how it changed during the almost 40 years she lived on the ranch. She explained how it had been expanded to manage the growth of the extensive business enterprises of Robert Bazinsky and the Barnetts.

It was a typical hot June Texas day with the air already shimmering. Even though the house looked rustic from the outside, inside the HVAC system and the insulation were obviously of high quality. Dane observed how these people managed their lives and thought, "They run a class operation."

Watching Dane's fascination in the house, Catherine broke in, "You probably wonder why we just didn't have it torn down and start over. You just have to understand where Jack and Robert came from and how they got to where we are today. They have never thrown anything away or torn anything down. These guys lived in extreme poverty long before the Great Depression. Since Robert passed away it has been like a morgue around here. You don't realize how your coming has perked up the boys," almost talking like they were both her sons.

She related how Robert immigrated to New Orleans from Russia via Hamburg as a young man and how the owners of Wilson Oil Company in Beaumont asked him to move his food service business to the oilfields of south Texas several years later. Being frugal Robert did well and became rich within a few years. Several years later the brothers got into financial trouble and Robert soon owned a large share of the business, then sole owner after an oilfield explosion.

She went on to say Jack emigrated from Ireland in his teens and worked for Wilson Oil, which eventually became GLO Industries, after Robert gained full ownership the business and was stretched so thin he needed help managing his businesses. Most of the roustabouts were just that…roustabouts, with little ambition for bettering themselves Most did not have the intellect or the interest to play a major role. Robert spotted Jack as a hard worker and soon realized Jack was a bright young Irish immigrant full of himself. Robert saw Jack as a diamond in the rough and the rest is history."

Catherine continued, "Robert was the closest person little Jack had to a grandfather, but for some reason Jack always thought of Robert as his great uncle. They adored each other giving him the advantage of learning from Robert's incredible intellect, his father's common sense and the tremendous work ethic of both of them with every day like a day at a university for young Jack. Whatever you do Dane, never underestimate either of them."

As soon as the Barnett men exited from their office to rejoin them, the three men immediately returned to the conference room and continued the conversation of the night before. Both sides wanted to go forward with a professional relationship and they drew up a confidentiality agreement. Told he could get outside legal counsel if necessary, Dane decided to go ahead without an attorney, even though his wife was one. The Barnetts said they did not involve an attorney either due to the nature of what they would discuss. They drew up a simple four paragraph agreement: 1. Confidentiality statement, 2. What Dr. Madsen would do, 3. What the Barnetts would do and 4. How either side could end the agreement. This lack of complexity appealed to Dane, a great believer of Ockham's razor: the simplest solution is best solution. They eschewed bureaucracy to the nth degree.

SR said, "Neither of us is an attorney or a politician but we are technically oriented. JR has a petroleum engineering degree from the University of Texas and I have a degree in 'hard knocks' from one of the best teachers to ever walk the earth. You have very different education and experience than the two of us. We know the rough and tumble world of the energy industry and ranching. We see you as our bridge to the evolving technologies we know nothing about."

"Now that is out of the way," JR offered, "Let's talk philosophy. Many things are happening. We need a cadre of key players who will help us continue and manage the concept of Project NewLand, which is the name we have chosen for our future world. As we told you last night, we consider this our outpost for preserving the future of civilization. In effect, this is Ground Zero, physically and philosophically. Other than with you and few others, we will never use the word NewLand. Instead it is always referred to the code name Zeus, Robert's favorite member of Greek mythology because Zeus was the god of law, order and justice. We want to be ready to create a survival link for civilization as we know it. There are those, we are among them, who believe virtually all life, not just the dinosaurs, has been extinguished before. We want to protect against it happening again. It would take too damn long for evolution to recreate a workable civilization."

The conversation went through an overview of how their plan evolved since 1930 when Robert and Jack first believed someday they would have to dispose of their business interests in the Beaumont area.

They discussed their strong beliefs about how socialism and communism evolved. Both had enough of the royalty in their respective countries, too. But the Bolshevik Revolution proved to be the major factor in the development of Robert's philosophy, even though he left before it actually took place. They wanted to live in a free world. They also wanted to help others achieve success, too.

After over 10 hours of constant conversation, they nailed down Phase I. JR said, "I think this is enough for dad today."

"The hell I have you young pups," SR said and they broke for a nightcap before going to bed.

CHAPTER 21

ROLE DEFINITION

The next morning Dane joined them early. This pleased SR to no end. "This guy is no piker," he thought.

They discussed the history of the Cold War from the end of WWII to the present over breakfast. Then SR offered, "We need someone with the cajones to stand up to these 'Commiecrat' bastards. I am so sick of this chicken shit treatment by our politicians, and it doesn't seem much different if it is Democrats or Republicans running the country.

For example, this Watergate mess has not done us any good. My god, we've come to a dead stop over a 3rd rate burglary. No one has died. Nixon made some stupid mistakes, but look at some of the interesting things he has done, like opening up a relationship with China, thanks to Kissinger. No doubt the Kennedy assassination shocked our nation, but we have bounced back like we always have. Hell, look the political shenanigans we have seen throughout our history. Look at the tremendous burden LBJ's 'Great Society' has placed on the tax payers of this country. I'll bet this so-called 'War on Poverty' is going to end up costing more than all real wars. It is going to trillions of dollars spent with negative results and we will eventually have as many, if not more, poor people than when LBJ started the whole mess."

After an hour they decided they were only banging their gums and could not change things. They moved to the main conference room to continue their discussions. Their completely relaxed mood and sense of organization surprised Dane. He observed they apparently ran a well-oiled business organization. Few interruptions occurred to tend to the oil or ranching business operations during his entire stay. In time he came to realize how the Barzinsky-Barnett team operated so efficiently over the years and smoothly managed an ever growing business empire worth billions of dollars. How big? Nobody but the Barnetts knew. During their discussions, Dane learned how the organization could be so efficient and effective. Robert, up till the day he died, retained the extreme discipline in all he did getting to America and continually applied it to his everyday life. Not only that, he was such an effective teacher his methodologies were universally adopted throughout the organization.

They started the third day talking about the resources at their disposal. Then Jack, Sr. explained why they selected this location. He told of his exploration of the stream up through the valley to the hidden artesian well inside the old volcano which supplied the water for the stream. He then told Dane of exploring the array of large caverns along the south side of the extinct volcano. They could secretly store the vast amount of gold they accumulated over the years...it was their own Ft. Knox. Dane knew they owned a considerable amount of gold, but no idea how much.

More importantly they estimated up to several hundred people could be protected in these caverns for a significant period of time, perhaps decades. They also realized the nature of threats would most likely change over time.

JR then explained that was why they were so interested in Dane joining their efforts, "Dane, you have your ear to the world of technology. You understand the evolving technology end of the spectrum of human knowledge. You will no doubt need help in time, plus at some point we need flush out a full technology implementation team. That will take a unique individual to head up those operations in preparation for when all of us in this room, except maybe you, are dead and gone. Keep your eyes open for this person. Others, especially technical people, will be needed, too."

Dane thought to himself, "Hmm, this young guy Chip Faraday may fit the bill, except he is green and needs to grow a bit and we may be able to use Rick Christiansen, too."

Then JR told Dane of the secure small oil refinery they completed several years earlier. It took almost a decade to design and build without the effort being detected. He said it could survive a nuclear explosion if it doesn't get a direct hit, but he was concerned some other natural or manmade disaster would destroy their efforts, such as a pandemic disease similar to the Black Death of the Middle-Ages. They discussed several scenarios where contagious diseases could spread out of control. Earth could also be hit with a significant meteorite, although a remote possibility.

He continued, "Fortunately for the nuclear disaster scenario, we have the talent to deal with this with our staff which has managed the construction and operational capabilities within our organization going back many years. But if non-petroleum energy sources are required, we are going to need people of your ilk. Who knows what else in the way of weapons, could destroy civilization may be in the works?"

SR went on, "Do you know the name Joseph Schumpeter? He was a Czech born economist, at one time in the Austrian government back around 1920, but he spent much of his life as a Harvard professor. He was one helluva an economist. He believed Capitalism would be destroyed by Socialism and Communism in time if they are not checked. We don't want that to happen. He also expounded the concept of 'creative destruction' as new technologies and products evolve. For example, the automobile destroyed the buggy and buggy whip industries. We strongly believe we need to prepare a group of people to re-initiate civilization after it is destroyed by some evil force, including a natural disaster, Socialism, Communism or maybe some wild ass religious force. It is only a matter of when. Robert believed it would most likely not happen in his lifetime, but it did not dampen his belief it would happen someday. I agree. In fact, it may not occur in any of our lifetimes...but it will happen.

Schumpeter believed Capitalism sparked entrepreneurship and entrepreneurship was the key to invention. The competitive nature of Capitalism is what drives invention. The other economic systems are a drag. Looking at other governments over history, they always collapse and someday ours will, even if we are careful. This time it could be a very destructive collapse. We now have the means of destroying civilization. Greece and Rome were examples of the most successful governments in history, but they did not last forever. Look at Hitler and his claim the 3rd Reich would last 1000 years, instead it lasted less than a quarter of a century. I believe the United States is good for no more than another 40-to - 60 years."

Dane responded, "That is a pretty grim prediction, but I don't disagree with you. It may surprise you, but these two young engineers who were students of mine don't think much differently than we do. These are people I need to watch for future recruitment."

They ended their third day with a couple of rounds of single malt scotch, a few jokes exchanged, and then JR asked his dad to tell Dane about the early days in Beaumont. "Dad, tell Dane about your first impression of Robert."

SR took a long sip on his scotch looked up towards the sky, as if to ask Robert for permission, and said, "He was the most unusual man a person could ever know, a pitiful physical specimen. Obviously he lived through severe beatings as a child or young man, but he had a look in his eye that immediately told you this was no normal individual. I have no doubt Robert Barzinsky was the most intelligent and driven man I have ever known. He certainly did not have much in the way of formal education or personal appearance, but he could grasp concepts better than almost any Ph.D., no insult intended Dane. Even though he never lost his rich Russian accent he could speak at least seven languages. His ear for understanding a foreign tongue was just plain incredible."

He went on, "I have not known anyone as well read as Robert. Our coming here has been an absolute boom for this little town.

Before you leave, you must visit the local library I mentioned yesterday. The townspeople wanted to name it the 'Robert Barzinsky Memorial Library', but he would have nothing of it. Since his death that has been rectified. Knowing Robert as well as I knew him, he is probably cursing us from his grave. Currently it is one the best libraries in Texas west of the Dallas Public Library. Hell, it may be better stocked and it is still improving.

Robert turned into a wild animal whenever a new opportunity arose. He took the Chinese approach. There was danger in every opportunity and opportunity in every danger. In our partnership, he was 70% concept and 30% action whenever we faced a new situation. By contrast, I am 30% concept and 70% action. Robert's death has left a big void in our operations, but now JR is filling the gap. It is joy to have such a savvy young partner who also knew my old partner so well."

With a quick nightcap they went off to bed. They left the meeting with a sense of satisfaction with what transpired the past three days. When Catherine asked her husband how things went, he responded with a broad grin.

Dane got up early on the 4th day to expound his philosophy and what he thought the future would bring. As usual the Barnetts were already at the breakfast table when he arrived.

Catherine joined the meeting being interested in what Dane had to say. Dane started his presentation by giving his family history and how he evolved into such a conservative. He explained his growing up in a liberal home and that his parents married at the onset of the Depression which impacted their life immensely.

At the end of this introduction he said, "Even though I am a product of the Depression I have always felt out of place with liberal philosophy, something I confirmed when I got to college and started meeting people with a wide range of political views, even though I was immersed in a technical education."

He went on, "This change of philosophy took several years. It created a large amount of stress with my family and to this day I am told by some relatives I violated my family's liberal ethics. When I began to study the interaction between the development of technology and civilization, I found technology advances on a fairly regular basis. On the other hand, it was obvious to me civilization does not evolve at the same rate. In fact, often civilization devolves to an earlier state, and then some outstanding leader comes along to get things back on the right track. I consider National Socialism or Nazism as a prime example. Germany reverted to the barbarism of a much earlier time when they killed anyone not fitting their warped philosophy. Just look at the Crusades and the wars leading up to them?"

Catherine interjected, "Are you saying the Christians were so brutal? I find comparing the Christians of the Middle-Ages to Hitler and the Third Reich a bit extreme."

Dane came right back, "Study wars throughout history. Most were fought in the name of religion. For example, Muslims waged many wars against Christians for several centuries before the Crusades began. Life was miserable except for a privileged few. Not until technology allowed a better life for the masses did the life of man improve. Poverty and misery have been the lot of the common man throughout most of history. I believe this has only changed with the onset of the industrial revolution, regardless of whatever perceived problems it has caused. Now this does not mean many bad things have not resulted from new technologies. In many respects, wars today are more brutal than earlier wars. They are more brutal on a grander scale. But look at what people have today compared to just a hundred years ago. Even the poor today are almost always better off than the poor of two hundred years ago and the poor in our country are better off than the so-called middle class of many other countries."

JR asked, "What is your point? What are you driving at?"

"I am trying to say the evolution of technology must be monitored for a number of reasons. New technologies can definitely improve the life of man, but bad things can happen, too. Just look at what the discovery of electric light bulb has done. There are those who believe in the long run our use of electricity has led to evil applications and results, for example the electric chair. Atomic energy is an interesting example.

Granted its initial use inflicted incredible damage to two cities in Japan. As terrible as those acts were, those bombs played a major role in the ending of WWII. Just think of how many more millions of people would have died if the war had not ended at that time. Conversely, just think of the horror if Hitler developed the atomic bomb first.

Now we have a number of great applications of nuclear technology, not only nuclear power in our submarines, plus space and similar applications which have evolved. Consider the medical applications. I have a number of thoughts about what role nuclear power could eventually play for NewLand, whoops, maybe I should continue to use the code name Zeus. On the other hand, there are those who will vigorously oppose the use of nuclear power for any use. This opposition comes in many forms. For example, the anarchists will probably join with the left-wing political philosophies since they are against capitalism improving the lot of the common man. The trouble with these kinds of movements is there is always some tyrant who won't play by the rules. Just look at the horrors of the Communist regime in the USSR during the 20s and 30s. It could happen again and again. Also remember Adolf Hitler was a member of the Workers Party, not a right wing movement the leftists want you believe."

"What I am driving at is I believe the evolution of technology must be monitored constantly to make sure no more dictatorial regimes use these advances to dominate civilization," Dane added.

The three Barnetts looked a bit perplexed, wondering, "What is this guy trying to say?"

Dane continued, "I see my role within the organization is to keep up the organization up to date with a broad range of technologies, from energy to food supply to shelter to assure our long term survival. We must be constantly diligent. We need a turnkey approach to managing our future. We must incorporate new technology at the same, if not at faster rate than the rest of society. This will not be an easy task, but I believe it is an important task to be done on an ongoing basis."

JR jumped to his feet, "Right! Right! You are exactly right. You have no idea of what a nerve you have just hit. We have constantly worried about how we keep abreast of the rest of the world. It makes me think of the Middle East. Hundreds years ago the Arabs led in the development of science and technology. For example, they created our number system. Go to the New York Metropolitan Museum's Middle East wing and you will be amazed by their culture, architecture and technology over a thousand years ago. But then something went wrong. For some reason the advancements stopped. Why this happened I don't understand."

Dane went on, "I have never been there and I don't have any experience with that part of the world. I did know a Sudanese man who went to Saudi Arabia to work for the oil company Aramco as a young man back in the fifties. An American doctor who worked for Aramco realized this young man was bright and arranged for his immigration to the United States, and then paid for his engineering education. Mohammed told me several anecdotes of the backwardness of the average Saudi. It bothered him to see the wide economic and social gap between the upper class, specifically between the royalty and the common man. He never mentioned the lot of women, but I noticed he didn't take long to meet and marry a young blond woman from a small Minnesota farming community and have a number of kids."

Dane then stopped and took a long drink of water, "I also had a college friend who married an American educated engineer from Jordan. They went back to Jordan for a while. This gal had a strong personality and a few years later I heard they returned to the United States. I think in retrospect it must have been frustrating for a person raised in America to go to that part of the world, particularly a woman and just as remarkable, if not more, for this young Jordanian to make the move to western civilization."

Catherine excused herself to go to the kitchen to check on lunch. SR said, "My butt is sore, how about we break, too."

The night before a front with good rain blew in from the southwest and it was quite cool for a June day around Kursk, Texas. Catherine set up on the large patio in the shade between the two wings of the house.

The ice tea tasted great to Dane, thirsty from the long presentation of the morning.

SR began the luncheon conversation with, "See the barn, bunkhouse and sheds off to the east? Those were the first structures we built back in the 30s. Then these two houses were built side-by-side, one for Robert and one for me. Over time they increased the length of each and joined the two houses across the front at the beginning of World War II to form the J configuration you see today. We first fenced this section of land and grazed our first herd here. This is also where I proposed to Catherine, totally frightened expecting her to turn me down. Hell, she had so much class being college educated and me nothing but an uneducated ruffian from Ireland."

"Jack, I heard that, you were not uneducated, even back then. You just needed a little spiffing up. As I got to know him, I realized formal education didn't mean much to a guy like Jack. He has always had this burning desire to learn. It is just one of the qualities I fell in love with years ago."

They obviously still loved each other.

After a relaxing lunch they returned to the conference room and Dane began to delineate what he thought he could do for the project. "Allow me to outline some of the considerations I think are crucial to the success of Zeus. The major categories we must consider are: 1. Food and other supplies necessary to sustain life for the population of the enclave. 2. Energy requirements for the long run, which may mean more than just oil, natural gas and, even nuclear and solar power. 3. Safe shelter for the population, any food animals and pets, plus storage for equipment and tools, as well as vegetable growth and storage for all foods. 4. A range of scientific laboratories, including medical personnel and facilities, to continue developing new technologies, as well as the required shops and repair facilities needed. 5. A complete program for the physical and mental health of the population of Zeus. And last, 6. A complete library stored on at least two, preferably three types of media which probably haven't been invented yet. This last one, as you mentioned earlier, is critical to long term success, as well as helping us tough our way through the period of potential confinement in the caves. We must also be able to create a new 'norm' for civilization."

He took a break for a sip of water, while the Barnetts sat there in silence. They knew they just found a new member who would prove essential to their success. JR spoke first, "Dane, I am in awe of what you just said in so few words. It is obvious you understand the job at hand. I welcome you to NewLand. In fact, I wonder how long before you find it imperative to join us here in Kursk."

"Thank you. I wonder the same thing. There is much that needs to be done before I join the project here in Texas, but someday it will be my home," Dane responded.

It had been a long, but important day. Dinner consisted of large T-bone steaks and vegetables cooked on an outside grill, with an ample supply of ice-cold long neck bottles of Lone Star beer which they drank to the music of Marty Robbins' *Streets of Laredo* blaring out from a series of outdoor speakers. They were exhausted, but satisfied with the discussions of the day. The next day, day five, they would introduce Dane to the extensive series of caverns and the camouflaged power plant.

The evening ended with a discussion of religion. Jack, Sr. retained much of his reverence for religion even though not a practicing Christian from the time he left Ireland until he met Catherine. Over time he converted from his Roman Catholic childhood to be a German Lutheran like his wife and in many respects more religious than Catherine. Jack, Jr. lost interest in religion when the young Hispanic woman he loved was raped and killed when a bunch of drunks from Valley Center came upon her stalled car. They left her body along the road. Jack, Jr. never recovered. His mood turned dark, his humor caustic and his demeanor all business.

He met Maria Santiago during his senior year of petroleum engineering at the University of Texas in Austin. She came from a Hispanic family living in San Antonio since before the Alamo. Her great-great-great grandfather fought against Santa Ana and his men. He returned to San Antonio to start a grocery store after the war with

Mexico ended. Maria had excellent grades in high school and received a full scholarship to the University of Texas where she studied political science.

The county prosecutor tried and convicted these men. They ended up being executed Texas-style, but Jack, Jr. never recovered from his grief. To survive he threw himself fully into the company's oil exploration and production operations where he excelled. Within a couple of years he had total responsibility for energy operations. Many who got to know JR did not know what happened. Little did they know of the guilt and sadness he carried with him, since he blamed himself for letting her drive alone at night. He always kept in contact with her parents until they died many years later.

Jack, Sr. and Catherine worried constantly about him. After several years he came to the realization Robert's and his dad's gigantic business operations and would eventually be his responsibility. This meant he needed to carry his share of the load.

CHAPTER 22

WRAP UP

As soon as they sat down for breakfast the next morning, the cook placed a large tray loaded with breakfast tacos on the table. During his few days on the ranch he became a fan of the food of the south, in particular, Mexican food.

"How did I ever live without the wonder of the jalapeno?" he thought as he took his first bite. It seemed like there was something magical about life in the presence of these fascinating people who lived a much different life than his.

The Barnett men and Dane started out in a Jeep about 9AM. They first traveled through the major oil fields and explained their exploration, drilling and production operations in straight forward terms, with much more detail than the brief tour of the first day. Periodically he would ask, "What is that over there? Why do you do this this way?"

Each time one of the Barnetts would answer in a way Dane felt like they made him a part of their organization. Next they explained how they collected and transported crude to the railroad in Kursk. At first hundreds of trucks transported oil. Outsiders had no idea of the vast array of materials and equipment brought onto the property. Pipelines changed the entire operation in the 1960s. No one who was not a part of the operations knew of the infrastructure being built for a future time.

They made a quick stop back at the ranch house for a cup of coffee. Catherine placed a lunch basket with sandwiches, fruit and coffee in the Jeep. Dane's realized they were going to be out for a number of hours.

JR got back into the driver's seat and said, "Dane, we are now going to show you the heart of our future." Without any further explanation the Jeep sped off towards the south side of the range of hills he wondered about since his arrival just a few days earlier.

"Back in early 30s, Robert and I decided ownership of considerable land in a remote area was the key to our future. As so often in our many years of working together, we didn't know how it would end up. Robert always attacked the unknown. This approach always seemed to work as long as we didn't panic when something didn't work as planned," SR said.

He went on, "Robert planned constantly even though most plans never work out the way they should. He always planned so when something went wrong he had a frame of reference for going forward. He believed, if you did not plan, you faced a continuous series of re-starts. He established this approach when he first left his home in Russia. He knew he could never go back home again. He knew it would mean prison or something worse. Knowing he could never go back once he left, that is how he lived his life.

I spent most of a year wandering around Texas looking for places for us to settle and restart as ranchers, but always with the intention of re-entering the oil business in the new location. I just had a burning intuition oil would be found here just like in southeast Texas around Beaumont. I remained frustrated until I found Kursk and Valley Center. Frankly, at first I thought Valley Center would be where we settled, but fortunately the bank there owned a considerable amount of foreclosed land around Kursk and we chose to establish our base here, much to the chagrin of many of the people of Valley Center, especially the local bankers."

He laughed and said, “That was an interesting experience. I found a large number of parcels of land around this strange string of hills owned by these two banks as the result of a number of farmers going bankrupt. The region fascinated me and as I explored the area, I met a number of the German Russian settlers and their families. A strange kinship evolved as I started buying pieces of land. To this day most of our original employees and their families still live in the area and are almost all land owners again. We always made sure we took good care of them. Not all situations worked, but most did.”

SR then explained how excited Robert became when told of his exploration of the area around where the stream emanated. “During my first four day trek up the valley I discovered a large pool of water fed by an artesian well inside a long extinct volcano. It was such a mystical experience,” he offered with a smile, “Now let us show you some of the other secrets of these amazing hills. It was not until well after WWII we solved many of the mysteries these hills held. There are things we still have not resolved.”

Jack, Jr. drove the jeep along the southern side of the hills. Just a couple of miles into the drive they passed the strange geological formation SR named ‘The Hull’ with its strange similarity to the back of a large ocean going ship. It stood a good thousand feet tall with a width of about 400 to 500 feet.

“See anything unusual?” SR asked Dane.

“Other than the large outcropping from the side of the hill is shaped like the stern of a ship?” Dane responded as JR parked near the rocky structure. SR led the way to the southwestern side of the hill along a twisted pathway. Suddenly an entrance to a cave appeared. Much to Dane’s surprise they were able to walk into the cave. Bright lights turned on as they entered and a large cavern appeared, so large he could not see the other end. JR explained the entrance normally remained closed and camouflaged.

SR said, “Later you will see another large opening I discovered early into our investigation of this land. What is surprising is there is a series of these caverns, all of which are interconnected and run for approximately 7 miles. We are installing a tram line from one end of the caves to the other.

At first the caverns were just a curiosity and a place to securely store gold bullion, but as time passed we stored more than gold. We used the caves for storage of critical materials and equipment during the war. Government visitors kept asking us where our materials were stored. We told them we had bunkers hidden in the desert. Little did they realize they were literally standing next to the storage areas. After WWII, we finally had the time to develop the caves as our place for long-term survival."

They got back into the jeep and drove slowly for the next thirty minutes dodging rocks, large pot holes and thousands of holes dug by prairie dogs.

"It is almost impossible to ride a horse through this land or have cattle grazing here. There are so damned many holes dug by these furry little bastards a horse or mule is always breaking a leg. Driving a Jeep through much of this area is a real experience," JR offered.

They finally arrived at the base of the ancient volcano. Here they entered what appeared to be a narrow opening in the rocks at the base of the hill which then opened enough for a large semi-cab and trailer to enter. Obviously this entrance was used to deliver a tremendous amount of materials and equipment to the small but sophisticated oil refinery inside, one large enough to supply the needs of NewLand on a continuous basis for a number of years.

JR explained, "There is an extensive supply of natural gas. We also have a small oil refinery to produce enough fuel for our diesel generators and other needs. What you don't see is our system of pipelines from our oil and gas wells which supply a series of underground storage tanks. Over five years of crude oil is in storage to supply our forecasted diesel and gasoline requirements."

"How did you accomplish this without the outside world ever learning what you were doing?" a stunned Dane asked.

"We started the two storage systems during the war. Robert devised a sophisticated system for bringing in materials and equipment. For a number of years, dozens of trucks arrived daily to haul crude oil out of our oil fields to refineries along the gulf coast. We had two pairs of two identical trucks, identical right down to dents and license plates, a pair of oil tankers and a pair of flatbed trucks. The identical twin Grauman boys drove the trucks. Their farm was the first parcel of land we purchased. The family has been a key part of our project for over 40 years. The parents passed away a number of years ago, but the sons are still part of the community. It fact, today they are successful ranchers starting with a portion of the property we deeded to them early on."

He went on, "Kurt and Kris devised a smooth system where one would drive one truck onto the property and deftly slip away from the other trucks by pulling into a cave. At the same time, the other twin would drive out of the same cave as if he had a load of crude oil.

SR went on to tell a speechless Dane how they designed and implemented the scheme, "Obviously we had many problems along the way. The design of the truck suspension system was difficult, but we made it happen. Early on during the war, Harry Truman and his small group of Senate investigators came to visit us unexpectedly. He wanted a tour of the operating oil fields."

"Thank goodness the twins were both on the property. They did a magnificent job of deception so we could take Senator Truman to all of the parts of the property he wanted to see and not expose our system," SR continued.

Walking back towards the truck, JR added, "As we work together, I want you to become intimately aware of what has been done. We have covered a lot of ground over the past five days. We now need to go back to the house and lay out our near term action items."

Upon return to the house, Dane went to his room and made notes of what he had seen and thought about what projects he should be pursuing. So much had happened the past five days. The next morning Jack, Jr. would fly him back to Dallas for his return to Minneapolis.

That evening a strong breeze blew in from the north with dinner again served on the north patio. Dane tried more Mexican food than he had ever eaten before and enjoyed every bite. "I am going to miss this.

Hey Jack how do you keep so thin eating this great food?" he said. JR just smiled and pumped his arms vigorously into the air to signify the key was physical activity.

Dane excused himself early saying he needed to pack and wanted to be prepared for the morning meeting. As he sat at the desk in his room, he made a list of the significant things he observed over the past five days, especially the day trip to the far southwestern end of the ranch. Amazed at what Robert Barzinsky and the Barnetts accomplished, he also saw many more possibilities. By bedtime, he had three lists: 1. Review of their discussions, 2. List what he saw and 3. A proposed list of what he could do for the Project NewLand. Then, exhausted, he fell into a deep sleep, but again waking at the first crack of dawn.

As usual, he came into the breakfast room to find everyone at the breakfast table. He apologized for being late. "No, you are not late, we are always early. You have to realize this family consists of two supercharged Type A personalities and someone who has to look after them and control their throttle from the time they first bounce out of bed in the morning," Catherine laughed.

"Pork chops for breakfast?" Dane thought back to his early days on the farm and commented, "I haven't seen any pigs around the ranch."

Catherine responded, "We have never raised hogs but a number of the German families do, so we always have a supply of good pork, as well as beef and chicken. We sometimes have wild turkey or some other critter. We often eat pork chops, eggs and raw fried potatoes for breakfast. May not be the most healthy breakfast for us, but we are great believers in eating a wide variety of food. No one in this family believes in any of the diet fads on the market. We are physically active and believe that to be the key."

The two Jacks came into the room having a big laugh about something. Apparently they watched their blue heeler dog Scout having a bird trying to catch a couple of prairie dogs. She loved to go into the pasture and try to dig out a prairie dog or two but did not know what to do with the one she caught.

After breakfast they moved to the conference room. Dane asked if he could speak first so they understand how he viewed the situation and what needed to be done over time. He started out, "First and foremost I want to thank all of you or should I say y'all? I believe security is a primary concern. We don't want an overzealous government agency getting on our case. Then there are the anarchists and left wing groups which would like to claim they took out a 'right wing conspiracy' organization. They still have their nighties in a bind over the Joe McCarthy hearings from many years ago. I agree we must keep up with technology trends, but I strongly believe my first task should be to create a secure data base system and communications system with state-of-the-art cryptography."

JR knew the term from his college days. Neither of his parents heard of cryptography before, but once Dane explained the term they fully understood.

Dane went on, "Earlier I mentioned a young engineer, who is a specialist in this area. I would like to budget hiring Rick Christiansen as a consultant to create a secure database and cryptographic system. He would be given a set of parameters to develop a product we would be able to customize in a way our security is not corrupted. This can be accomplished by setting up an encryption key, possibly 32 binary bits long which gives us over 2 billion combinations. Someday we should hire him. There is also this other engineer who is developing as a top notch business manager you may want to hire in the future. It would be best, if we have the time, to have him get at least another decade of management experience before we bring him on board."

Completely over the heads of Jack, Sr. and Catherine, she asked her son, "Do you understand Jack?"

He nodded yes, "Good advice, please go ahead with hiring him for this project if you have complete confidence in this guy. Just don't let him know anything about our operations. I am going to set up a consulting fund for your time and effort. We will fund efforts of this sort through another account than your consulting account. We've had several programs of this sort in the past and we have considerable experience in setting up secret accounts. You may be able to help us improve our system and help us protect our assets."

JR thought, "If Dane only knew there is well over 100,000 pounds of gold hidden on the ranch he would probably crap in his pants."

Dane continued, "Good. I see my main mission to keep up to date with electronics and computer technology and much more, not just my field of physics. I also have a fairly good background in aeronautics. My understanding of mechanical engineering is pretty good, as well. Somehow I need to get tied into subjects far afield from my background, for example, food and animal sciences and, of course, chemistry and the related sciences. Chemistry has never been my strong suit, but we must be tuned into pharmaceuticals, as well as other aspects of medicine. With what we expect to happen, I intend to spend only a little time on aeronautics, especially any thoughts of space exploration.

Last, in time, I think you will be interested in Chip Faraday, the other young engineer, to be your potential successor as the head of the project when you and he are both ready."

As he finished with his presentation, he asked if there were any questions, to which they said, since they videotaped Dane's presentations, they would like to listen and watch his presentation several times.

Dane suggested they pick a series of code names. Just in case a code name got compromised, they would have other alternatives to contact him without being exposed. They decided Dane would use names from Norse mythology, Jack, Sr. from his being Irish, Catherine from her German heritage and Jack, Jr. from Hispanic culture in memory of Maria Santiago.

By late morning they finished and JR took Dane into Kursk for a brief look at the library he mentioned earlier. Then they were off to the airport in the middle of the vast property using the Lear Jet to return Dane back to DFW Airport. Dane fell into a deep sleep as soon as the American Airlines jet took off and he did not wake up until the plane touched down back in the Twin Cities at Wold Chamberlain Airport. He first wondered if the experience in Texas was a dream, but as soon as he unlocked his briefcase he knew it had actually happened when he saw the pay package they offered him, never expecting to earn that much during his entire career.

THE TECHIES

CHAPTER 23

CHIP AND RICK

1976

As usual, on a Thursday night, Rick Christiansen and Chip Faraday met at Manning's, a longtime family owned beer and burger restaurant not too far from the University of Minnesota. It opened at the end of prohibition in the early 1930s. They had been going there on Thursday nights ever since their junior year in college when they were first old enough to buy beer legally. They kept up the practice most weeks since they graduated from engineering school. This practice continued until Chip moved to Silicon Valley in 1980. It just didn't feel right for Rick to go there alone after Chip left the area.

Having grown up together in the same town, they thought it natural for them to go the same college and to drink together, but they never worked together. Rick called it their weekly "bitch session". They always discussed a range of subjects, starting with the news of the day and their current work projects, but normally talking about Rick's passion for studying disasters and tragedies and Chip's favorite subject, the end of civilization as we know it. Tonight the conversation evolved around a *Newsweek* cover story published in 1976 which proclaimed: "*To scientists, these seemingly disparate incidents represent the advance signs of fundamental changes in the world's weather. The central fact is that after three quarters of a century of extraordinarily mild conditions, the earth's climate seems to be cooling down. Meteorologists...are almost unanimous in the view that the trend will reduce agricultural productivity for the rest of the century. If the climatic change is as profound as some of the pessimists fear, the resulting famines could be catastrophic."*

"Stupid media! What bung hole did they dig that out of?" Chip exclaimed, "The whole media mess is getting worse and worse. I'll bet you in 20 to 25 years it will be proven to be a wrong prediction. We put up with this guy Paul Ehrlich and his 'Population Bomb' book a few years ago and now we get this shit. Where is it going to end?"

Rick said, "It is not going to get any better. At least Ehrlich's prediction of over-population probably has some validity, but hell, we are still waiting for Malthus' prediction to come true. Maybe it would if we double or triple world population. There were about 2 billion people on earth back in the 30s and now there are close to 4 billion. It'll keep going up unless we have a major war or some other type of disaster."

They each ordered another schooner of beer. "You know, Chip, I can go through my data base and find a disaster happening somewhere in the world thousands of times during man's existence on earth. People bellyached about the cold and snow back in the 1960s when we were in college. Hell, my great grandparents lived in this ice box back in the winter of 1888 with snow so damned deep they cut off the tops of trees for fire wood. They even lived in a dugout for a couple of years on their homestead with a bunch of kids until they could get the sod house built. Kind of reminds me of the Donner Party disaster. Only my relatives and their neighbors didn't have to resort to eating each other."

Chip chuckled, "Rick, you have the damnedest perspective on life. You get a big kick of nothing but misery, you have a sick mind. I guess it is better than this guy Charlie I work with. He came into the office one day complaining if the weather gets any better it is going to crap. His problem is he came to this tundra from somewhere in the mid-Atlantic or south where it never gets this cold and the snow thing is a seldom occurring event. How much worse it can be? And I remember you telling me it even snowed in Boston on the 4th of July in 1816."

"My way is better. You are like the kid always looking for a dead pony in a manure pile. Someday you are going to find it. What would you do with it? You worry about the end of civilization over which you have no control. I just like to list the problems man has faced over time and observe how stupid the responses have been." Rick dove back into the subject of 'global cooling', "If my reckoning is right, in 20-to-25 years some idiot non-scientific dumb cluck politician will be crowing about 'global warming'. He will get some politically oriented so-called scientists to play into the whole concept. Hell, they'll be claiming the north and south polar caps will melt and we will float into the sea and be eaten by starving polar bears. I can just hear some stuffed shirt Dumkopf, probably a fat assed politician, venting his spleen. Be just our luck he is treated as some sort of the second coming. I'll bet $100 and a case of beer I can prove them wrong. Weather is constantly changing, that is what climate is all about. Why do you think Leif Ericsson called it Greenland in the 11th Century when he discovered it?"

"Are you ever going to get into politics?" Chip asked.

"Are you nuts? Never! Christ, let's face it we're technical guys. As far as I am concerned engineers and scientists simplify the complicated while attorneys and politicians complicate the simple, and the way we are breeding lawyers these days, the world is heading straight for the toilet."

Neither of them cared much for politics, but Chip got involved during the whole Watergate blowup. Ever since LBJ and his Great Society he had been disenchanted with the Democrat Party his father so dearly loved. "They supposedly were concerned about Negros, but weren't they the party of the KKK?" Chip queried. He thought the whole Great Society to be nothing but a big economic redistribution charade.

"What about the likes of Senator Fulbright and Senator Byrd, both Democrats? I'll bet there are KKK members in Congress?" he asked his buddy, then said, "I can see the campaign poster: Vote for your favorite KKK member for Congress spelled K-o-n-g-r-e-s-s," Rick chimed in.

Chip had gotten involved in his local Republican precinct but soon was disenchanted dealing with a whole bunch of 'wannabes'. The egos of some of these people, particularly this one bitchy housewife, totally frustrated him. He knew of a few guys and gals who went all out to help the party, but he could not stand the infighting. He did get to be a district and state delegate one year, but that was enough.

He knew a young conservative black engineer, a state senator. Roe vs. Wade, ruled on a year earlier by the Supreme Court, concerned him because he believed it made black baby abortions much easier. "You didn't want to get him turned on about Planned Parenthood and its founder Margaret Sanger. He was sure history would prove him right. He despised LBJ and those of his ilk," Chip added.

Rick then went off on his whole disasters and tragedies scenario, "Does anybody realize how many people have died from wars, floods, disease epidemics, earthquakes and volcano eruptions? Just take the Black Death. It decimated much of Europe. Or look more recently like the Spanish flu of the late teens. My god, somewhere between 25 and 100 million died in just a couple of years."

Chip laughed to himself and knew Rick would be on his favorite rant for the next hour. He would just let it peter out as Rick went through his usual litany of floods, tornados, ship wrecks, plane crashes, etc. He even quoted how many ships had been lost in the Bering Strait.

As usual, he next went through his list of Lockheed Electra crashes years earlier. He remembered being in high school when the Tell City, IN crash occurred. The wings fell off of the Northwest Airlines Lockheed Electra and killed all aboard shocking the airline industry. Just over a year earlier on February 4, 1959 the first Electra crashed in Boston killing 63 the day after "The Day the Music Died" when Buddy Holly, Richie Valens and The Big Bopper died in a private plane crash in Iowa. Then a Braniff Electra L-188 crashed near Dawson, Texas on May 3, 1968. The Electra crashes fairly well reduced the commercial aircraft business for Lockheed, which has thrived in the military aircraft and space business since then. The cause was later determined to harmonic vibration in the wing assembly at certain power settings.

These events affected the young Richard Christiansen greatly. His interest in disasters and tragedies evolved from following these events. He spent several hours each week in the library digging through microfiche and created one scrapbook after another. Regardless of these crashes, Rick wanted to be a military or airline pilot but could not qualify due to his nearsightedness.

Finally Chip got his chance to vent. "You know Rick, this kind of idiocy is going to get Jimmy Carter elected. President Ford is a nice guy. Met him once briefly just a week before Nixon resigned and he became president. In my opinion, he did not fight enough when he ran for his own term. These Demon nutcases will drum up every stupid cause you can think of and the U.S. of A is going to suffer in time. As someone said, 'if the U.S. has the sniffles the rest of the world has a cold, and if the U.S. has a cold the rest of the world gets pneumonia'. I think we need to go head-on after these Democrat bastards."

Then Chip, with his dark side, would go into his end-of-the world scenario. He did not have to look back at the disasters and tragedies that fascinated Rick so much, but rather look at the current conditions and trends of the time, and the history of war...especially religious wars.

"For example, we had the Korean War when we were in grade school and now we're finally out of this horrible mess in Vietnam, but the Cold War continues to loom. If the Democrats win we will not only have the Cold War get worse, but look at the other possible problems? Our energy policy is non-existent. We'll probably have gasoline shortages. I believe the Republicans could do some good if it were not for the Watergate stigma Nixon caused. All over a botched burglary! Hell, I believe there have been much worse scandals in the past. And I still remember years ago when this guy Khrushchev came over from Russia and pounded his shoe on the podium telling us the Commies planned to bury us. I believed him and still do, if we don't watch out. Now there is so much subterfuge and dishonesty in our political system I am concerned about our government's ability to respond."

"Chip, you worry too much," Rick said with a big grin, but he knew Chip really felt that way. Rick knew Chip's dark side and believed him to be much too serious. Maybe he would be the same way if his father died when he was young. By contrast he was a big overgrown happy kid who collected disasters and tragedies history along with his toys, including a snowmobile and an old truck with big wheels. He figured man is such a screw-up he is incapable of doing things right, so why worry about it?

About 9:30 they decided they analyzed the problems of the world enough and went home. Chip married several years earlier, with a baby and a two year old at home, but his wife believed her husband needed time with his childhood friend. Even though she had a Ph.D., Sue decided she wanted to be home for her children when they were young. She worried when Chip came home depressed sometimes because of his time with Rick, but he needed to vent his work frustrations. Rick was still single. His 'sorority sister' girlfriend was still going to the U. Chip doubted the relationship would last, but they finally married.

CHAPTER 24

TECHNOLOGY INFRASTRUCTURE

Not long into his association with Project NewLand Dane realized it was time for him to make his move to Kursk. He and his wife Beth discussed when to make the move on a regular basis. Much to his surprise she wanted to move from the beginning. She practiced law at a large firm in downtown Minneapolis. Although she enjoyed the practice of family law, she longed for a slower pace of life and one not so wrought with the backbiting nature of the partners in the firm. She also wanted to have a family, convinced she would rather raise a child in a small town like the one where she grew up than in a big city.

On his monthly trip to 'RJ Ranch', Dane decided to broach the subject with JR and his dad. They were both surprised and pleased. Both believed he had made considerable progress in developing his technology evaluation process and thought it would be a good time for the move and time to start the implementation phase.

When they placed their house on the market, people around the university wanted to know where they planned to go. He proudly announced his being named Director of Research for GLO Industries. This created considerable confusion. What would a Ph.D. in physics and college professor with tenure be doing for an energy operation like GLO Industries? They were nothing but a bunch of drillers and pumpers in the energy business managed by a bunch of real oddballs and right wing nuts. They believed his decision to be career suicide. Why someone would so well connected and respected move to a god awful dump like Kursk, Texas, even though none of them had ever been there? Dane would only say they made a lucrative and challenging offer and they both missed small town life. Most who knew him believed he must have had a nervous breakdown.

People also wondered why his wife, a well-like family law attorney, would join him. The local community wrote them off and soon they were forgotten. Dane's move clearly disturbed Rick, who could not understand why an energy operation would need such a sophisticated encryption system and why Dane would go there. By contrast, Chip totally erased Dane Madsen from his mind.

Once they moved, Beth joined the only local law firm in Kursk. The change in environment fit her well and she soon became key member of the firm. The area never had an attorney with her expertise and experience before.

Dane immediately integrated the work done remotely in Minnesota into the Texas operations. He reviewed his progress on a weekly basis with the two Jacks which proved to be a real tonic since they were still mourning the loss of their longtime friend and partner. They always believed they had done a good job of providing an integrated plan for evolving technology for Project NewLand, but soon realized how much more needed to be done. Dane's patient approach of keeping them informed about his projects made it made it easy for the father and son team to understand. Their lives were regenerated, Catherine repeatedly told Dane and Beth how much she appreciated what Dane being there did for her husband and son. After Robert's death, she worried about their mental welfare until he joined the organization.

He soon created a completely new approach to technology evaluation. He could explain complex concepts of various technologies and integrate this information in such a way the two Jacks understood. Dane evolved into a master in predicting how a new technology would evolve and determined with great accuracy the success or failure of various developments. For example, when 'Bluetooth' technology came on the scene in the early 1990s, Dane predicted wide usage of the technology, but thought it would be frustrating to make reliable. Dane called it 'marginally applicable' much to the chagrin of the Swedish developers. For years users found Bluetooth technology frustrating with many limitations. He cautioned new technology always must be used properly or it could be passed over by another breakthrough. He could cite dozens of examples, but was always puzzled by the staying power of Bluetooth.

The security programs implemented by GLO Industries and Project NewLand seemed to work. However, their knowledge of the dangers of espionage remained meager until Dane Madsen came on the scene. They later realized the tight management of data and communications developed by Dane put them in a strong position when dealing with government agencies and sinister organizations trying to spy on them.

When email came on the scene, Dane's inherent suspicious nature and his knowledge of DARPA (Defense Advanced Research Projects Agency, founded in 1958 in response to the surprise launching of Sputnik the year before) resulted in his directing the development of a separate secure communications network. Working with Rick, first as a contractor and then as part of Project NewLand, a sophisticated encryption algorithm was developed. Dane then built a unique communications system between them and the outside world. By the end of the 20th Century his engineers designed an enhanced version using a 64 bit code. They also devised a scheme that prevented determining the location of an email address used by anyone on the inside. It took Dane over five years to map out and design his program completely, a task only someone with complete self-discipline could accomplish with so few technical and human resources.

In time he and Beth had a son named Hans in honor of his grandfather who braved the unknown to come to a strange new land many years earlier. Dane believed he, his wife and his son would be representative of a new type of 'immigrant', only the environment would change around them and they would experience a new kind of new world in one place rather than changing their location.

Dane found it necessary to develop a plan for updating technology on an ongoing basis in preparation for the implementation of NewLand at some later date. He turned more and more nervous worrying the Cold War with Russia would spiral out of control. With the onset of the Iran hostage situation they became more concerned. The election of Ronald Reagan in 1980 resulted in the management team having many discussions about whether the risk of a catastrophic event improved or worsened. They agreed to a man President Reagan would force a binary result: Either the state of world tension would get much worse or be greatly improved. They believed there would be none of the waffling of Carter years.

Dane also said new dangers would evolve as time went on, with the methods of warfare more and more lethal with time. No one knew where it would end.

The question JR always posed, "When will it blow up? And what horrific tools of war will be used? Or will there be a natural disaster of catastrophic proportions?"

They worried more and more as the Soviet Union fragmented and the threat of radical Islam arose. Ever since the creation of the Geneva Convention there was concern over the use of such terrors as chemical and nuclear weapons by belligerent countries. They soon realized terrorist organizations had no intention of following international accords. The world had seen radical religions over the centuries, but up till now even the worst were self-limiting. They began to realize political unrest bedded in religious fervor would become much more dangerous to world stability than the Russian Bear and last many years into the future. Historical events were often referenced to make their point.

CHAPTER 25

END OF AN ERA

1980s

Dane made considerable progress by the early 1980s and the technology infrastructure for NewLand was established. They were preparing for an ever more unstable world. Dane and JR spent many days worrying about the new threats facing civilization. After President Reagan's successful release of the US hostages from Tehran in 1981, everybody gave a sigh of relief. Little did world leaders realize how dangerous the world would become over the next 50 years due to religious radicals. Year after year he and his team adapted to new threats facing the world. JR and Dane were so involved they missed the physical deterioration in SR, in his early 80s, and to a lesser extent, Catherine in her 70s. His many years of hard work resulted in a totally worn out body. Worrying about SR's health caused most of her problems.

One morning in 1986 SR disappeared after spending a restless night dreaming about and mulling over what all happened since he left Cork, Ireland so many years earlier and how meeting Robert and their friendship completely shaped his life.

"What would I have done in my life if I had not met Robert? I had no real education and no resources. He made my life and created the environment that led me to Kursk. What would my life have been without Catherine and our son Jack?" he wondered in severe pain with his chest hurting and head pounding. He feared being an invalid as he left the house and walked towards the original barn he built on the ranch 50 years earlier.

Writhing in pain Jack's mind flashed back to 1945 when WWII ended. The demand for GLO Industries ranching and energy businesses ramped up rapidly. When the government offered many excess products for sale at the end of the war, just as after WWI, particularly the materials left over on their property, Robert jumped at the opportunity to acquire everything available. Why not? They owned tens of thousands of acres of remote property, plus the vast array of caves for storage. Pennies on the dollar bought expensive equipment abandoned by the government. The materials and equipment were stored near where the products and materials were purchased in places with good highway and/or railroad access. This gave the partners the opportunity to discretely continue the building of structures inside the series of caves along the south side of the range of hills, often with resources few knew existed or even remembered.

Their goal was to create over 3 million square feet of usable space by building a series of two-to-three story structures inside the caves, with some of the space being built for the residences, offices, schools, and storage of materials and machinery needed to survive for a long period of time. Some caves were wisely reserved for future needs.

They prepared for growing and storing food with long shelf life and other products related to maintaining a group of people for a period of several years, even to survive for several decades, if necessary. Technology changed rapidly and it weighed heavily on him. SR continued to manage these efforts until Catherine and JR finally convinced him to slow down. From then on JR managed the effort, incorporating the technologies Dane identified.

Still in pain, he had another flashback to how they built the structures. The 7th transport truck just made the quick exchange at 'The Hull'. As soon as Kurt Grauman rolled into the opening in the camouflaged hill, his identical twin brother, Kris Grauman, rolled out onto the roadway in an identical truck, down to the license plates, dents and scratches, on its way to the storage tanks several miles further into the expansive oil field.

The spring assemblies of both trucks made them look empty when they were fully loaded and vice versa. Then trucks proceeded like any other trucks in route to a refinery hundreds of miles away. Along the way a truck would exit onto a rural road and head for a one of a series of railroad sidings. There it would be loaded with more materials for project NewLand. This routine occurred five or six days per week, depending on the demand for oil. After each exchange, the hill closed.

This intricate exchange, as devised by Jack Barnett, Sr. and the Grauman twins, provided the means to bring in almost any type of material required undetected. Interspersed were large flatbed trucks, including a pair of identical flatbed trucks, and closed trucks carrying the oil exploration and production equipment. But here, too, materials ended up inside 'The Hull' by the indirect means of being unloaded somewhere on the property, then in the dead of night moved into the appropriate cave.

He then thought back to the time he first found 'The Hull' when he found the first cave nearby. At the time he did not realize there were a series of caves running for miles along the southwest side of the hills. He often wondered what kind of geological phenomenon could have created the strange formation containing the artesian well and this extensive series of caverns. He opined there must have been volcanic and earthquake events millions of years ago.

Catherine awoke early and realized Jack's absence. Not unusual, because her husband often wandered around the huge house during the night, but was startled when after searching the house she could not find SR. She ran to JR's wing in a fright. JR thought it strange; the vehicles he normally drove were in their normal places, except for his original old Chevrolet he kept since his early days of exploring the area around Kursk and Valley Center. A newer vehicle would have had a tracking device installed as part of the integrated security communications network for NewLand.

JR and his mother thought of places where his dad liked to be alone. Catherine told JR to go where SR first kissed her. He jumped into his Jeep and drove to the opening to the valley from where the stream flowed. As he came over the edge of the hill at the mouth of the valley he first saw the old car, then Jack on the ground. He ran to his father's side.

He called for an ambulance, hoping something could be done, but his father had suffered a massive heart attack and died immediately. Telling his mother reminded him of Maria's death at the hands of the monsters from Valley Center many years earlier. No longer JR, he was now the Jack Barnett who would run GLO Industries and head up Project NewLand, just as his father had for a number of years after Robert Barzinsky's death. They both died alone from massive heart attacks; an appropriate ending for such a dynamic pair. Fortunately, Catherine and Jack did not have to see either of these active individuals to suffer long slow declines. They were now both at peace with Jack challenged to manage his dynasty and prepare for the future.

The funeral started out as a solemn affair, but soon friends and family were reminiscing about his accomplishments and what Jack Barnett provided for the people of the area. Most in attendance had at least one Jack Barnett story, often combined with memories of Robert Barzinsky. Soon a combination of laughter and tears filled the large pavilion at the county fairgrounds in Valley Center, the only place large enough to hold such an event. What started being a one day shutdown of Kursk and the surrounding area ended up lasting well into the next day. People were exhausted at the end, but it proved to be a proper sendoff to the hero of Kursk who not only saved the village, but who brought renewal and growth.

Jack and his mother vowed to continue the fight to keep NewLand prepared for the fateful day they both believed would come. When disaster would occur, nobody knew. To handle her grief she involved herself with the database developments headed up by Dane Madsen. She had always been the major benefactor and inspirational donor to the city library in Kursk. Now she dedicated herself to be the one who would head up efforts to assist Dane in the conversion of the NewLand library to a total digital format with multiple backup systems. Together they planned for the massive increase in data storage they believed necessary to handle the rapid growth in data with the onset of the Internet.

CHAPTER 26

CHIP GOES TO KURSK

July 1987

Chip Faraday arrived at Barzinsky-Barnett House, so named after SR's death, on a very hot day. He took the first flight from San Jose to DFW, was met by Jack Barnett and flown to the GLO Industries airport in a new Gulfstream jet, arriving about 3:30PM. As with Dane Madsen over a dozen years earlier, Jack gave him an overview of their operations and plans during the flight. They landed at the airport located far inside Barnett's property and were driven to the ranch house headquarters by Len Girard, Jack's close friend and ranch manager. Little did he realize he was about to be surprised and would realize how completely he was vetted. Shown to his room in the Barzinsky wing of the building, he soon joined them in the conference room four doors up on the left side of the hall.

As he walked into the conference room he was surprised. There sat his old professor and friend Dane Madsen. He quickly realized how Jack Barnett knew so much about him when they first met.

"Dr. Madsen, is it you?" Chip exclaimed.

He replied, "Yes, but it is no longer doctor to you, please call me Dane. We will be working together. In fact, I will be working for you."

The confused Chip said, "How can that be? You were my professor. Why didn't I make the connection between Kursk, TX and you? I am so stupid!"

Dane spent 30 minutes bringing Chip up-to-date on what the nature of his work since they last met. He went on to explain his role as Director of Advanced Technologies. He said he recommended Chip to be Jack Barnett's successor, leaving Chip in a state of shock with his life charted out for him.

Then Jack entered the room. "Surprised?" Jack shot at Chip.

"Overwhelmed," Chip replied.

"You up to the task?"

He shot back, "I am your man. I am pleasantly surprised to have Dr. Madsen, I mean Dane, here. How the hell did you pull it off?"

"Getting to know Dane was an interesting outcome due to his curiosity about Robert Barzinsky's death," Jack said with a Cheshire cat smile. "He contacted us and the rest is history."

"Jack and I were worried you would figure out the connection after your meeting in San Francisco. Intelligence is darn good these days and we pretty well know your whole life story, but we had to be careful not to let the cat out of the bag," Dane offered, "Now we want you to do some recruiting and, if you agree, let's go after your buddy Rick. You game on that?"

"Sure but give me a bit of time. Rick gets a bit rambunctious. I want to be damned sure I am ready for him full time. He can get out of control, but this is an environment he would enjoy. He would be a heck of a contributor, especially if he works with Dane. Also, he and his wife broke up and got a divorce a couple of years ago, so he probably is ready for a change. Thank goodness there were no kids. Rick was just a bit too country for Shirley. She is a hotsy-totsy sorority girl while Rick is a small town good old boy. I told him they should have never gotten married, but he did anyway.

Surprised it lasted for five years. I think he is still doing some sort of consulting gig. He has been real hush-hush about what he has been doing for the last two or three years."

Rick Christiansen walked in, "You snarky bastard! You are a helluva friend ripping me apart. Dane and I have been working our tails off to get you recruited so you could be my boss?"

"What do you mean?" Chip said sheepishly.

"Well, you are my boss." Rick said.

"What?" Chip responded.

"Dane is your Director of Advanced Technology and I am your Director of Applied Technology, if you can put up with us?" Rick shot back as they noticed Jack standing in the corner with a big grin on his face.

Jack's cook yelled, "You guys ready to eat? Good beef is not as good when it cools off. Who wants beer and who wants wine?"

They agreed it was too hot for wine and by time they got to the dining room table an ice-cold mug of draught Lone Star beer was at each place at the table.

Chip found out Dane had been trying to recruit Rick for several years but was not successful until Rick realized he could not save his marriage. There was no way his wife would have ever considered moving to a rural town in Texas. He told Dane he needed a new life and thought the open space of west Texas would fit his outdoor life style. He loved to hunt and fish. Rick said would miss the fishing of Minnesota, Wisconsin and Canada, but they convinced him he could go to the gulf coast and try deep sea fishing and there were plenty opportunities to hunt anything from rattle snakes to deer. Rick owned a Harley and a couple of ATVs, but realized he could not keep the snow mobile.

He asked, "Why did you recruit Rick before me?"

Jack's answer made a lot of sense, "Dane and I have discussed this many times and we came to the conclusion we needed you as the overall manager of the project, but we needed Rick's technical expertise first. I didn't want you to be buried down in the minutia of one area or another and I wasn't ready to give up my control, but now Dane and Rick have convinced me we have progressed enough to have a dedicated CEO for the NewLand operation. Also, we wanted you to have as much seasoning as possible. Rick knew of your problems with Ryan Smith and the board. He told Dane and me you were on your way to China faced being forced to do something you definitely did not want to do, so we put whole plan put together about 10 days before we met in Tokyo. Make sense to you or are your feelings hurt?"

"No way, I just wanted to know how you made the timing of the decision. I should have been more suspicious when you gave me the crypto scheme. Rick and I played around with this kind of stuff a number of years ago. Damn, I must be dense and feel like a fool. I am just glad you still want me. You guys played me like a violin," Chip responded.

Dinner was great with prime beef of unbelievable quality. The conversation casual and not about the challenge they faced which would start in the morning. Chip could not wait to tell his wife what transpired. He just hoped she could adjust to the strange new world of Kursk.

At midnight the group finally gave up for the night. They all drank a bit too much. Concerned about Dane, one of his ranch hands drove him back to his house on the edge of Kursk, and then picked him up in the morning. Dane's wife worried about his tendency to drink a bit too much when out with a group of guys. He never drank more than one or two beers or glasses of wine at home. He always got nervous when in a group of more than two or three people, probably due to his being shy as a child, but it never seemed to bother him when lecturing his students. He would always wake up the next morning with a hangover and vow he would never do it again. Dane always seemed happier being home at night and year or two after they moved to Kursk, Dane developed his department to the point he seldom traveled, much to his liking.

Dane and Beth had a good marriage. They not only loved each other with great respect for each other. Much to his surprise she found Kursk to be a comfortable place for her. She never liked big city life. First an attorney with a local law firm, she later ran for county district attorney and surprisingly won. For years there had been a battle between the Valley Center people and the Kursk people. This reserved likable Midwesterner just seemed to have the right personality to minimize the rivalry between the ranchers and the immigrant farmers. They wanted children, but remained childless until Beth was almost 40 years old. Young Hans was the joy of their life and Beth decided she would rather be a mother than a district attorney after two terms, so she resigned her position and doted on their son.

All except Chip and Rick retired for the night. They were not only happy to see each other again, but more important they were anxious to work together. They brought each other up to date. For the first year, Rick periodically flew back to Minneapolis, via Chicago, where he told people he consulted with an organization from Europe as a front. Since his parents had both died and being an only child, he found it easy for him to disappear.

He moved to an abandoned adobe house far out into the GLO Industries property on the south side of the hills. After making a pitch, Jack gave him the property on the basis he would improve the house. He did in spades.

Chip was not surprised Rick wanted to be isolated. He cherished the lifestyle. Most people did not realize the old house was an extensive home laboratory where he did much of his work.

Two hours later Rick left. Chip went to his room and called his wife to discuss the strange turn of events. They were careful not to discuss anything that could compromise anything. So typical of critical events during their marriage they were well prepared with a series of code words, so Sue understood what transpired. She didn't say anything to their kids when she got off the phone since they were already in bed for the night and they decided to tell their kids jointly. When they moved from Minneapolis to the Bay Area several years ago, their children were small. Now it was going to be a more difficult situation to explain why they were leaving the hubbub of a large metropolitan area to a place as remote as Kursk.

CHAPTER 27

RELOCATION PREPARATION

The next morning Chip met with Jack for an early breakfast. Jack apologized for the curtain of secrecy they used to recruit him, but explained there was so much at stake they could not take any chances. He went on to assure Chip they needed him to also run GLO Industries in the future and told Chip he would have to learn a lot about the energy business. He noted if the catastrophe they expected happened there would probably be little need for an energy business, other than to supply their meager needs. This would be further exacerbated with several years of crude and refined oil in storage.

As expected, both men came to the meeting well prepared. Per their discussion the previous night, each prepared a draft of what Chip's job description should be. Not surprising their descriptions synched.

"Chip, I want you to spend at least three months and no more than nine months before you move. President Reagan has been putting extensive pressure on Gorbachev for the past several years. When Reagan walked out on him last October in Reykjavik, I thought our time had to come. I think George Bush is up to the task but there will be a time of definite uncertainty. Then we have the elections coming next year, too. I realize they are trying to put together an agreement, but these negotiations could blow up in the next couple of months. My biggest concern is Reagan's health," Jack said in a somewhat worried voice.

"I am fully aware of the risks our president is facing and I will do what is necessary to I can take over Project NewLand as soon as necessary," Chip responded.

For the next four hours they worked out his job description and created an extensive list of action items. Chip said he had a pretty good idea of Rick's job description after their conversation the previous night, but wanted to spend at least a half of a day with Dane and Rick.

After lunch, Chip, Dane and Rick met in Dane's office for the rest of the afternoon. Dane showed a computer generated spreadsheet of technologies vs. actions with the status of each technology. Dane reviewed each line item making sure Chip realized which technologies evolved the most rapidly. Several times Chip looked at Rick to see if he was in agreement. Typical of Chip he got a bit irritated being drawn into some of the minutia, but caught himself as he remembered Dane's attention to detail. He thought to himself, "I can see Dane asking someone to hold the legs of a gnat apart so he could zero in on the gnat's rear end!" However, this character trait made Chip completely comfortable with Dane in this role.

Chip, Dane and Rick headed into Kursk for dinner, first stopping by Dane's house to introduce Chip to his wife and son and to drop off Dane's car. Rick then drove the three of them to dinner. During dinner they brought Chip up-to-date with some of the non-confidential aspects of Project NewLand. After dinner, being fully aware of the need for secrecy, they drove back to Dane's so they could talk business in private. The meeting ended long after midnight. Rick and Chip drove to the local hotel where both took a room, being too late for the long drive back to Barzinsky-Barnett House and Rick's adobe house far into the GLO Industries oilfields.

The next morning the two of them drove out to Rick's house, which Chip found to be about what he expected: A lot of equipment and toys. Obviously Rick was a big kid at heart…a very talented big kid, even in his early 40s. Chip wondered if Rick would ever grow up and be a normal human being. Over a cup of coffee, Rick reviewed a map of the cave system with Chip.

"We are going to visit a number of the caves during which I can give you an idea of where we are today. Right now we are fairly well prepared for the more traditional disasters, including both man-made and natural catastrophes. We think we could withstand even a nuclear disaster, providing it is not a direct hit within ten to twenty miles. What is beginning to worry us are some of the previously undefined dangers.

For example, we are beginning to monitor the field of EMP, electromagnetic pulse technology. Do you realize that Nicola Tesla started discussing this phenomenon back in the mid-30s? Someday this technology is going to be weaponized. Not only that, solar flares could basically create a similar level of danger. As you remember from our physics classes with Dane, major solar flares have hit earth throughout history. None of the sensitive electronics we have today existed. Now we could have our lights turned off on a major scale," Rick cautioned.

Chip knew of some of the other dangers that loomed, volcanos for example. The Krakatoa volcano eruption of 1883 killed about 36,000 people, mostly by the tsunami that followed the eruption. The explosion was said to have been heard as far as 3,000 miles away. During one of their 'disasters and tragedies' discussions back in Minneapolis years earlier, Rick said the earth got its bell rung by the eruption and said the shock wave probably circled the earth several times before dying down.

Rick expanded on the history of Krakatoa which is located in the Sunda Strait between the islands of Java and Sumatra in Indonesia. "There were serious eruptions during the 5th, 6th and 17th centuries and as late as 1927 an island arose from the caldera of Krakatoa and this baby is not done acting up. Furthermore, look at other major activity around the world in places like South America, particularly in Chile and Argentina, and then we know that Iceland is a virtual minefield of future volcanic activity. Look throughout history and you will find multiple occurrences of how Icelandic earthquakes affected the lives of Europeans, sometimes other parts of the world like during the Little Ice Age.

There are also major volcanic dangers right here in North America. For example, just look at Mt. St. Helens in 1980. Besides the west coast, we could also see major earthquake activity here in the middle of the U.S. Major eruptions occurred along the New Madrid fault in Missouri in the early 19th Century. The one we should worry about in the U.S. is the extreme volcanic danger that lies below Yellowstone National Park. Chip, you should research that one. The last major eruption 600,000 years ago spewed ash as far to the southeast of Yellowstone as Alabama. Take a look at what would happen if four or five major eruptions would occur around the world at the same time. Eruptions of the Krakatoa magnitude have even caused severe climate change in the past. If something like that happened, we would really find out what 'global cooling' is. Also, some nut could use a natural event as an excuse to trigger a much larger man-made event."

Chip jumped in, "Another area of concern is what happens if our anti-bacterial medicines become ineffective or some virus comes out of Africa and destroys much of mankind just as the Black Death came out of Asia into Europe hundreds of years ago. Also, what about existing families of viruses? Many drugs are being compromised from overuse. We know the deadly results of the influenza outbreak towards the end of WWI. Mass migration of people who have never received the vaccines received in countries like the U.S. could be a real future problem."

They were back in 'Minneapolis Mode'. These scenarios were remote, but they realized if they were going to be able to assure the continuation of their community, they needed to be ready for any potential disaster. They agreed there was no better trio of people to prepare an organization for such a future than the three of them.

With that, they took off on Rick's motorcycle, which Chip thought was strange until Rick drove into the remote area of the hills. Systematically, Rick and Chip toured six of the major caves and several of the minor caves. By using the motorcycle they were able to travel from cave to cave along the tram line that ran from 'The Hull' to the hidden oil refinery, something that would have been impossible with

Rick's truck. The tram system provided the primary transportation through cave system.

As they passed through each of the major caves, Rick explained its function, for example, equipment storage or residential, with some reserved for future use. Two hours later they ended up at the secret oil refinery at the far end of the string of caves.

When they returned to headquarters Chip asked Jack, Dane and Rick if there were any further questions or comments. Jack spoke first, "You have spent your career in the rapidly evolving world of high tech markets. If fact, you have been closer than any of us to the epicenter, pun intended, since you live in Silicon Valley. We realize once you leave the Bay Area, we will lose some of your technology market currency. That is something we will have to work on. Dane believes the three of you will come up with a methodology to keep us up to date."

Jack added, "We must make sure you are able to travel in-and-out of technology organizations around the world. It was well known Dane has been here in Kursk for a number of years, but they still have not caught on Rick is located here."

"I guess I am just nobody!" Rick quipped.

Dane offered, "You have always been fairly low profile, but it does not mean you are not a key factor with your design expertise."

Jack continued, "On the other hand, Chip has always been high profile, especially after his stunt with the Primary Pacific Capital people. I still think it was funnier than hell. I can just see those stuffed shirts' mouths dropping as you stuck it to them. Obviously, Dane can continue as he has. He will probably travel the least of any of you going forward. Rick can continue his consulting engineer cover quite easily, but Chip will stick out like a sore thumb wherever he shows up. Maybe we'll just keep you as a floater as far as the outside is concerned. Someday the technical business media will catch on. We just have to deal with that when the time comes."

When they completed their meeting, Jack flew Chip back to DFW. On the way he asked, "What do you think?"

"Right now I am overwhelmed, but committed to the project. When I get home, my wife and I will break the news to the kids we are moving. We will start the clock on getting the house sold sometime during the next 4-to-6 months. Within a week I will try to have a business structure scenario coordinated with what Dane has done. As important is how to determine the importance of one technology versus the next. How hard will it be to find a house in Kursk?"

"You will be amazed what you will be able to buy for half of what you get for your California house and your kids will have wide open spaces to enjoy," as Jack waved Chip goodbye.

Chip found an office as soon as he returned to California. He leased a 1,000 square foot space on the third floor of a four story building near the Gateway Center in San Jose and hired someone to paint a sign for 'Technologies International, LLC' with his name and the title of 'Managing Director' on the door.

The space consisted of three offices and a reception area. Observers never saw anyone other than Chip enter the facility and for a good reason. No one else ever used the office. An answering service advised callers to leave a message. Chip never answered the phone and seldom returned messages. He first thought of having a recording to stating he was traveling, but then realized too many people in Silicon Valley would recognize him when he was in the area, especially after the attention paid to his explosive departure from his previous company. The leftwing bias of the Bay Area media fervently tried to discredit him. He knew the story of his mysterious new venture had national, if not international, interest. Then he set up a set of fake online files with some traps and within a month he discovered his security got attacked both physically and electronically by some nasty organizations. Just another game of cat and mouse he loved to play.

The ruse completely fooled the media and others interested in his activities. Chip often flew into the Bay Area from different locations than DFW, each time spending some time in his San Jose office for the first year. The organization's business jets took him from one location to another and then met him at another city.

The cover perfectly fit his evolving role in Zeus, a word which someone in the local media uncovered accidently. The media and government agencies tried to understand the significance of the term. Occasionally Zeus would be mentioned, but no one ever uttered or printed the term Project NewLand. Government agencies and the media constantly tried to figure out what the organization did. The company, soon known of as TechIn, a nickname created by a local reporter. The company publicized itself as a technology monitoring organization, but nobody knew by whom. Aware of the company itself being monitored by a number of organizations, including the U.S. government, the UN and several sinister fringe groups, Chip always kept his guard up.

During his time in Silicon Valley, he established rapport with several venture capital firms, but not his old nemesis Pacific Primary Capital. He made it known he wanted nothing more to do with his former organization, part of his ploy to establish his role as his own man. Working with both Dane and Rick via their secure communications system he integrated his findings into the sophisticated monitoring and tracking system Dane devised. Once he re-located to Texas, he expanded the monitoring of new technology markets worldwide. A year later he did not renew the lease for the San Jose office. Chip Faraday disappeared long before that happened.

Years later, when the media knew he relocated to Kursk, Texas, they realized he had joined the secretive GLO Industries, but never could determine his role. Later Chip started several companies in this remote spot. The various venture firms thought they would be approached for investment, but he kept his distance once he left the Bay Area. The seed money came from Jack Barnett and the new product ideas were generated by the trio of Chip, Dane and Rick and their staff. The products and services were primarily oriented to the needs of NewLand. In time several products were licensed for manufacture and sale to outside ventures.

Dane continued to evaluate and compare technologies as they evolved, while Rick determined which ones fit the needs of Project NewLand and implemented them. The rapid progress pleased Jack.

Shortly after his relocation, Chip started a total organizational review process. The process started with evaluating the status of each area then planning the required actions. The biggest surprise came when they evaluated the project's weapon inventory, which turned out to be nothing but WWII surplus with a bit of Korean and Vietnamese era weaponry. This equipment accumulated because Robert and Jack thought their future would result in physical attacks. Chip soon realized the real dangers were in the areas of intelligence and environmental attacks, but they still needed some defensive capability. Weapon systems were as automated as possible. By early 21st Century most defensive weapons were based on drone technology. They believed any serious catastrophe would result in massive reduction of population around the world, thus they needed to monitor and protect the periphery of NewLand continuously. Time proved this to be the correct strategy.

They systematically reviewed each area. Dane used the evolution of various storage technologies and how closely they followed Moore's Law as a model for following technology evolution. Moore's Law states that over the history of semiconductor technology, the number of transistors incorporated into integrated circuits doubled every two years and costs declined dramatically. Dr. Gordon Moore, one of the founders of Intel Corporation, described this phenomenon in a 1965 paper he wrote. Moore's Law did not have to be revised until well into the 21st Century when semiconductor manufacturing technology approached line widths of 10 nanometers (10 billionths of a meter). Dane expected this. The diameter of a hydrogen atom is only 0.1nanometer. As so often with Dane's proclamations, this left the non-technical people at NewLand scratching their heads.

Dane noted one of the early computer designers he knew back in Minneapolis created a simplified version of tracking the evolution of storage technologies in general. He often pulled out a rat tailed sheet of paper showing this data. This engineer defined his findings as the basic 'rule of doubling', consistent with Moore's Law for the use of projecting evolution of various storage technologies from main memory to peripheral memory devices way back to the late 1950s.

They observed the ability to predict the increased rate of information they could plan on storing over time. Dane predicted within a couple of decades they would be storing more information in digital form than in the entire Library of Congress. At that time the upper extent of memory capacity terabytes, i.e. 1000 gigabytes, Dane believed by the turn of the 21st Century mass storage technologies could be at least 4-to-8 orders of magnitude larger. Rick liked to kid that someday Dane would be talking about 'yottabytes', which is one septillion bytes or 1 followed by 24 zeroes or 10^{24} bytes.

Rick said "That is a lottabytes".

As result of this review process, Dane and others considered the possibility using DNA as the ultimate storage medium. Many areas of medical science, from medical diagnostics and procedures to drugs to medical devices and materials for designing and building a state-of-the-art hospital, were also considered over time as part of the technology review process.

During the next ten years they documented information on all aspects of human medicine and stored it for future use. Granted, they knew they may not always have the trained personnel to do operations such as open heart surgery and similarly critical operations. They would have the information required to teach such procedures and were convinced many procedures could done by robotics.

Even they were amazed by the rapid evolution of technology. For example, early in the 21st Century they were pleased with the development of 3-D printing technology allowing the manufacture of unique spare parts…even replacement parts for the human body. They also adopted the use of drones for applications the oil field maintenance and surveillance and as the basis for their weapons system.

By the turn of the century on January 1, 2000, they were prepared for the 'Millennium Scare', the concern over the numerous computer system problems expected as the 20th Century faded into history. They also predicted that sometime in the future that systems based on 32 bits would become obsolete, and in many cases inoperable. Only a bit over 2.1 billion combinations existed. Dane believed systems should be based on at least 64, if not 128 bits. He noted by going to a 64 bit numbering system, the number of combinations would be over 18 quintillion combinations.

Typically Dane selected a technology to be incorporated it into their operations only after rigorous evaluation. Then Rick and his technical staff determined which available alternative should be adopted and whether or not it should be developed internally or with one of their ventures.

Over time Chip proved he was the seasoned executive they needed running Project NewLand, especially in maintaining secrecy. The federal government agencies were frustrated they could not find out how his crew operated. They approached the United Nations for help. As a result, the UN formed the UNMS (United Nations Monitoring System) in total violation of United States laws, but it still operated within the United States with the help of leftwing legal organizations and some rogues in the federal government. Dane uncovered its existence a couple of years into the new century while tracking some mysterious patterns of hacking and monitoring techniques used by a previously unknown organization. When the Republicans took over, the US government found the horse left the barn long ago with no way to slow down the spying by the UNMS, much less stop it.

By the time the 2008 election took place, most media and technology people forgot the mercurial Chip Faraday, but the spy agencies from around the world had not. They knew where to find Chip Faraday, but nothing more. The media just assumed Chip and his merry group of technologists failed and decided to pull in their horns and became harmless survivalist nuts. As far as they were concerned the little town of Kursk was the home of a bunch of technology dropouts who joined the rightwing cult of Jack Barnett, Jr. They barely noted the technology companies started in the area, which remained as low-profile as possible even though several of their developments were economic successes through licensing. None of these companies were very successful by design.

Dane continued to believe wind energy would never be practical in the scale needed to make any difference due to serious maintenance and replacement cost issues. It required traditional major transmission systems as backup. He also warned that solar energy could eventually be a major source of global warming. He noted collected energy remained on earth rather than be reflected, thus, raising the temperature of the earth, i.e. global warming.

He supported the use of solar energy anyway, but believed in a distributed approach. He always kept a sign in his office that read "Reflect not Collect!" and would make reference to how ancient Mediterranean societies white washed buildings with thick earthen walls. He believed while collecting energy makes sense, it made more sense to reflect energy whenever possible. For emergency backup, they purchased and stored a significant number of solar panels for future use, if needed in the future. He continued to remind everyone wind and solar would always be intermittent and would only be useful if adequate battery or capacitive technology evolved over time.

No one outside the inner circle of Chip's personnel knew Chip's wife Sue had developed a nuclear power generation facility based on nuclear sub power systems and the work done by various companies around the world. Over eight years Sue directed the design and manufacture of the facility which they buried several hundred feet underground for future use if and when needed.

Oil and natural gas would continue to be the major source of energy unless the future catastrophe destroyed most oil fields around the world. If that happened, the nuclear power source they developed provided enough fuel to last for approximately 20 years. Rick would joke they would kill each other long before the 20 years passed if they were stuck in the caves that long.

In time Chip believed the infrastructure sufficiently in place and was confident they could routinely handle new threats as they arrived. He decided to implement a major procurement program. This role fell mainly on Rick Christiansen's shoulders and Chip realized he needed a 'right hand man' to support his efforts. This person did not necessarily have to be technically experienced but a person who could continue procurement efforts when he traveled meeting with vendors. No one in the organization appeared capable of doing the job. They needed a hyperactive self-starter who could be aggressive. Rick felt the available people were either too laid-back or just too nice to deal with vendors. The frustrated Rick stomped into Chip's office one morning and said, "Chip, I need to take a couple of days off or my head is going to explode."

Having known Rick for so long he agreed, "You are like a monkey in a banana ranch just picked clean. Get the hell out of here for three or four days."

The next morning Rick took off for Abilene on his motorcycle to see some of his hunting buddies.

CHAPTER 28

RICK MEETS MARY CATE

It was mid-July as Rick rode his motorcycle on the way back to Kursk after visiting friends in Abilene. He'd met them two years earlier while rattlesnake hunting for the first time and enjoyed the experience so much he went back. He found a bunch of guys and gals who liked to hunt anything you could legally hunt and they were planning a major deer hunting trip for the fall.

About 10 miles east of Kursk, he came upon a white Chevrolet compact with the hood up and a steaming radiator with an exasperated young woman standing with her hands on her hips and tears running down her face. He stopped and got off and asked, "Do you need help?"

"What do you think I need? A chopped liver sandwich?" she barked back in a definite east coast accent.

"You from New Jersey?" he asked.

"You stupid or something? Does that look like a Jersey license plate? I am from New York City, the Bronx," as she pointed to the front New York license plate.

"Sorry, but do you need help?" he responded. He thought to himself, "Man this broad has a real attitude."

Then she said in a much nicer voice, "Yes, I need help. I need a lot of help," as she went on to explain she left the east coast when she could not find a job and now was on her way to Phoenix to find a new life.

"Why didn't you stop in Dallas?"

"I did and spent a month there, but found nothing. They are still trying to get over the savings and loan disaster. The economy there is the pits. I used to work in banking and insurance. Nothing!" she offered back. "I have nothing left," and she started crying.

"Hey, hey, let's first get control of the situation. How about riding into town on my bike? We can get a tow truck out here and get your car into town."

"Why, I don't think I can pay for the repairs. I have less than $100 left to my name," she replied, "Do you expect me to ride on that contraption in a skirt?"

Rick told her his name and said he would help her. He said he would take care of her car repair expenses and put her up in the local hotel for the evening. She looked at this guy, wondering if he would take advantage of her. "Why is he doing this? Am I about to be raped and murdered?"

Unshaven and sunburned wearing an old 'West Texas Is Winning' t-shirt he looked like a bum, but he did have a nice motorcycle.

"I have never ridden on a motorcycle. Oh by the way my name is Mary Cate Riley. Actually it is Mary Catherine, typical Irish Catholic name, but I am also a half Italian Catholic," she said as she got on the Harley behind this country hick. It came off almost as a confession for being so different than the people in the area.

As they rode to Kursk, Rick shook his head and thought her attitude would piss off Mother Teresa, but he got kind of a kick out her. She had a pretty face. Not his type of woman, but then he found his sorority sister ex-wife definitely not his kind of woman either. She held on tight fearing she would be thrown off and come face-to-face with the asphalt highway. Ten minutes later they stopped at the local General Motors dealer and arranged for the car to be towed in and serviced.

She remembered she left her belongings in the broken down vehicle, "What about my things in the car? They will be stolen. Will the tow truck driver rob me?"

"You are not in New York City anymore. Jake will protect your belongings. He has a strong German Lutheran upbringing. Nothing will be missing. Let us go have dinner and we can come back to the garage when your car gets there. Then I'll get you a room at the hotel. It is not fancy, but it is clean and comfortable."

Dinner was difficult. At first, all Mary Cate could do was cry. Rick finally calmed her down with his goofy humor and she was finally able to talk about her situation. He assured her that everything would work out for her. She was not convinced, but put on a good front.

After dinner, on the way to the hotel with her belongings from her car, she asked, "Why are you doing this for me?"

"You need help. This is the way we do things around here. Have a good night. I'll contact the shop on Monday and see what has to be done. Then we will decide what we have to do to get you back on the road. What are those weird cigarettes you smoke? I have never seen anything like them."

"They are Capris. Don't worry I have five cartons in the truck of my car, as long as they are not stolen. I can buy more when I get back to civilization." she shot back defiantly.

With that he shook her hand and told the desk clerk to put her meals and other expenses on her hotel tab which he would pay.

"Where do you live?" she asked him as he turned towards the door.

"Out in 'the boonies'," he laughed.

"What the hell can be more 'the boonies' than this place?" she joked.

9AM the next morning he called her room to find her still distraught. "Don't worry. I am taking care of your expenses," he offered. She again wondered who this guy was and why he would do this for a complete stranger. Mary Cate did not know Rick sometimes got bored and enjoyed doing things for other people, plus he got a charge out of the brashness of her personality. "Must be a New York thing," he thought.

"Hey, would you like to see some of the area, like 'the boonies'? I have nothing going on today. I am harmless. By the way, I am single so you are not dealing with a guy cheating on his wife," almost pleading.

Mary Cate said, "Why shouldn't I do something while I am waiting for my damn car get fixed but I need a couple of hours so I can go to Mass. I need to pray and meditate over my problems." She worried through the night and needed to get her mind off her problems.

Rick picked her up a bit after noon for a quick lunch. At least this time he didn't have the motorcycle, instead he drove a new Dodge Ram pickup. They talked about growing up in totally different environments. She had never been to Minneapolis, much less rural Minnesota, and Rick didn't think he had ever been to the Bronx.

Mary Cate wondered why this guy lived out in the middle of nowhere, with an expensive Harley Davidson and a fancy new truck. Why didn't he live in the civilized world? Obviously not a poor yokel on welfare, but he still seemed a hayseed. She mused over what kind of engineer he might be. She would soon find out she was dealing with no ordinary guy.

As they headed out to the country, he gave her a quick overview of the people who ran GLO Industries where he worked for the past three years. He made no reference to Project NewLand. They traveled primitive roads beyond anything she ever saw before thinking they would be attacked by Indians around the next bend.

Looking at the wide open spaces she said, "Hell, Minneapolis is the end of the world, this place is somewhere out in the universe, at least on some foreign body like the moon or Mars. How does a technical guy like you get stuck in a place like this?"

"Would you believe there are three of us guys from Minnesota working here? The other two guys are married. One has three kids and the other one boy. I was married once but she was too fancy for my life style. Fortunately there are no kids and I am thankful for that," he added almost mournfully. "This place grows on a person."

"Yeah, like a goiter. God, I would go nuts living here. There is more excitement in a convent getting bruised knees from kneeling while praying than in this place. Where are the buildings, where are the people, where is the noise? My god, nobody is getting robbed. Haven't heard one siren or seen a fire engine or an ambulance since I got here. I feel like I am at the city morgue," she sarcastically answered as they drove past a herd of cattle.

Rick got a big charge out of Mary Cate. The first time they drove over a cattle guard she jumped thinking they were about to go off the road, "What the hell is that thing?"

He ignored her, then pointed out the big house and gave a brief history of it and why it was built looking like a giant letter 'J' with the northwest leg much longer than the southeast leg. He gave her a brief history of the Robert Barzinsky, the two Jacks and Catherine. Rick told her Robert came from Russia, Jack, Sr. from Ireland and Catherine a local of German Russian heritage. Except for Catherine and Jack, Jr. they were all gone. He told her Jack, Jr. now runs the entire operation, which is a ranching and petroleum exploration and production business. He told her he worked for his childhood friend Chip Faraday.

"Then why are you here? You don't sound like a petroleum engineer or a rancher type," she quizzed him.

Rick stared forward as he drove, pondering how to answer her questions. "Let's say I am here on special long-term project," He immediately knew he made a mistake to say it that way.

That piqued her curiosity, "What the hell do you mean by a 'special long-term project'? I can read all kinds of crazy things into what you just said. Are you a mad scientist? Are you some sort of a survivalist or religious nut? What are you trying to do, overthrow the government?"

No, he told her, not being convincing. Wanting to change the subject Rick said, "Let me show you some of the property. Let's drive down to where I live and do some of my work. When I came here I found this abandoned adobe house on one of the properties. They gave it to me on the condition I fix it up."

They drove for about six or seven miles through more herds of cattle, dozens of oil well pumps, storage tanks and past a series of barnlike buildings. She told him the hills seemed so out of place out in the middle of this barren land.

"Oh my god," she nervously blurted out as they got further away from any sign of civilization. "Now you are going to rape me and cut me into little pieces?"

"Heavens no, boy are you weird. I just want to show you what I do and how I live."

"I'm getting to know a bit of how you live. You have all kinds of toys, motorcycle, truck, you hunt and you probably ramble around this god forsaken place like a little kid on a 4-wheel buggy."

"So, what's wrong with that? I work hard and play hard. Like Dr. Dane Madsen, my freshman physics professor at the University of Minnesota, who is responsible for following advanced technology. He is totally into the theoretical aspects of technology and his hobby is astronomy. It is a great place for astronomy. The skies are so dark at night and in the dark of the moon you can see millions of stars. My job is to apply these technologies in a way to achieve our corporate goals. We work for our boss who works directly for Jack Barnett. Chip is from the same farming community in Minnesota as I am. We have known each other since kindergarten."

Again Rick knew he said too much.

"Sorry if I got you to talk about things you don't want to talk about," she apologized as they drove up to the old adobe house covered with a black structure about 4" thick instead of a traditional tile roof. "The adobe house looks nice, but why the ugly roof? It seems so out of place. Ugh! What a weird looking structure."

"It is part of my system for generating electricity. The sun heats water in pipes running through the black thing on the roof and drives my electric generator along with the wind mill over there. I know it is not elegant but it runs my appliances, air conditioning and heating. I have a bank of storage batteries buried deep underground where the soil temperature is much lower and very stable. The system doesn't have to work very well to satisfy my needs. The adobe house, which is estimated to be over 100 years old, has solid walls over 12" thick and maintains almost a steady temperature all year. Let's see, the temperature outside right now is about 90 degrees. When we go inside you will see I left some of the windows wide open and there is a cool breeze flowing from the northwest. The system only works because we have a considerable amount of wind and sun. One of my next projects is to play with geothermal energy."

"Is this your job?" she asked him, completely perplexed.

"Naw, this is one of my hobbies, along with hunting, fishing and electronics. Many companies are trying to build photoelectric semiconductor arrays to generate electricity. Takes a lot of expensive processing equipment and nasty chemicals, but probably is the way to go where you don't have the abundant natural resources I have, such as water, wind and sunlight. I am more into alternative energy than the liberals who beat their chests bragging how environmentally aware they are. Most people don't realize the first photoelectric was developed way back in the 1890s and they still are not economically feasible, maybe in 25 to 30 years. Did you know that back around the 1920s much of Los Angeles used solar water heating? They probably never should have changed. Just my view."

"You talk about water, where in hell is the water? The only water I have seen is the little piss ant stream we crossed over miles back," she returned to her sarcastic mode of talking back to him. Then she said, "I don't mean to be so nasty."

"Your sarcasm doesn't bother me a bit. There is a huge aquifer about 200 feet under us. Did you notice the windmills we passed by? They are typical water wells, except for mine which is both a well and a wind generator," he responded and thought, "I like a woman who is not a goody-two-shoes and she certainly isn't."

She gave him another dirty look as they entered the old house she noted a large room with a rudimentary kitchen on one end, a dining area in the middle and 'den-like' living area on the other end. Then he told her he also installed the indoor plumbing and then pointed to the old outhouse out back.

"I was either build an indoor bath room or put an air conditioner and heater on that thing," he joked.

An old beat up television covered with dust sat in the corner. Apparent this guy didn't watch TV very often even though she noted a satellite antenna at the side of the house on the way in. The house fit a guy like Rick.

He pointed to the doors to his bedroom and the one across the hall, and then motioned her towards a door to the southeast side of the house that led to his laboratory. He punched in an eight digit code into the keyboard pad on the wall by the door. The door popped open and he motioned for her to enter the room.

Having little technical knowledge she stared in disbelief. "Is this Frankenstein's lab? Are you going to use me as a lab rat? I'm kidding, but what the hell is this stuff doing out here in the middle of nowhere?"

"These are my real toys. I spend hours communicating with people worldwide using different techniques, such as ham radio and satellite communications," he offered with a look of satisfaction, "But I also use this same type equipment, and some much more sophisticated, in my office and lab in a building back near the ranch house to do my real job."

"You are a strange one. You get your kicks out of this? Wow."

They got back in the truck and drove for another half dozen miles. Rick told her Jack Barnett owned most of the land they drove through, but various parcels were owned by some of the original farmers who settled the area, as well as some of the people with whom he worked.

"How rich is this guy?" she asked.

"Nobody knows, maybe not even Jack himself. There are thousands of acres of oil fields throughout the ranchland. Rumor is there is gold stored in these hills. Maybe some mined locally, but the majority purchased over the years and stored here in secret places throughout those hills starting back in the 1930s. Sorry, I should not have told you that, please don't repeat any of this. There is good evidence the U.S. government and even the United Nations snoops have been trying to break into their circle and figure out how to steal it from them for decades. There are many rumors about their wealth. We do know the people who created this financial empire have been secretive going back for almost 90 years when Robert Barzinsky started his first business in New Orleans selling food from a hand push cart after jumping ship."

Mary Cate became more and more fascinated during their long drive.

"Those hills seem to be so out of place. What about the strange looking rock of a hill over there," as she seemed to note the tallest part of the long string of hills poking up from the surrounding flat lands.

"It is a special place. How about going back and getting some dinner?" Rick asked, but did not say any more about the hills.

"Are you sure? You appear busy. I can go back and take care of myself," she answered.

"I am sure. Let's talk about how we are going to get you on your feet financially. Would you like a job?"

"What the hell are you talking about? What would a girl like me from the Bronx do living in a place like this? I would go nuts within a week. Are you crazy?" she fumed.

"Sanity has never been my strong suit. I enjoy being who I am. I don't intend to give you a job forever, just long enough for you to get on your feet financially. Maybe for two or three months so, you can leave with enough cash in your purse to get established in Phoenix," he persisted.

"That is going to take a few martinis to mull over such a prospect and I would probably need several every night if I lived here," Mary Cate laughed as she took another draw on her Capri cigarette.

Rick wondered where in the hell she bought those things. They certainly are not available in Kursk. The name sounded just too chic for Kursk.

"Deal!" and off to Kursk they went.

CHAPTER 29

MARY CATE'S SURPRISE

Mary Cate woke up with a nasty headache. "Damn martinis. I know better than to have more than just one. I wonder how many I drank. For me, one martini is just right, two are too many and three aren't enough," she mused as she started to recollect the events of the previous day and the night before.

They had gone to a steakhouse at the end of town and she enjoyed it, much to her surprise. They both had several drinks, Rick did not show any sign of being tipsy, but she definitely got drunk. All of sudden she thought, "My God! Did he take advantage of me?" She soon concluded he did not, almost disappointed.

She remembered they talked mostly about their childhoods. He grew up on a farm in Minnesota while she grew up in the hustle and bustle of New York City. He was the only child in a happy home, but she grew up in a broken home with two siblings. They were so different except in one area. They both grew up knowing how to do hard work. Rick helped his dad on the farm, but Mary Cate needed to work to survive. During their conversation, she got abrasive and sarcastic at times, but would soon stop and apologize. Rick would always tell her not to apologize and said he enjoyed her sometimes abrasive personality.

She then remembered he made no further mention of a job during dinner the night before and assumed it just a ruse.

Rick called the still woozy Mary Cate just after 9AM, "You ok?"

"I don't know. My head feels like it is going to explode and my mouth tastes like used cat litter. How many martinis did I have last night?

"I think maybe five or six. Not sure. I wanted to let you know your car will be done later today, but I wanted to know if you wanted to talk about the job I mentioned." It got real quiet on the other end of the line.

"Are you serious and this is not just a bunch of bull. If you are serious, I want to know what kind of a job you have. You can't justify a BS job. It would not be right. There is no way I want to remain out here in nowhere land long term. Sorry, I didn't mean to be so caustic," she responded apologetically.

"I have a real job which could last at least three or four months, maybe longer, if you like. With your experience, you would be a good fit for the job. Over the couple of years I have been analyzing products needed to accomplish what our project needs. We are in a major procurement mode and I need someone to interface with a whole range of companies with products and services we need. There will be a large number of suppliers to deal with and shipments will be made to a variety of places around the country. I think you might find it interesting," he offered.

Puzzled she came back with, "Why do you think I could do the job? There is probably nobody more low-tech than I am. I have a hard time making my coffee maker work and what the hell are people going to think when they hear my Bronx accent coming from the middle of nowhere?"

"Simple. You are intelligent, have good instincts and won't let people buffalo you. You have banking and insurance company experience, which will be helpful. Furthermore, few people you would be dealing with know what part of the country they are working with and we like to keep it that way. As I mentioned, few of our purchases are ever delivered here. We have developed a sophisticated re-delivery system, where products are shipped to one place, then transferred here. You are perfect with your accent. These people have been dealing only with us hicks with either a Midwest or a Texas accent. The thought of their confusion trying to figure out where we are located is hilarious and just what we want. You will have to have to sign a non-disclosure agreement."

"Sign a non-disclosure agreement? That is a joke. What could somebody like me know anything that is any risk to your project? Are you sure what you are doing is legal?" as she let out one of her loud chuckles.

She continued, "What will you pay me and how often? You realize I am too broke to afford a place to stay. I don't even have the money to feed myself for more than a few days."

"I have that figured out. Can you show me a pay stub from your last job? I'll pay you the same amount for three months, and then review the situation, if you decide to stay longer. Your living costs will be low. There is a farming family that lives about two miles from my office with a nice apartment over their garage. Your gas expenses will be almost nothing, unless you find yourself going into town a lot. You can live with them for a reasonable amount. Their kids are away, one is career army and the other lives on a farm about 10 miles away. They would love the company," Rick offered.

"What! Are you out of your fricking mind? I would die like a beached whale. How can a city girl like me exist for a week, much less three months, in such an environment?" she screamed back at him.

"Don't be so damned childish. As soon as you get a bit of cash you can find a place to rent in town and as soon as you feel you have enough to move on, you will be free to go, but don't come back once you leave."

"Too bad I am devout Catholic. Suicide is out. Okay Hercules, when can I start so I can start my trip back to civilization?"

"I'll be in late afternoon to get you when your car is ready and then take you out to meet Kurt and Bertha Grauman. They are in their late 60s and are a really nice couple. Kurt, his father Franz and twin brother Kris were the first people Jack, Sr. hired when he started fencing the first sections of land for cattle back in the 1930s. You will like Kurt and Bertha. Tomorrow I'll pick you up about 7:30AM and take you home at the end of the day so you will know how to get to my office and back starting Wednesday," Rick said without giving Mary Cate a clue the Graumans lived in a virtual mansion of a ranch house of over 6,000 square feet. He couldn't wait to see the look on her face when they got there.

They picked up her car and she followed him to the Grauman family's house. She could not believe her eyes when she saw Kurt and Bertha's house. "Holy crap! If these people have this kind of money, why the hell do they live in a place like this?" she thought as she almost ran off the road.

Rick set up the arrangements with Bertha earlier the day before even though he did not know if Mary Cate would accept the job offer. The meeting went well except for her trouble understanding the couple's west Texas drawl with a tinge of German accent which remained since childhood. She could not believe the separate apartment built over the garage, with its own kitchen and bathroom and two television sets would be her temporary home.

"Damn, this is pretty darn nice. No place I lived back in New York looked like this," thinking of where she lived in growing up. Then she found out the Graumans were happy to have a younger person around and they did not even intend to charge her rent, but she would be responsible for her own meals. Later she found out a number of free meals seemed to come with the deal. They liked having someone to talk to, especially someone with her accent. Rick explained they stocked the kitchen with enough for her to get started.

At 7:30 the next morning Rick arrived and took her to work. They entered a non-descript building which contained his office, as well as the offices of Chip Faraday and Dane Madsen, plus about a dozen other employees. Chip, Dane and Jack were all there to welcome her. She took an immediate liking to Dane and Chip, but seemed overwhelmed by the tall weathered Jack. "My god, there is a real Texas redneck," she thought.

After brief introductions, they went to her new office and got to work. Four hours later she already had a list of over 60 suppliers she would be working with on the procurement and shipment of a wide range of products and services. She thought she would be over her head but these people had developed a series of effective procedures and processes. She soon learned the whole world was not a bureaucratic cesspool.

Surprisingly by the end of the day, with Rick's help, she already dealt with four different vendors. Mary Cate blew people away with her Bronx accent. When people asked her where she got her accent, she would answer, "Down the road a piece." Obviously they were trying to figure out where she came from and how she could end up with this bunch of people with Midwestern and Texas accents.

The day exhausted her, but she woke in the morning looking forward to the day. She realized she hated getting up for her last three jobs. They were boring and her co-workers were mostly jerks. She liked working with these guys and gals.

Over the next couple of days she got to know the other employees and what their jobs were. Mary Cate quickly became friends with Liz Housman, a native of Kursk, who came back to the area after getting a business degree at Tarleton State in Stephenville, TX. She started to realize this special project was building and outfitting something quite large. Rick noted her curiosity, particularly her noticing the steady stream of trucks coming and going from the property. Most appeared to be oil tankers, but there were also a number of flat bed and closed semi-trailers. While some trucks obviously carried products like drilling pipes and oilfield equipment, she couldn't understand what the other trucks were transporting.

At the end of the first month, Rick invited her to go to the "Big House" as she named it. They were met by Jack, Chip and Dane. "My god, what have I done? Am I in trouble?" she thought."

Jack started the conversation, "Mary Cate, up front, let me be clear. You are not in any sort of trouble. I know this crew can appear quite ominous, especially an old fart like me. We like your work, but I know you are most likely here on a short term basis. Regardless of how long you will be here, your curiosity is obvious. You are concerned we are doing something illegal. Let me assure you we are not. I am going to tell you some things we do not want to go beyond this organization. For decades my family and others have been dedicated to being ready if some sort of major threat endangers the continuation of civilization as we know it."

"What?" she exclaimed.

"Ok, we could easily sit back and enjoy life. I am extremely rich, but I am compelled to continue the work of my father and his senior partner, both of whom were poor immigrants back early in the century. You probably wonder why I just don't go off to some remote island and live out my life. Frankly, I somewhat enjoy being in this position and, since I have no children, I intend to spread most of my wealth among those who continue this effort after I am gone. I am getting older and my health is not as good as it used to be. I have assembled a cadre of accomplished people. You know the three in this room, but there are others who manage our ranching, energy and other operations, as well as those who you work with on this project."

"Why are you telling me this? I could leave here tomorrow and blabber what I know." she answered with a puzzled look on her face.

"But you won't! And I doubt anyone would believe you," Jack said as he stared his beady eyes directly into hers. It sent a chill down her spine, but as she looked at the other three men she relaxed a bit as Jack continued, "You can be the key to our procurement process and you are better at it than you realize. We are telling you we want you to continue being as effective as you have been as long as you remain." With that he rose and walked towards her chair. As she stood up he gave her a fatherly hug and walked out of the room.

After Jack left, Chip asked Mary Cate, "Are you ok?" She explained her mixed emotions. She never felt as needed as she now did, plus she felt bowled over by the amount responsibility they gave her.

"Ok, then let's go back to work." Rick barked out with a big grin on his face.

As they walked back to their offices, Mary Cate tore into Rick with a vengeance. He laughed at the whole barrage.

"You jackass, why did you put me through that?" she spat at him.

"Just part of our test and you passed with flying colors," he responded.

"So I am some sort of guinea pig you can play your silly game with and expect me to take it? Ok, so you proved I can take it. Let's get back to work." She continued with a bit of a grin on her face.

As time went on Mary Cate interfaced with more and more of their suppliers, but Rick still had not told her what they did with the products they purchased ranging from such things as dozens of storage cabinets and shelves to large pieces of industrial, medical and computer equipment. They also needed for a continued supply of food and medications, as well as other products, to buy to assure inventory is kept fresh.

Over the next month Chip and Rick spent more time with her explaining that over the years they developed what he called an 'earthship', a place where a limited number of people could live and enjoy life for a fairly significant period of time in case of a major world-wide catastrophe.

Rick went into Chip's office one Monday morning about two months after Mary Cate joined the organization, "Mary Cate isn't here today. She called in sick. She has never done that before. I tried calling her and no one answered the phone. Then I called Bertha and she told me she had not seen Mary Cate all weekend. This is totally uncharacteristic of her. She has not missed one day since she has been here. I hope there is nothing wrong with her."

"You are worked up. Do you need her here on the job or do you really need her?" Chip noted Rick seemed to be almost in awe of this woman.

"What do you mean?" Rick shot back.

"Just making an observation, you seem to be comfortable having her work for you. You got a crush on her? Let's face it, you have had a number of girlfriends, but you have never seemed as discombobulated as you are right now. Boy, opposites must attract each other. I don't know any two people with more different personalities than you two. Also, she is nothing like your ex-wife," Chip smiled at his old friend.

Rick stomped out of Chip's office got in his truck, drove to her apartment and knocked on the door.

"Go away you bastard," she screamed. "I want all of you bastards to go away."

For the next hour they bantered back and forth through the door. Finally Rick got her to open the door. She had been crying but now just plain angry totally puzzling Rick. She sat down and stared him in the eye, "Why did I have to have my car break down in this god forsaken place?"

"What is the matter? Do you hate your job? Do you hate us? What is going on?" he pleaded.

"I like my job!" she bawled.

"What the hell is going on?" Rick asked totally blown away, "If you like your job why are you so upset? Don't you like the people you work with? Is it me or is it Chip or Dane? Does Jack scare you?"

"No, I like all of you, especially you," she blurted out. "It is just I hate this place. It is so dull around here when I am away from work I sit and listen to the paint peel."

"Do you want to stay or do you want to leave?" he asked trying to make sense of her behavior.

"Yes I want to stay, but yes I want to go. I don't know what I want. This is the first job I have ever liked and the people are so nice, but it gets so boring around here. I am afraid I will go crazy if I stay here."

"What if you could get out of here and go back east or to the west coast or other places several times a year?" he posed.

This brought Mary Cate to a total state of awareness. She wanted to know how could be possible with Kursk so far from the rest of the world with even Dallas seven hours away by car.

"Within the next couple of months, it is going to be necessary for a couple of people to visit a number of our vendors. With some training, I believe you could visit some of the less technical vendors. It would take some of the load off me and could get you to visit around the country, even get back to New York once or twice a year. And you wouldn't have to drive to Dallas-Ft. Worth either. You would travel back and forth to DFW on one of the corporate jets. Not a bad way to travel and then you get to fly First Class." Rick offered.

He went on to tell her she would have to be brought into the secret nature of Project NewLand if she decided to stay. She never heard the term before, but she had heard the term Zeus. He said she would have to go through some interviews to be sure she wanted to stay.

Stunned, Mary Cate wondered what she could be getting herself into and realized her life would never be the same again.

With that he said, "Think about it. Take some time. When you are ready to make your decision, call me." He then got up, gave her a hug and walked out of the door. In total shock she didn't even return the hug. This made her upset with herself. She liked the people she work with, especially Rick. At the time she didn't realize how much she cared for him.

GETTING READY

CHAPTER 30

FINAL PREPARATIONS

At 8AM the next morning Mary Cate walked into Rick's office and announced, "I'm your gal. Let's get with it. I'm a day behind with my work. Tell me what I have to do."

"Get caught up and then we will meet with Jack and Chip. I am happy you made the decision to stay with us. You will not be bored," he joked.

"That is what worries me," she laughed back at him.

The next three days were hectic. Not only did she have to make up for the missed day, but a couple of shipments got lost. After much consternation she determined the destinations for the shipments got switched. "Hell, this may queer the whole deal for me," she fretted.

Instead she proved her mettle when she recovered from the problem with a quick re-direction of the two trucks. Fortunately, the two rail stops were only 35 miles apart, but she was still worried.

Unbeknownst to either Rick or Mary Cate, Chip just completed doing a serious background check on Mary Cate. He asked Dane do a second check to be sure she could be trusted and dependent. Rick would have really been pissed if he knew this had been done, but Chip wanted to be sure.

On Friday morning she received a call from Chip, "You able to come to my office?"

Ten minutes later she sat in front of Chip trading small talk as they waited for Jack and Rick. Jack came in last with a big grin on his face, "You want to be a fixture in this nuthouse?"

He went on to tell her what they were going to be discussing proprietary information for the next several hours and that when they finished, she needed to make a decision quickly. If she decided to leave, she had to promise not to divulge anything she knew about NewLand.

Jack spent the first hour explaining the history of Project NewLand and then Chip explained the current status of the program, "We are at the point we have to do some major purchases of goods and services before doing a complete test of the system in case of a major disaster. New applications are being developed by companies like Apple Computer and a bunch of newer startups at an accelerating rate."

He explained their goal was to not only keep up with the latest technology advances but remain in a position to adapt these advances to applications on a real time basis. Mary Cate's head reeled, "I don't know if I can keep up with what you are talking about!"

"Don't worry, we all are overwhelmed at times," Chip responded. With that Jack let out a roar, telling her she should just think what it must be to be an old relic like him trying to keep up. He wondered what Robert and his dad would think of what has been done to what they thought initially was just a project to get away from it all. As they aged, they constantly were wowed by what happened to their simple beginnings many years earlier.

After four grueling hours, the meeting ended. The three of them congratulated her on her decision and welcomed her to the inner circle of Project NewLand. She became the 48th person to know the whole story out of approximately 100 involved in the project. One of the next steps was to expand the number to over 80, and then to about 120 with a well-defined vetting process to qualify the people involved. There was a considerable amount of work ahead of them. Any additional population beyond that would be family members not directly involved in the operation.

Chip's assistant brought in lunch and the business discussions ended. Obviously these people liked each other and enjoyed working together. Mary Cate wondered how many organizations operated this cordially. Then she shuddered when she realized, if a major catastrophe happened, she would probably survive, but then she would be stuck at the edge of the world for the rest of her life. Not a pleasant thought for her, but her decision was to stay.

The next several months were busy getting familiar with the products needed and the subsequent vendors selected.

At noon on a Saturday Rick and Mary Cate just finished a grueling week. As they walked towards the parking lot, Rick asked, "What are you doing today?"

"What do you mean? During the weekend I never do anything but sit in my apartment and watch the soaps I have recorded during the week. What else is there to do here in Dullsville?"

"Wanna go for a motorcycle ride?"

"A motorcycle ride? Are you talking about me getting onto that thing of yours again? You want to put me in a full body cast? Why not your truck?" she responded with her usual sarcasm.

"I want to take you some places you have never been before and it is not possible to take the truck to some of them."

She reluctantly accepted his offer. An hour later Rick came to her apartment and off they went to the south, first passing company headquarters and then headed off to the southwest. Mary Cate said, "Oh good, I am going to see some more of your toys."

Rick did not respond as they rode past his adobe house, then past a number of oil wells and storage tanks. He slowed down when the road turned into a couple of tire tracks. As they approached 'The Hull', Rick explained Jack, Sr. first discovered it back in the early 1930s. He said he wanted to show her the series of caves that ran inside the bank of hills.

Mary Cate asked, "Why are you showing me this?" Rick responded by telling her the products they were purchasing end up in these caves and he wanted to show her the results of what she had been doing for the past nine months.

After they passed by 'The Hull', the road deteriorated to a pock marked trail filled with prairie dog holes. It puzzled Mary Cate and she asked, "How they could get the equipment and materials they bought into these caves without better roads?"

"It gets a little involved, but there is a good set of roads at various places along the hills running perpendicular to this road. They are so well camouflaged you did not even notice when we passed over two of them. We will cross over another four before we get to our destination. Tell me if you see any of them. Right after WWII Jack, Sr. hired several ex-military people, Corps of Engineers guys, who could build almost anything. They were so clever they could camouflage Main Street of downtown Dallas so you wouldn't recognize it," he exaggerated.

"These roads were also keys in the building of the structures inside the caves which are used for storage, open areas and residences. It is an amazing thing to see. Some of these structures have some unbelievable characteristics I'll tell you about when we get inside."

The road soon became nothing but a cow path. Rick slowly guided the motorcycle around prairie dog holes and rocks, finally reaching a wall. Mary Cate identified one of the intersecting roads but missed the other three. The roads were not visible from the air and they never allowed visitors anyway near the hills after WWII.

Rick dismounted and helped her off of the bike. She rubbed her butt and said, "I am going to have to sit in my bathtub for the rest of the weekend. "Does our health plan cover massages?" She gave him a nasty look, fully aware of their good healthcare insurance at little cost. As usual, Rick ignored her complaints.

As they approached the base of the hill, Rick pushed a button on a device he held in his hand and a portion of the wall opened. Rick told her if a large truck approached the area, a much larger opening would appear. Once inside, the lights came on so Mary Cate could see a large area with a number of structures.

Rick began to explain what they saw inside the cave, "This is an industrial area. Behind these walls are the offices and warehouses supporting the oil refinery in the next cave. In another cave, a nuclear power plant is buried deep in the ground. It can supply the power we would need for about 20 years. It may seem strange to have these sitting here in reserve for a time they may be needed. Once a month the systems are tested.

You have no idea how difficult it is to keep this system in tip-top condition. It is just one more example how committed we all are to be prepared for what many of us think is inevitable. Other caves have residences, schools and whatever else is needed to house a couple of hundred people for a long period of time. A number of these caves have been fortified to survive anything but a direct nuclear blast. It turns out two of the Corp of Engineers guys were instrumental in building the silos used to contain nuclear tipped missiles and other fortified structures."

"You know I like you people and enjoy the job, but I still think y'all are as nutty as a grove of pecan trees." Mary Cate commented, surprised to hear she could speak like a southern gal. Rick just ignored her as he did many of her comments.

As they left the cave, he told her there were caves of various sizes the length of the hills from 'The Hull' to where they were. Mary Cate then says, "Ok cowboy where are we going next? You could have used the truck to get here along this country road."

"You will see when we get there. Don't be so damned impatient, we are going to travel back along the tram system inside the caves." As they did, Rick stopped at several more caves to show her the work done and then they rode on and exited back at 'The Hull'. From there Rick drove along the side of the hills to the opening at the end of the valley and slowly made their way uphill along the stream.

"Are we supposed to be here? Isn't this some kind of secret place?" she asked. As usual, Rick ignored her fully aware it ticked her off to be ignored. He went around to the right saddle bag and pulled out a blanket and spread it out on the grass and then he went to the other side of the motorcycle and got out a bottle of white wine packed in ice, plus some cheese and crackers.

"Wow, John Wayne is turning into Cary Grant. What's the occasion?"

"Well, we have made considerable progress the past nine months and I wanted to celebrate a bit. Also, I wanted to be alone with you," Rick said sheepishly and with a red face.

"Are you blushing you big oaf? I didn't think you had it in you," as she put her arms around his large frame and gave him a big kiss. "I have wanted to do this for a long time."

They enjoyed the late afternoon sipping wine and munching on their cheese and crackers. What happened next surprised both of them. They made love.

They crossed the Rubicon, in reverse. From then on their relationship became more gentle and loving, instead of cantankerous and sarcastic like it had been since they first met. Neither of them fully realized what happened. Rick noted it began to get dark and the ride down the hill. It would be real dangerous if they did not get going.

Back at his house Rick put a frozen pizza in the oven and opened another bottle of wine which they enjoyed before falling to sleep on the couch. They woke up in the next morning still sitting next to each other.

Mary Cate spoke first, "That sure as hell was not the way I thought it would happen!"

"What do you mean? How it supposed to happen?" Rick shot back.

"A woman has this fantasy of how she would realize when she found the man she wanted to be with. Yesterday certainly wasn't my fantasy. Sorry, I didn't mean to offend you."

"You didn't. I hoped yesterday would be the day we would express how felt about each other and it was. I am very happy and hope you are too."

She nodded with a smile.

CHAPTER 31

REACHING STABILITY

1990s

Mary Cate sat in the dark on the porch behind her apartment above the Grauman's garage after returning from a week's trip to New York City. At the end of the first year of her new role of working with critical vendors, she was now the organization's medical services procurement specialist. Little did she realize what additional duties would be thrust on her over the next several years. She drew on her Capri cigarette in a state of deep thought. Rick often tried to get her to quit smoking, but no dice.

"Another fascinating experience," she said to herself realizing she just finished a big job, satisfied to the point of considering west Texas as her home, something she never thought possible.

The Kursk hospital's medical staff consisted of Dr. Samuel Benson, a GP, and a young orthopedic physician named Pete Watkins. Both were part of Project NewLand, as well, but several more specialists were badly needed before anything catastrophic happened. For example, they were concerned about the mental welfare of the populace if they ended up trapped inside the series of caves due to radiation resulting from a nuclear war or some other condition. They were also concerned about the physical damage resulting from being denied sunlight for an extended period of time. After much discussion, they decided they needed an experienced medical director. Chip had a candidate in mind: Dr. Ronald Lansing, head of heart surgery and on the board of directors of the New York hospital where he practiced.

Chip met with Dr. Lansing several times, but being concerned about being too visible, he gave Mary Cate the job of approaching Dr. Lansing in person. The next morning Mary Cate caught a ride on the corporate jet to DFW and flew to New York. There she met with Dr. Lansing, ostensibly to discuss heart medications Dr. Benson should stock in case of an emergency.

The doctor, a strong conservative looking for a change, had long been interested in the work of Jack Barnett, Jr. and Chip Faraday. When Chip Faraday met with him earlier in the year, they immediately found out their philosophies were similar. After a long discussion, he agreed to sign a non-disclosure agreement. Mary Cate gave him a snapshot of the recent activity at their headquarters in Texas.

He spent his entire career working in the New York City area, but wanted a new challenge since his wife recently passed away from a long bout with cancer. With no children and after her death, Dr. Lansing felt an increasing urge to leave big city life. In preparation, he moved most of his assets to a blind trust under an assumed name in the Bahamas. At dinner Mary Cate, at Chip's direction, suggested he join them in Texas. He said he might be interested.

The next Monday Jack and Chip met Dr. Lansing in disguise when he arrived at DFW. On the flight to the ranch they realized the good doctor, being a conservative and an outdoorsman, was primed to join their project. Discussions progressed so well over drinks and dinner Jack and Chip decided to see if he was interested. By the end of the next day, the deal closed. The doctor decided to fake his death disappearing while fishing in the Catskills and joined the program. There would be some serious suspicions if this famous doctor showed up in a burg like Kursk. He got a real charge following the search for him over the next several years.

He immediately became the project's heart specialist and medical director for both the recently completed NewLand hospital and Kursk hospital. The other two doctors were excited to be working with 'Dr. Ron Lawrence', his assumed name, who immediately grew a beard and dyed his hair. How he kept his credentials no one except Jack and Chip ever knew. Did he really have a license? No one knew for sure. Within a year Dr. Lawrence completely outfitted the project's hospital and prepared the staff to leave their jobs at the small Kursk hospital with their complete staffs and patients on a moment's notice. Dr. Ron had a former medical school friend who was a conservative psychiatrist unhappy with the trend of medicine in the state of Oregon. Within 3 months Dr. Dean Dickson and his wife, a clinical psychologist also joined them in Kursk.

During this time, Dane and Rick made considerable progress in updating the data collection and storage system, thus allowing for Dr. Ron, as he came to be known, and his crew to map out a plan for establishing a state-of-the-art medical library, including an extensive array of medical school books, just in case they were in a situation where the staff required considerable on-the-job training. It also resulted in a major upgrade to the hospital in Kursk, which few realized had been duplicated in the caves. Dane and Rick were pleased when they found the technology they developed was transferrable to each major area of their operations from energy technology to food growth to the manufacture of products and to the medical needs of the community.

Jack and Chip were so happy with the work of Dane, Rick and Mary Cate they were given bonuses and major raises. They realized when a catastrophe occurred money, even gold, would have little value, while the food and supplies preparations made over the decades would have tremendous value. They told three of them to go and enjoy life for a while.

Chip told Dane to take a month's vacation with his wife and son before the school year started and strongly suggested to Rick I was time for him to marry Mary Cate and go on a long honeymoon after Dane returned from his break. On the spot Rick proposed to Mary Cate and she accepted. So typical of these two, they never did anything typical. Afterwards Rick told her he would have been devastated if she turned him down, to which she gave one of her classic chuckles.

Six weeks later they were married in the county courthouse instead of the Catholic Church since Rick was divorced, with Chip being Rick's best man and her friend Liz being her bridesmaid. Dane Madsen and Bertha Grauman were also attendants. They spent their honeymoon in the mountains of Colorado on Rick's Harley Davidson. Much to Mary Cate's surprise, she enjoyed the entire trip having never seen the wonders of the Rocky Mountains before. She completed her transformation and now was a country girl who loved the boonies as much as she loved Rick.

All the while Chip became more concerned about the world situation. Those in the inner circle knew, if a major catastrophe occurred, Jack had devised a system to take those involved in the project into the cave system, but it needed to be expanded to cover other residents of NewLand. During the late 1970s many of the people of the area around Kursk worried about the direction of the country's politics and economic policies, so they formed the Conservative Club of Kursk. As expected, it proved to be somewhat divisive and the group was strongly damned and criticized by the local liberals, who were a distinct minority. A number of other people remained uncommitted.

The CCK became the vehicle to recruit and qualify individuals and their families to be members of Project NewLand, thus assuring their inclusion in time of a catastrophic event. This turned out to be a fairly straight forward program since they used the same system they used to bring new employees into the fold. The program first tested the local police, fire and hospital personnel making sure procedures for bringing their families to safety were in place.

While always concerned about people defecting and the rabble rousing by the liberals in the area, Jack, Jr. found it best to fight fire with fire. He read Saul Alinsky's *Rules for Radicals* for the first time shortly after it was first published in 1971. He re-read it often, always with a copy on his desk and he kept a summarized list of Alinsky's rules tacked the bulletin board above his desk.

He used Rule #5 regularly: "Ridicule is a man's most important weapon." Having been associated with Robert and his dad for so many years, like them he was a master of ridiculing his critics. At one time or another, he used every one of Alinsky's rules against liberals. They were so successful left-wingers complained conservatives were stealing their thunder, proving they were accomplishing their goals. Even with this in mind they knew they always had to be diligent.

One of their biggest concerns was how to handle exceptions at the time an emergency occurred. A set of guidelines were set up to handle these exceptions fully knowing any late admissions would add to the potential mental problems the sequestered colony would face. Unfortunately, they never found a way to test guidelines, but they were prepared for immediate action at the time people were brought into the cave system.

Once the 1988 elections were over and the new administration prepared for taking over the government of the United States, Jack and Chip held their periodic strategy meeting with their staff. They reviewed the past administration and looked forward to the next four years. Although happy with the fall of the Berlin Wall, which happened about a year into the George H. W. Bush administration, they began following a couple of new issues.

Dane began to track the Middle-East following the 1990 gulf war. Rick remembered being in Ireland at the time of the response to Saddam Hussein's attack on Kuwait. He laughed at the Irish reaction to how fast the U.S. military got things done. They had not seen battlefield leadership like General Schwarzkopf since General Patton during WWII. The people at Project NewLand were frustrated President George H. W. Bush did not continue the battle until the military defeated Saddam Hussein and removed him from leadership of Iraq.

Although the Reagan years resulted in higher spending, Project NewLand's management believed the tremendous growth in the economy, after the doldrums of the late 1970s, justified the additional spending levels. With the 1992 election, they believed the Democrats would take the country more towards a socialistic form of government, resulting in dramatically increased federal spending and more bureaucracy.

They were particularly concerned about Hillary's ranting about socialized medicine after Bill Clinton's election. Jack immediately re-read Saul Alinsky's *Rules for Radicals*, happy his parents and Robert were no longer alive. It would have traumatized the little man and depressed his parents. In general, the Clinton years turned out to be relatively positive…except for Clinton's scandals which hung in the air for years like a dirty blue dress in a crowded closet.

At one staff meeting, Mary Cate brought up the subject of health insurance. "What do you mean health insurance?" Rick asked. The others looked puzzled.

"Look, we have been coddled by Jack and pay hardly anything for our health insurance, but we have car insurance, homeowners' or renters' insurance and, who knows, how many other kinds of insurance requiring the payment of premiums. What happens when disaster strikes? There will be no State Farm, Farmers, Liberty Mutual or any other insurance company around. And what about those of you who have been paying for life insurance or any other type of insurance? There will be no Prudential, no Met Life or John Hancock, not any insurance company," Mary Cate added.

She continued, "But what is of most concern to me is health insurance for the people around here not covered by Jack. What about those who will need health insurance? There will be no Blue Cross/ Blue Shield, no United Healthcare. Nobody! I spent several years in the health insurance business. With the crap being proposed by Hillary Clinton, who knows what we are going to end up with. We could be in big trouble. I hear Parkland Hospital management in Dallas is in bed with the concept of HillaryCare and they want the employees to kiss ass with Clinton and her merry gang of Socialists. I don't care for it at all. It is just going to be European Socialized style medicine all over the place…only worse. I am sure there are an increasing number of people looking at the government taking control and saying 'Hey that is a neat idea. It is free'. That is bull shit." She became embarrassed and blushed.

She never had sworn that much in front of management before. Rick roared.

Recovering her composure she continued, "Also, friends of mine were in London several years ago and were disturbed at what they saw at an orthopedic hospital near Paddington Station. They told me there were people milling around this hospital waiting for some type of treatment, with some of these people apparently deteriorating for a long time waiting for medical attention. We have also heard horror stories out of Canada, such as waiting 6 months for a CAT-Scan and a year or more for an operation. People die while waiting in line. Just wait, we will have that happening here, too. I don't like the prospects one bit. This is not health care.

Unfortunately this is where our system is going to end up if we do not prepare. It is just one more way for progressives to control the population. If you can't get treated you can't work, if you can't work you are then a ward of the state. All we will get is more government, but fewer satisfactory results. It is just that simple."

She obviously struck a chord. They immediately understood what she said. Jack then spoke, "Mary Cate is exactly right. GLO Industries has been taking care of the personnel of both the petroleum and ranching employees and those of you involved with Project NewLand. That is fine, but what about the other people who will join us in time of disaster. And what happens if I am gone?"

For the next two hours they discussed only healthcare insurance. Chip ended the discussion, "I want Mary Cate, Dr. Ron and me to attack this issue. Mary Cate just blew the lid off a very big issue. I cannot believe with all of the planning over the decades not one of us thought of this problem before."

They knew they would not need auto insurance for a group of around 300 people living inside a set of caves. They also did not foresee much danger of crimes like robbery or property insurance either. Maybe it would change once they were able to leave the cave system, but not in the beginning. And no way did they want to develop a 'government does all' situation.

Chip constantly insisted when they implemented insurance NewLand would continue to be a Capitalistic organization. Over the next several months, the three of them spent a number of hours discussing how to protect themselves properly, primarily in the area of healthcare and life insurance, which proved to be tough problems to resolve.

At the end of six months, Mary Cate presented the concept of 'mutual insurance' organizations where the subscribers were the shareholders. Chip decided it best to establish the health insurance organization first and not surprisingly named Mary Cate to run the operation. She was overwhelmed at first, frightened by the prospect of accepting so much responsibility.

Chip said, "Look. You are my choice and it is not my practice to make such a major decision and not support the people I select for the job. Big jobs make big people, not the opposite. Unfortunately, the federal government never has and probably never will understand the concept. We have these 'big men and women' in DC and they do nothing but create bigger problems. They have never learned how to develop people and create solutions. We will take it slow and make certain we do it right."

As so often before, Jack Barnett knew he made the correct decision in hiring Chip Faraday as his replacement. Everybody in the room assured Mary Cate they agreed with the decision, as did the other employees when Chip made the announcement of her promotion. Now Mary Cate needed to deliver again as another big job was thrust upon her and this one would not be completed over night.

The next few years went better than expected. Even though quite liberal, Bill Clinton had been a governor for a number of years and over time he moved towards the middle enabling Republicans to compromise on a number of issues. Also, HillaryCare never developed. Chip believed the 'Young Turks' and Newt Gingrich's 'Contract with America' in 1995 forced him into this position. As a result the late 1990s were quite prosperous.

Late in the 1990s Catherine was diagnosed with breast cancer and Jack concentrated on her welfare. Unfortunately she did not survive and passed away shortly before the end of 1998. Her funeral was a solemn affair the entire area attended. Even the people of Valley Center loved and admired this gracious lady. Jack took his fourth serious blow very hard. Chip stepped in as acting CEO of GLO Industries for almost a year, but just before the end of 1999, Jack bounced back to his old self. As usual, he surprised them.

CHAPTER 32

DECLINE OF JACK, JR.

2000s

Early in the new decade the dot-com stock boom split at the seams and a major price correction occurred. The NASDAQ hit its peak of over 5100 in the spring of 2000, a level not surpassed until early 2015. The NYSE went down also and did not achieve new highs until 2012.

The rise of radical Islamic groups around the Middle-East, particularly the Taliban in Afghanistan, and the continued atrocities of Saddam Hussein in Iraq concerned the people involved in Project NewLand. The last decade of the 20th Century saw a group called Al Qaeda come on the scene with the son of a rich Saudi as its leader. In fact, most regions of the Mideast and much of Africa developed their own radical Islamic group. Rick and Chip both thought about the 1983 movie *High Road to China* starring Tom Selleck. Although supposedly set in the 1920s, Rick felt the tribal chief character in the movie glamorized people like Osama bin Laden. The movie made the tribal chief look like a happy hero. To Rick, the response to this character demonstrated the naivety of the American populace.

The horrible attacks of September 11, 2001 or 9/11 by Al Qaeda faced George W. Bush less than eight months after his inauguration. Most believed Osama bin Laden selected the date because of the use of '911' as the emergency number in the United States. Rick noted the expulsion of the Moors from Spain started around September 11, 1492. He said historians and the media ignored this fact on purpose and instead highlighted the arrival of Columbus in the western hemisphere later the same year. He also firmly believed it was the Islamists' revenge for the Battle of Vienna which started on September 11, 1683 when King Jan Sobieski of Poland helped the Austrians defeat the Ottoman Turks and pushed them back to the Middle-East.

Early in the decade the health insurance program for NewLand was fully operational. Mary Cate spent several years developing and operating a health care model including the employees of Project NewLand. It also provided insurance for any people brought into the cave system at the time of an emergency.

Early on, Mary Cate and Chip considered the issue of funding and made the decision to wean employees off the company teat as soon as possible. This seemed to be a move in the wrong direction by many, but Chip explained if and when a disaster occurred, GLO Industries would be their virtual government in the form of NewLand and the result would be socialized medicine. The conversion process began soon with employees paying an additional 20% of their premiums to the mutual healthcare insurance company each year, with the conversion completed in five years. Again taking a mathematical approach to solving a problem, they decided to increase premiums by 25% for each doubling of a family's income. A decision some did not approve of without complaint.

Taking the lead from Dane and his experience with health insurance as a young man back in the early 1960s, they established the plan as a major medical program, with a sizeable deductible. This minimized the amount of paperwork and bureaucracy, thus reducing to overall cost of medical care. Knowing there would be times when a policy holder could not pay his or her medical bills, Chip established what he called a 'slush fund'. When additional funds were required, the policyholders would be assessed on the basis of percentage ownership of the insurance companies. This impressed Jack and he provided initial funding of $10,000,000 in gold bullion for emergency coverage remembering Robert's opinion of paper money. They next established a process for bringing future outsiders and even non-quals, into the mutual insurance program. The level of ownership was based on the amount of premiums paid over time. Policy holders knew with quick access to the plan's website the value of his or her holdings.

Along the way, they created a mutual life insurance company using the same guidelines. Chip selected Mary Cate's friend Liz Houseman as the CEO. Again Jack presented the company with an initial investment of $10,000,000, also in gold bullion, for unexpected damages, making it fully clear it would not cover any property outside of NewLand. Once they were able to leave NewLand after a disaster, they were aware the scope of the insurance programs would have to be expanded.

As usual Rick added his two cents, "What do you think the liberal feminists at Code Pink would think of this? Women in charge! Wow! What a novel idea."

Chip continued to advise people the intent of the two companies was to provide insurance and not a way to create wealth. Wealth was to be created by the Capitalistic system and every possibility for creating wealth through capitalism would be encouraged with significant seed funding for new products and services readily available.

He knew he would be accused by critics of trying to create Utopia, assuming any critics survived. He acquired the attitude of Robert and the Barnetts: "Who gives a damn what you think? Anything built on Capitalism is superior to the trash heaps of history created by Socialism, Communism and Fascism, as well as any royalty throughout history."

Jack also decided it was time to create a system of currency for NewLand, primarily based on gold and silver. Since Robert and his stored gold coins and bullion for decades, minting gold coins created no problems. Minting silver coins for smaller face value created a problem.

No significant silver inventory of consequence existed, so a program of buying silver bullion was initiated being careful not to be noticed in the metals markets. A series of designs were created for values from a dime, quarter and dollar equivalent minted from silver, as well as five dollar through 1000 dollar equivalents of gold. This was done even though most transactions done in NewLand would be done electronically and realizing that many of the higher value coins would be collectors' items.

Concurrent with these actions, Jack and Chip created a bank, with Kristian Grauman's son Gerd as bank president. This was a natural move since he had been on the board of directors of the Kursk bank for the past 20 years. With this in place, NewLand would be able to operate financial transactions as soon as it was necessary to retreat into the cave system.

During the year 2002 they determined their preparations for long term survival were in place and the job going forward was more of maintenance and periodic upgrade. Jack's health started declining mid-decade and Dr. Benson told him he needed to back off his 50 years of non-stop working. At this time Chip also added the position of CEO of GLO Industries. This proved to be a natural time for this change. Chip, with Jack's full support, began to use more GLO Industries assets as a source of funds for new ventures based in the area, a move Jack supported with the anti-carbon sentiment bubbling up across the US. Typical of Jack he said, "Burn the bastards at their own game."

Jack slowed down after giving up the CEO position. A new role for the active man and it caused some difficulties for him. Mary Cate, who recently retired as CEO of the health insurance company although she remained an active consultant, took it upon herself to help the hard charging man to develop some hobbies. He started doing water color paintings of the land he loved so dearly for so many years. Mary Cate also convinced Jack he had a fascinating story to tell and he should be an author. Introspective about his life and the lives of his parents and Robert Barzinsky, he started writing the history of GLO Industries and the people involved. The first book of his planned trilogy was a biography of how his father emigrated from Ireland and became a partner with the mysterious Robert Barzinsky and how they developed their incredible wealth. Volume II told the love story of his parents, a labor of love for him. By the middle of 2006, Jack finished the first two books, neither of which made any mention of Project NewLand. Both books were successfully published at the same time.

He then set about writing the history of Project NewLand to be published far in the future, a date when the secrets of their saga of over 100 years could be told for the sake of history. Unfortunately, later in the year Jack's health declined and the complete story was never written by someone so intimately involved. He passed away during the summer of 2007 at which time Chip lost the man who recruited him from Silicon Valley. For the rest of his life Chip remembered the fateful day he drove from Dallas to Jack's deathbed. There was so much more he wanted to discuss with Jack, but time ran out.

He realized the towering figure of Jack Barnett was no longer there support him. As the head man, Chip grew into the job, just as Jack expected. By this time, his three children were long grown up and ventured out in their own lives. After the attack of 9/11 they moved back to Kursk. His daughters both married local men and his son Michael married a young woman from another Texas town he met at Texas A&M. While at A&M he was a member of the Corps of Cadets and received substantial military training during the four years he spent at the university. Coming from Kurst, Michael had no philosophical differences with the conservative and highly patriotic atmosphere of the Corps.

After graduating with a BS in Physics he entered the Air Force as a 2nd lieutenant, assigned to flight school at Sheppard AFB in Wichita Falls, TX. He excelled as a fighter pilot which he did for 5 years before resigning from the Air Force as a Captain. He decided he needed some additional education and returned to Texas A&M where he earned a Ph.D. in Applied Physics in only 3 years after which he returned to Kursk to do research in what he called "optimal integration of energy resources", the subject of his Ph.D. thesis.

Michael grew up in awe of his parents, especially his mother's experience with and knowledge of nuclear energy. Once he moved to Kursk as a child, he began to understand the role of different sources of energy and thought about how to optimally combine their use. Dr. Madsen provided him with a theoretical approach to analyzing the role of carbon based, solar and wind energy, as well as nuclear energy. He also spent hours tagging along with Rick while he tinkered with his energy systems at the old adobe house. Later he watched the construction of the small nuclear plant near the existing oil refinery inside the NewLand cave system. He observed a major problem existed with the energy infrastructure of the United States, especially the burden of the energy grid's dependence on an extensive distribution system. As a result his Ph.D. thesis explored his theory "The United States must reduce its dependence on an extensive and expensive transmission system" in order to survive long term.

He approached his research with the question: "How can we eliminate or at least dramatically reduce the need for high voltage transmission systems?" Although fascinated with the extremely large 'solar farms' and extensive wind power installations, he treated both of these applications as future dinosaurs. Both energy sources promoted further use of extensive high voltage transmission systems, both increasingly expensive and causing further visual blight to the environment. He pondered the value of the real estate that could be recovered by the elimination of much of the transmission infrastructure of the United States. He also worried the power grid could be severely damaged by sabotage or a solar storm.

Michael agreed with Dr. Madsen and his belief wind power systems were expensive and unreliable long term. He hypothesized the source of energy is the most effective efficient when as local as possible. He watched as solar panels became economically feasible for applications such as road signs, remotely located applications, such as farms, and believed the best approach used small solar systems as locally as possible.

He concluded the optimal solution to be combinations of clean natural gas power plants supplemented with small nuclear plants and local solar panel and battery storage systems, combined in such a way to minimize transmission lines. For example, he believed burying small nuclear power plants several hundred feet underground provided a viable long-term solution. These would be based on the design of early nuclear submarine power sources and capable of supplying power to urban populations of 20,000 to 50,000 people and provide an approach to dramatically reduce the need for high voltage transmission lines. He modeled a simplified electric grid consisting of hundreds of these compact nuclear power plants requiring no high voltage transmission lines coupled with local solar collection and battery storage.

Michael was also interested in the environmentally safe use of coal and consulted with pro-carbon energy researchers in several northern states highly dependent on the use of coal. He believed the development of various coal cleansing technologies could be developed resulting in small clean and competitive local power generation systems, but it would take at least a decade or two to become competitive and private industry needed to fund the research.

Fortunately, he attended a university in a large energy producing state and with a Ph.D. advisor who agreed with his philosophy.

Michael returned to Kursk a couple of years shortly after Jack's death and to be the technical advisor to a number of local company startups in addition to pursuing his interest in energy storage research. Chip always planned for Michael to succeed him as CEO, but Michael's real interest remained in physics research. He proved to be an avid apprentice to his father, but said he would only consider filling the position for a year or two. They were co-CEOs a couple of years before the long feared catastrophe occurred. Yet he continued to spend most of his time in his research and advisory positions.

CHAPTER 33

THINGS GET WORSE

Much frustration existed with the constant conflict between the George W. Bush Administration and the heavily Democrat Congress over the evolving situation in the Middle East. The people involved in Project NewLand were disturbed with the 'Weapons of Mass Destruction' controversy that hung on after the second Gulf War. Chip and his senior staff always believed the WMDs in question would someday rise out of the sands of the Iraqi and Syrian Deserts. What frustrated them the most were the Democrats, who at first fervently supported the belief WMDs existed in Saddam Hussein's Iraq, then later reversed their positions. The main stream media helped them complete the ruse and the lemming public allowed it to continue.

The selection of Senator John McCain as the 2008 Republican candidate frustrated the people of Project NewLand. Although a war hero who spent 5 ½ years as a prisoner in Vietnam's Hanoi Hilton and years as a senator from Arizona, they felt he did not have the drive to win and believed he tended to be too liberal. Although they did not like either Democrat candidate in 2008, they believed the country would have been better off with Hillary Clinton as president rather than her opponent, Barack Obama. At least her husband operated for 12 years as Arkansas governor and 8 years as president. Did she have the intelligence and instincts of her husband? Even more important, could she be trusted? As time went on more and more concerns about her trustworthiness and veracity, as well as her definitely leftist views, arose.

Barack Obama bothered them immensely. To them he was an inexperienced rabble rouser with no real experience with traditional American values and institutions, other than being a community organizer. They were also concerned with his coming out of the Chicago political machine and were bothered by his Chicago associations with people like Rev. Wright, Father Pfleger, Bill Ayers and Tony Rezko, plus he an affinity for the views of Saul Alinsky. They were frustrated with the result of the 2008 elections, but even more discouraged four years later after the 2012 elections.

They deemed the entire presidency of Barack Obama a failure and considered the so-called "Affordable Care Act" a total disaster. Unlike most members of Congress and the media, Mary Cate, Dr. Ron and Chip poured over the more than 2000 pages of the act as soon as available. They believed the healthcare insurance industry in the U.S. was destined for a major negative change, resulting in the animals treated by veterinarians often receiving better care than humans due to the bureaucracy. Only time would tell if most Americans would be able to protect healthcare insurance. When Jack died, Chip gained control of the tremendous wealth created by Barzinsky and the Barnetts. He made the decision to protect those not covered by the GLO Industries' mutual insurance companies, by deftly creating a 'buffer' to keep the onerous aspects of Obamacare off their backs.

Another area of concern was the amount of discrimination against conservative businesses and political organizations, plus smaller businesses, experienced during the 8 years from 2009 through 2016. They found the company constantly under attack by the IRS, the EPA, OSHA and other alphabet soup organizations in the federal government, as well as being harassed by the United Nations with their "American oil is bad" mantra which turned into "America is bad". There were even instances where it appeared that some government agencies were spying on various Congressmen and other government employees.

They considered the Department of Homeland Security particularly troublesome. A steady flow of illegals kept trying to pass through GLO Industries properties. An effective network of surveillance drones was able to detect and deter encroachments through an excellent system of misdirection. The UNMS or United Nations Monitoring Services also increased its attempted incursions. Other anti-American foreign countries, plus NGOs (non-government organizations) pursued them. While the 2014 midterms resulted in a large congressional win for the Republicans, the expected fruits of the election never materialized.

When email, originally known of as electronic mail came on the scene, Dane immediately thought back to the early ARPANET, started in 1958, a year after the successful launching of SPUTNIK by the Russians. "The Advanced Research Projects Agency Network" or ARPANET, led to the development of the Internet, contrary to popular liberal belief Al Gore invented it.

The introduction and rapid growth of the Internet made Dane nervous, and for good reasons. Working with Rick, they developed a sophisticated system which encrypted any messages in or out of the Project NewLand system. Originally based on 64 bits it was expanded to 128 bits early in the 21st Century. They also created a method preventing anyone from knowing the source or location of an email from within the project. For example, Chip's email always appeared to be based in the Bay Area while Rick's in Minneapolis. Just for fun they located Dane's address somewhere on a small island in Denmark, even though they all lived in Kursk. Dane predicted that at some future date, the exponential growth of the Internet would be its eventual demise, another reason for maintaining a separate network. Dane also constantly worried about increased governmental control of the Internet.

A few minor news stories were written about how GLO Industries funded a number of high-tech startups in the area. The remoteness of Kursk led to a lack of interest by the 'Coastals', i.e. the effete elites of the east and west coasts. This allowed these companies to pursue research and development with little media attention since they considered themselves to be above traveling to such a desolate remote outpost.

One reporter snidely referred to Kursk as Fort Courage from the 1960s *TV series F Troop.*

As usual, Dane monitored technological, political, economic and social trends. He became increasingly concerned with what he saw as the first decade of the 21st Century came to a close. As political unrest grew, it was obvious an increasing amount of government resources were being used to counteract terrorist activities, but not effectively. This drove Chip to increase the frequency of emergency drills.

Being concerned there could someday be a nuclear war, they initiated nuclear radiation monitoring on a continuing basis, reminding Chip of two books he read in his younger years. The first and better known *On the Beach* by Nevil Shute, published in 1957 and, the second, *Level 7* by Mordecai Roshwald, published in 1959. Both are Cold War accounts of the results of nuclear war. In *On the Beach* life ends in Australia as radiation spreads south from the populated areas of the continents to the north. In *Level 7* a multi-level survival system is established, with Level 7, the lowest level, being reserved for the most elite as the last hope for mankind. In both novels, humanity did not survive. Project NewLand was developed to effectively prevent the total demise of the human race.

Dane and Rick proposed a method for detecting and preventing radiation leaks into their cave system like what happened to destroy civilization in *Level 7.* Residents were required to always wear radiation measurement tags Rick's engineers developed a wearable tag to monitor radiation. Tag data were monitored both on an individual and collective basis at regular intervals. They did not want life on earth to end from radiation. They were aware of the Chernobyl disaster in April, 1986. As a reminder, Chip always kept a button his wife Sue got during a technical seminar on nuclear power held in Germany back in the early 1982. It touted the "Safety, Culture, Effectiveness and Social Progress" of the nuclear facility in white bold letters on a green ring that surrounded a map of the world highlighting Chernobyl.

"Just more Communist bullshit! Yep, their lack of safety effectively blew up their culture, killed a lot of people and destroyed any hope of social progress," Chip would always remark as he looked at the button, thinking of the comments of an American civil engineer he knew who visited the disaster zone years after the disaster who said it was the most godawful mess he ever saw.

The next step was the installation of a matrix of monitors external to the cave system, 64 in total. These were mounted in nuclear hardened bunkers surrounding the set of hills with the closest near the well-sealed entrances and then spread out over an area 16Km in diameter and transparent to anyone who did not know the exact location. Rick's staff monitored them on a continuous basis and the data integrated using an algorithm determining the direction and level of radiation increase. Each camera monitored a full 360 degrees.

The system was tested every time they detected a nuclear test anywhere in the world. The true measure of its accuracy came as a result of the Fukushima Nuclear Power Plant meltdown in March of 2011. This ongoing test proved the sensitivity and accuracy of the system.

One of Dane's software engineers, Warren Mercer, made this all possible by merging a detailed world map of trade winds data into their radiation monitoring system. They were able to determine the origin, magnitude and rate of movement of radiation patterns worldwide on an ongoing basis. Nuclear explosions could be identified before the communications systems around the world could respond. Any time they started seeing increased radiation levels on their monitoring system, they could test the accuracy of their critical algorithms.

Warren's performance on this project impressed Dane, much to Dane's surprise. Warren had been kicked out of MIT, but certainly not due of a lack of intelligence. He was expelled for testing pipe bombs along the Charles River in Boston and was given the opportunity of leaving Boston or going to jail.

Being a free spirit, he took off for California in his beat up VW bus using back roads to see as much of rural America as possible. He just happened to stop in Kursk for lunch on his way to California and recognized Dane Madsen sitting across the room from him in the restaurant. As a high school student, he read about how the esteemed Dr. Madsen gave up his professorship for the small town life of west

Texas a number of years earlier. Never a shy person, Warren introduced himself to Dane and asked him for a job.

"What can you do?" Dane asked.

Never the shy one, Warren responded, "I am one helluva good programmer."

"What is your educational background?" he asked further.

"Not much formal education. I got kicked out of MIT for experimenting with pipe bombs. No, I am not an anarchist, although they tagged me as a potential revolutionary. Frankly, I'm too conservative for those panty waists in Boston. I hear you are supposedly quite conservative. People claim you could not stand the political pressure of academia and had a nervous breakdown when you moved down here."

Pissed off, Dane said, "That is a damn lie. I just got sick and tired of the left-wing BS a conservative college professor had to put up with at the university. Furthermore, I was raised near a small town. I like the relaxed life style down here. So you must think you are pretty good?"

"Damn right. Give me a chance," he shot back at Dane.

"Look we do some fairly secret work in our business. I don't think I can bring you on site but I will make you a deal. I have some non-proprietary programming I need done quickly. I will give you a contract to develop the program but you will have to find a place to do it."

"Great. I live and work in my VW camper. I have a DELL PC with all of the memory and programming tools I need." Warren responded.

The next day Dane brought a work order describing what he needed and gave Warren three days to complete the work. Much to his surprise he received a call from Warren less than 24 hours later saying he completed the project. He was not only amazed at the performance of the program but also how few lines of code Warren needed to complete the project.

"You are pretty good. Where did you learn to program?" Dane asked in awe.

"My dad had an early Apple stored in the attic for about 20 years, a 1980 model with only 64KB of memory. He gave it to me when I was 12. He thought I could do little damage with it because of the slow speed and minimal memory. I learned to be creative and efficient with such an antique. I figure a good programmer can write approximately 100 lines of code a day, but an excellent one can write 10 lines to do the work of a 1000. I would rather think, then write than write and then think," Warren remarked with an air of superiority.

"You are pretty arrogant, but apparently damn good at what you do," Dane added.

"Yep, when can I come to work?"

Dane told him there may be a job for him, but he would have to go through a series of interviews with various members of management. He told Warren how to get to his office at the ranch and said he should be there by 8AM the next morning. He then paid Warren for his work and left.

Perplexed Warren wondered what kind of scientific work would be done in such a remote area. Being a committed conspiracy theorist, his mind considered a range of possibilities which excited him. He wondered if they were planning to overthrow the current government which he despised or were they building some type of secret weapon.

At 7:30AM the next morning he parked outside of the building Dane described. Employees approaching the building were wondering what this beat up old VW bus was doing there and people were surprised when Dane and this scraggy bearded young man entered the building. He looked like a hippie and seemed out of place.

Chip and Rick soon joined the two of them. Chip asked, "What the hell are you doing here?" trying to shock Warren, fully knowing why he was kicked out of MIT and with a fairly good idea of his political bent.

Without blinking an eye, Warren responded, "I recognized Dr. Madsen at the café in Kursk. I read an article about how he left the academic world unexpectedly years ago. I have been an admirer of his since age 15 and a freshman at MIT. God, what a boring place! Got kicked out after two years when I blew up a couple of trees with a pipe bomb I built. What a beautiful sight, but they didn't appreciate what I did with things I bought at the local A&P store. The whole thing cost me less than $2.50, plus about $2.00 for the piece of threaded pipe and caps I got at Home Depot. I tried to explain I was only trying to see how cheaply I could build one. The campus cops hauled me away from the Artificial Intelligence lab while I was doing homework. Bastards kept my books and anything else I had on campus. Fortunately, I left my computer in my VW van. Parking is so damned bad around there I had to walk almost two miles to campus and didn't feel like lugging it along."

Then Rick asked, "Are you some kind of left-wing nutcase?"

"Hell no! You guys appear to be conservative. I am probably as conservative, maybe more conservative, than all of you. I am looking for my niche in the world. You guys may be what I am looking for."

Dane said, "We are involved in a long ranged project. Do you have the patience to stick with us or will you just flip off and go barreling down the road the first time you get upset?"

Without waiting for Warren to respond, Chip took over the conversation, "Do you want a real challenge? Dane told me you were pretty damned full of yourself. If you are as good as you think you are, we can give you all of the challenges you want. Just remember you won't have any of the amenities of a big city. But you will be amazed at our resources, such as our scientific library, and our computer resources. Dane and Rick make sure we always have the latest equipment and software available. Does this interest you?"

The rest was history. Warren soon was a major contributor to the success of Project NewLand. That was made evident by the development of the NewLand's radiation detection system. Due to his work, the 'cave people', as they named themselves, felt safe years later as he monitored the ebb and flow of radiation in the air passed over the set of hills and they realized the effectiveness of the alert communications system he designed.

CHAPTER 34

VIRTUAL REALITY

The staff often discussed the potential mental health problems of eventual residents of NewLand when disaster finally occurred. Dr. Dickson, the psychiatrist of the medical group, and his wife, a psychologist, were concerned there would be a large portion of the population having mental problems. They pointed that approximately 20% of the population was mentally unstable in one way or another even in normal times. He wondered what would happen in a confined environment after witnessing most of the world's population destroyed, followed with a long period of being confined in the series of caves. Would a lot of aggression occur? How about depression? How much of an issue would suicide be, especially with the oldest, youngest and sickest members of the population? What about person-on-person crime like assault, rape and murder? The problem could be worse than space travel. Astronauts go through extensive training. This could not be done on a population of an approximately 250 – 300 person mixture of adults and children, particularly when a portion of the population would not be aware of what happened until the disaster occurred.

Dr. Ron and Dr. Dickson believed keeping the population of NewLand fully occupied was the key to their success of the managing mental problems that would arise. Neither worried too much about the management except for Rick who had a tendency to throw a tantrum once in a while and the possible excessive drinking by Dane and several others. Dane retired the previous year and was having a hard time adjusting to the new way of life. When Beth, Dane's wife, discussed the situation with Chip, he agreed. Mary Cate agreed Rick also needed to be continuously challenged. Chip decided to keep both of these individuals overloaded with creative work challenges.

He engaged them jointly to solve the concerns of Dr. Dickson and others by creating the proper environment working. Knowing what to do would take a considerable amount of creative system software development. They also assigned Warren Mercer to work with them, just another fun challenge for Warren.

They made a commitment to create an active environment with a good set of choices to keep people occupied, both at the onset of confinement and then for the long term. Chip knew once the situation stabilized the various high tech ventures in the area could use all personnel once recovery began. Job creation to keep people challenged was a major goal. They did not have a shortage of computing resources, but they needed to build a reason to live in the population.

Per usual, Rick had his normal smart ass comment, saying like in *The Brave New World*, they would be kept on *soma* or something worse yet. Rick often referenced Stanley Kubrick's *Soylent Green* where the old people were ground up for food. Falling back into his old 'disasters and tragedies' mode, he started his typical rant. Michael Faraday laughed having read *Brave New World* as a teenager and being a big fan of the Kubrick movies, but Chip told everybody to shut up.

After a couple of months of studying the situation, Dane suggested they create a virtual reality system allowing the survivors to live as normal an existence as possible while in confinement. He, Rick and Warren came up with an approach and worked on it constantly for over six months. Dane kept Chip aware of what they were doing. Dane, the penultimate perfectionist, finally was prepared for his presentation to the management group.

When Dr. Dickson and the others were told of the project, they could not understand how a realistic virtual reality system could be created. He was convinced trying to create virtual reality by projecting images on flat screen TVs was unworkable. It would be eerily like the telescreen in Orwell's *1984*. He then added it would be impossible to project images on the uneven surfaces of the cave walls and ceilings and even if they could it would not appear realistic. Dane disagreed.

This confused the medical staff with the exception of Hans Madsen, Dane's son, who just completed his residencies in internal medicine and radiology at the Southwestern Medical School in Dallas. He was aware of his father's project and its status, but was sworn to secrecy by Chip and Dane.

Dr. Ron said, "What you mean? How are you going to do create an alternative reality capability of any value? How are you going to project images on the uneven surface of the cave walls?"

Dane explained, "A number of years ago, several friends of mine were involved with a U.S. Navy project where they mapped a rough section the bottom of the ocean off the coast of a small island in the Pacific with an electronic matrix to simulate underwater conditions in order to play submarine war games. Despite the limitations of the technology of the time, the project achieved its goals. And that was done over 40 years ago. I believe it is now possible to successfully do this simulation totally in software and create realistic situations.

The naval project made the bottom of the ocean look like a flat surface. This is the same problem facing us today, only we must make the uneven surfaces of the cave walls and ceilings appear flat and then develop a number of scenarios that can be readily addressed and simulated. Video images are processed to simulate more than simple flat screens. What we have done is create a set of algorithms enabling us to make the walls and ceilings of any cave look like seamless 3D images using a matrix of high definition projectors. This approach allows us to simulate any venue. In addition, we will incorporate holography to project realistic images such as the players, coaches and officials for a sporting event or any other situation."

The non-technical people in the room were nonplussed, so Chip entered into the conversation and said, "Dane is right. This is a feasible approach. I have also read about this Navy project. Those guys were working with some pretty primitive technology compared to what we have today. In addition, holography is now considerably advanced, no longer a fantasy out of Star Trek. They are able to realistically present an event, such as a football game. Dane and Rick have shown me some early work on their project. Although not yet perfected, it is good enough to create a fairly realistic environment. They have mapped out several additional significant improvements which should be available within a year. In addition, various weather conditions can be created. Fortunately, the people of this area are used to a dry environment. Creating rain presents a number of problems, not only of having access to enough water, but also handling the drainage issues.

We have a vast inventory of video material, 1000s of terabytes of compressed video data, and the ability to organize it in any manner we want, thanks to the work being done by Warren's software group. I believe the simulation software we have makes it possible to create real scenarios for these caves. For example, cave number 7 is large enough to provide an outdoor athletic venue," he offered.

We have made measurements of this cave and it is large enough to serve as a football, soccer or baseball field. The ceiling in the center is tall enough to provide enough height for what appears to be a fairly high fly ball without hitting the top of the cave. There is also enough room to provide a substantial set of bleachers on the side of any field configuration. We would probably have no more than 250 or so people in the cave at one time, thus we could easily accommodate any sporting event we want to stage.

In addition, cave number 13 makes an ideal indoor sporting event and concert venue. This would be a great place for basketball games and such sports as tennis and handball, as well as recreate any videotaped concert from our files. Not every sporting event can be simulated from our sports database but most can.

Cave number 11 can be used for any number of smaller events," he added.

"Rick, Warren and I are ready to provide beta tests for management to observe. I believe these are good enough for the medical team to proceed with the psychological tools needing to be developed. How would next Wednesday work for you?" Dane asked.

The next Wednesday Dane provided a demonstration in cave number 13 by having the walls completely simulate the interior of the American Airlines Center in Dallas for part of an actual Dallas Mavericks basketball game on a simulated hardwood floor. He then simulated a complete Dallas Stars hockey game. This time he projected an actual game on a simulated ice surface.

Those present were visibly impressed, especially the medical staff. They immediately realized the potential of being able to create high level virtual reality situations not only for day-to-day activities, but also as a means of therapy for disturbed residents of NewLand. With the help of Rick and his crew they defined a wide range of scenarios they wanted available. Having a software genius like Warren Mercer helped the project greatly.

Concurrent with this effort, Chip and the medical staff attacked the physical and mental problems caused by not having access to natural sunlight for a long period of time. They started by studying research done on this issue for the past couple of decades. They knew sunlight deprivation increased susceptibility to a number of chronic diseases. They needed to find ways of providing the much needed vitamin D to enhance calcium absorption. They also were well aware the mental dangers of the lack of sunlight. Rick for one always believed his mental condition improved once he moved to sunny Texas. They studied research done in parts of the US, especially Washington and Oregon, and also northern Europe, with considerable cloudy weather and fog in countries like Scotland.

They researched diets knowing certain foods contained Vitamin D, foods such as fortified milk, egg yolks, fatty fish, juices and cereals since children are more vulnerable than adults, with a high risk of diseases like rickets. The dietician wife of one of the engineering employees helped greatly. In addition to creating a strong diet for the residents, she worked with medical staff and technical personnel to develop and implement an extensive network of artificial light to provide the needed UV light normally coming from the sun. A large purchase of UV bulbs and materials were acquired to assure sufficient inventory. They were also well aware artificial light could be as much of a source of skin cancer as natural sunlight.

Chip and the medical staff believed they were in good shape about the same time Dane had the virtual reality program ready for full implementation. Once done, Chip wanted to reduce his involvement and began to push Michael into playing a bigger management role. Dane decided to retire again, but Rick wanted to work for several more years. They promoted Warren, chomping at the bit to increase his management role, to replace Dane. Even though he did not have the academic credentials of Dane he performed well in the role.

GOSECURE

CHAPTER 35

"THAT GOVERNMENT IS BEST WHICH GOVERNS LEAST"

2020s

Years before Chip was promoted to the position of CEO of GLO Industries, he knew the title of CEO of NewLand would change to President of NewLand, a political position, when disaster struck and they entered the security of the caves. They did not want to be in conflict with any legitimate state or federal government functions when the problem subsided. This continued when Michael became the sole CEO, a position he wanted to hold as a short time as possible. Chip showed his age and was ready to give up the role, but he continued as a valuable consultant to help Michael prepare for a number of structural issues which would later have to be accepted as part of the NewLand Constitution to be created and approved by the citizens.

An Assistant President and two Representatives of the citizens of NewLand would first be elected by direct popular vote as soon as feasible to support Michael after the initiation of GoSecure. Warren Mercer and his staff of young programmers developed GoSecure shortly after completing the radiation monitoring system several years earlier.

The Assistant President would be elevated to President for a four-year term at the end of the first year after the election. During the third year of the new President's term, a new executive would be elected for five years, with the first year as Assistant President, followed by four years as President. The staff decided this would make the transition from one administration to the next run more smoothly than the current system used. No president would serve more than one term, at least until the writing and enactment of a constitutional amendment. This arrangement would be the Executive Branch of the government.

The Representatives would be elected for a term would also have a four year term like the President, but staggered by two and four years with the first year concurrent with Michael's last year as President, thus their elections would be staggered with the President's term. Thus, two elections never occurred at the same time. Elections would be done electronically and Representatives would serve no more than two terms. They would be designated the Legislative Branch.

They knew the population would at most be about 300 people at the beginning of the NewLand experience. They were confident the colony would survive and population would grow over time and additional representatives would be required. Being a bunch of techies, they decided to add representative on the basis of Fibonacci Numbers, i.e. 1+1=2, 1+2=3, 2+3=5, etc.

Rick, who proposed the approach said, "Why not? It is good enough for nature, why not for government? We know there have been a lot of unnatural acts done by various governments throughout history. It is time to change things."

Fibonacci Number Sequence:

#Reps.	>Population	#/Rep.
2	250	125
3	1,000	333
5	4,000	800
8	16,000	2,000
13	64,000	4,923
21	256,000	12,190
34	1,024,000	30,118

Next the President would appoint and the Legislature would approve the head of the Judiciary Branch, but additional members of the judiciary would be determined jointly by the Executive and Legislative Branches. At first two judges would be appointed with one the Chief Justice. In the case of a tie, the President would provide the deciding vote. All judges would be nominated by the President but approved by the Representatives. The legislature would pass a law, to be approved by the President, regarding the addition of Supreme Court judges.

They were well aware that all of these decisions would have to be approved as part of the NewLand Constitution. The staff also believed it would be best in the beginning to evaluate the entire American Constitution in order to write NewLand's Constitution at the time of a major chaotic event. He told the senior staff he wanted to establish a constitution which would fit their situation as soon as possible after the initiation of GoSecure. The entire population of qualified residents over 18 would review the Constitution, including the Bill of Rights, and the amendments following the Bill of Rights, as the basis for their new government. They wanted to exist as a true democracy rather than a democratic republic, at least until the population greatly increased. Since their population would be comprised of people of several races and religions, the staff decided race and religion were not the purview of the government. NewLand would be completely tolerant of the various ethnic and religious groups. Furthermore, religion would be personal in nature. They documented the history of all religions in the digital library.

Chip said, it fit his concept of minimum government and quoted one of Thomas Jefferson's more famous statements:

"That government is best which governs the least, because its people discipline themselves."

When the time for transition came, they did not want to create any type of dictatorship or monarchy and they definitely did not want government to sap the efforts of individuals. So they drew up plans for the implementation of a fully democratic town hall system. At town hall meetings, the President and elected representatives would discuss issues offered by the citizens. In addition, able citizens should contribute time and effort to developing businesses and it would be a capitalistic society, as they knew Robert and the two Jacks would want.

CHAPTER 36

IT WAS ON A TUESDAY

A bit after two years of Michael's elevation to CEO the world situation worsened. One evening Michael, Chip and the senior staff left their emergency headquarters where the senior staff of NewLand had been reviewing world events for the past eight hours. They were all exhausted and knew the preparations of the almost 100 years were going to face their first full implementation, not just a test. With the situation getting increasingly critical by the hour they decided they needed a break. Since the eight of them were always in contact electronically and lived close to headquarters, they knew they could reassemble in just a few minutes. They realized it might be time to initiate GoSecure, which meant qualified NewLanders would be notified to head with their families to the security of the caves.

They ran a number of dry runs of the system since the beginning of the 21st Century. At that time, qualified NewLanders were provided with a secure two-way communications system for their family which secretly alerted members to go into the caves. They knew what to do and where to go. The first real test was run back on 9/11 in September 2001 when the group of 19 terrorists made the horrible attack on the World Trade Center towers, the Pentagon and, potentially, either the White House or the Capital building, if it had not been for Todd Beamer and his brave crew who brought the fourth plane down in the field near Shanksville, PA.

The threat had been building for a number of years back to the 2010s, with the crumbling of peace and order in the Middle East, and the chaos running completely out of control around the entire world. The first real decline started in the first decade of the 21st Century, but it accelerated during the second decade of the 21st Century. America was so absorbed with its internal problems it lost its role as the world leader. The 'have-nots' became a major force. Not realizing they were destroying the social order, they began tearing at the fabric of American life. Not only would the many of the 'haves' have a lot less, but the 'have-nots' fared even much worse. The long touted American middle-class, built over more than two centuries through hard work and optimism, rapidly deteriorated over the past three decades.

"Is this what the liberal elites wanted to happen?" Chip had often wondered.

What started as a hopeful period with the decline of the Soviet Union years earlier evolved into a dysfunctional world order. Riots were rampant worldwide: Minority against minority, poor against rich, Muslims against other religions, Muslims against other Muslims, and Islamists against established governments. The situation became hopeless for many people around the world.

Six months earlier a major solar flare of a once in a 500 year magnitude caused extensive damage to the power grids in parts of the U.S., Europe and Asia causing considerable panic. Several rogue governments initiated a series of EMP (electromagnetic pulse) attacks, but had no sense of the devastation these weapons would cause. Israel's enemy's attacked it repeatedly and the country struck back with a vengeance, destroying of the electronic infrastructure in and around Tehran, resulting in an open war between the Sunni and Shia populations and both against Israel. No one knew who attacked whom. Meanwhile, starvation soon became a major problem throughout the Indian subcontinent and China where almost half of the world's population lived. This was also true throughout the Middle East and much of Africa. Australia, Japan and most Pacific Islands were ok for a while, but they, too, succumbed in time.

Mysteriously some country started blasting one communications satellite after another out of commission with powerful lasers. It was strongly suspected, but not proven either Russia or China made those attacks. The entire world began losing its communications infrastructure. Ham radio operators were the most important form of communications in many parts of the world, but soon were ineffective due to continued EMP attacks which destroyed so much of the electronics infrastructure globally.

The end game started a week before the NewLand emergency meeting when the Middle East completely blew up. Due to the extent of the damage to communications and infrastructure, no one knew who did what first or the scope of the initial damage. The area blew itself up with a series of nuclear and chemical warfare attacks throughout the area. Whatever population survived the initial attacks and the after effects of the radiation soon lived a Stone Age existence and did not survive for long.

NewLand management reassembled and decided the situation deteriorated so badly just a few hours later Chip activated the code word alerting all qualified members of the organization. Qualified NewLanders immediately collected their families and headed for the cave entry on the southwest side of the hills.

Emergency crews were sent to bring family members who were at work in Kursk and other places, including patients at the Kursk hospital. As had been tested so often over the past 20 years, vehicles were camouflaged so well and routes taken were so routine none of the non-quals realized what was happening. Patients were transported to the NewLand hospital, including family members, when possible. This created a problem. Some of the patients and their family members were not part of the NewLand system. Fortunately, the preparations of years worked perfectly.

It took less than 2 1/2 hours for all to be secured in the caves. Kursk soon was almost a ghost town. Those left in Kursk and the surrounding areas hardly noticed what happened. They were immersed in trying to survive on their own. Not a pretty picture. Panic set in and many of the people from places like Valley Center and other communities attacked each other. Many farmers and ranchers who were not part of Project NewLand were left to their own devices. With the social structure completely collapsing, people had to fend for themselves. In some cases family members even attacked family members. The same happened all over the country and throughout the world. Although some remote areas established a well thought-out survival plans, few were prepared to withstand the blanket of radiation which would possibly persist for many months, if not years. NewLand prepared and remained prepared.

Even in his old age Rick liked to exaggerate with his black humor and said much of the world turned into nothing but a bunch of highly irradiated large glass bowls. Many smaller countries were virtually destroyed. The extended war spread from India to southern Europe and throughout North Africa. What started as the "Arab Spring" many years earlier now spread into a wide area of "Nuclear Winter" killing an estimated 2 billion people in a matter of days during the initial series of attacks and no one knew how many in the long term. The total number would never be known.

No one knew the extent of the devastation. So much of the world had been destroyed to the point where almost no communications existed. It soon became an international problem as the trade winds spread the deadly radiation around the world. In addition, the trade winds over its location would result in long term radiation. They would be safe while in time most of the world's population died horrible deaths.

The economies of the EU had been destroyed over the past decade under the weight of its socialistic bureaucracy, uncontrolled immigration and nationalistic jealousy. The governments and infrastructures of countries around the world were systematically being destroyed by both internal and inter-country turmoil. Rioting throughout Europe had been rampant for over a decade.

The United Nations stopped operating when terrorists exploded a small 'dirty bomb' in the headquarters in New York City. The social structure of New York City, already under severe stress, completely crumbled. Los Angeles and Chicago were soon also hit. Politicians all around the country caved in and went into hiding or were killed. Many committed suicide. The turmoil spread like wild fire. Washington never initiated a nuclear response. The word went out to each state in the United States it was on its own. It immediately was evident even the individual states were ungoverned. The more conservative states fared better than liberal states. Their populations were more self-reliant, but in time they were also destroyed. Chaos set in across the country and in most parts of the world. Strangely, the populations of some of the most undeveloped countries seemed fare better due to being less dependent on technology, but their lack of social order allowed them to completely collapse over time.

In the midst of this, China and Russia, allies for years although shaky for the last decade, went at each other with a vengeance. Vladimir Putin's successor Vlad III, as he liked to be called, started the war. He could not understand why Russia's economy, which was decimated during the later teens due to world price of oil declining to $20 a barrel, spun into a total collapse. Oil was its only industry providing any international trade, other than arms sales. The situation became so bad they could not even produce enough petroleum for internal usage. Alcoholism and drug usage made Russia much worse than other countries. No one realized Vlad III, Vladimir Barzinsky, was the great-great grandson of Robert Barzinsky's father. Robert's often stated fears finally materialized.

Total panic took over the United States, as well as Europe. Major cities around the world devolved into virtual jungles where it became a case of kill or be killed. Survival was possible mostly in very rural parts of the United States, and in areas with a strong local government, but in most cases these factors only delayed the inevitable.

CHAPTER 37

INTRODUCTION TO NEWLAND

The first 18 hours after GoSecure activation were grueling. Staff members directed new arrivals to their living quarters. The people were disturbed by what happened and many were sobbing, especially the children and elderly. Dr. Dickson and his staff were available to handle most psychological problems and there were many. Residences were stocked with fresh food and supplies, including multiple WTVs (Wall Televisions) to serve both children and adults. Large quantities of entertainment, from movies to electronic games to educational programs were available to keep people occupied until a normal flow of life could be established. The world situation deteriorated with little news available, except for the sketchy hourly updates provided by Warren who constantly monitored available communications around the world.

281 people who were not on site before GoSecure were accommodated resulting in a total initial population of 316 people, 16 more than the facility design capacity. This infuriated Michael who realized last minute exceptions were made for special situations, such as extended family members and close friends.

The facilities and medical staffs constantly monitored the situation. Fortunately, other than a couple of minor injuries and number of people with severely upset stomachs and headaches, all were in relatively good shape. This was not unexpected. The pre-qualified residents had gone through a series of disaster training sessions over the past 15 years. The biggest problems came from the 27 individuals, mostly relatives and hospital patients, who were not pre-qualified. Five staff members assigned to this group kept them isolated from the others. This entire group needed to go through an extensive program to prepare them for their future before having more than superficial contact with the rest of the population.

Somehow they made it through the night, with few getting any sleep due concerns about the grave turn of events. Morning came with a realization of what happened to some, but others were still in a state of denial. Those who were trained to manage the transition started adopting the roles they were assigned, fully aware life would never be the same. Some of the staff cooked and served food. Others provided various services. Each person received an initial supply of NewCash, coined some time earlier from the extensive inventory of gold and recently purchased silver, to purchase goods and services. Not till later did most realize how well stocked and how extensive the resources were. People were given a quick course on the layout of the area around their residences and where purchases for goods and services could be made. No alcohol was served for the first 72 hours.

Warren continued to follow the status of world events, which became more difficult by the hour. One-by-one, the points of communication from around North America and around the world rapidly declined. By mid-afternoon, they were receiving communications from less than twenty locations around the world, down from over a thousand only 12 hours earlier. A steady flow of inquisitive data wondering what was going on arrived from the recently settled colony on Mars. Dane and Rick monitored the transmission time from the Mars colony to earth, with transmissions taking roughly 17 minutes per one-way transmission at the time, but chose not to respond. Dane, the consummate amateur astronomer, said transmission time could vary from about 4 to 20 minutes, depending on the relative orbital positions of Earth and Mars.

Rick and Warren both got a real charge out of the level of concern in the messages from Mars. Rick said, "What the hell are they going to do about it? Pop over and rescue us?" Only the two of them saw any humor in the situation.

Mary Cate responded with her typical pique, "Why do you two always have to be such complete asses?"

At 4PM the qualified residents, except for a small number of the staff and the children under 14, were directed into the virtual reality auditorium in cave #11.

When they settled down, Michael arose and cleared his throat, "Welcome to NewLand. For those who do not know me, I am Michael Faraday, formerly General Manager and CEO of Newland, but now President of NewLand. I will remain the CEO of GLO Industries, assuming there is still need for an energy exploration and production business anymore.

I am sorry we must gather under these conditions. Before we proceed with official business, allow me to introduce my father, Chip Faraday who came on board in 1987. Next to him are his two closest associates. Over here to my right in the first row is Dr. Dane Madsen who came to Kursk in 1974 to be Director of Advanced Technology. Next to him is Rick Christiansen, who joined the effort in back in 1984 as Director of Applied Technology. The three of them have known each other since the 1960s at the University of Minnesota, with Dane actually being my dad's and Rick's freshman physics professor. Dad, the floor is yours."

Bent with age, Chip leaned into the podium and said, "Ladies and gentlemen. Welcome to NewLand. We are in a helluva mess," his serious eyes scanned the entire audience, "Except we are better off than most of the rest of the world. Life will never be the same, but we will survive if we choose to survive. We are, at best, a microcosm of our past. In the worst case, we could fail and be lost to history. Our challenge is to maintain as much of our culture and society as possible for future generations, and to create useful and productive lives. We may be a major part of the future history of mankind. Our job is to survive, prosper and multiply. We are a colony, possibly not much different than the colony recently established on Mars. But we have the opportunity to control our destiny better than probably anyone else who has survived on earth.

The amazing story of NewLand, for the few of you who do not know, began with two immigrants from Europe early in the 20th Century. Robert Barzinsky, who left his home in Russia under the harshest of conditions in 1897, and Jack Barnett, Sr. from Ireland about 20 years later, conceived the concept of NewLand back in the early 1930s, after years of concern over the direction of the U.S. and the rest of the world. Robert never married. Jack married Catherine Gruenberg, a native of Kursk. Their only child, Jack, Jr., also never married. They have all passed away, with Jack, Jr. dying in 2007. Jack recruited me to first run Project NewLand and then take over GLO Industries as well when he no longer could manage. I became permanent CEO of both NewLand and GLO Industries in 2002 and gave up the positions two years ago to Michael, who is determined to leave the position within a year, if possible, to pursue his interests in education and research. Thus, we must initiate elections as soon as feasible.

Without their many years of hard work and the efforts by the people mentioned above, a number of other people who are no longer with us and others here in the caves, we would not be here today. Our challenge is our opportunity, especially if you are an optimist who wants to live a full life. If not, you will have a sad and difficult time. It is our intention for us to learn, contribute and thrive. Our goal is to create a truly democratic society, not one fraught with regulations and control. We must be the solution, not the problem. We can be the most educated people ever. However, we must survive for it to make any difference. This means residents must learn to think before acting. What we have seen for decades has been people acting before they think sometimes never really thinking.

I know you are concerned about those who came into the cave system who are not in this audience. As much as we regret having to do this, it is important all residents understand the challenges we face, thus those who are not part of our inner circle are being isolated for the time being. They have to be oriented to what has happened and who we are. It is obvious we will not all get along, at least not all of the time. That is ok. By being thinking people, I believe we can resolve our issues. Remember, we are a colony which must survive on its own. Before we take questions, I want Michael give an overview of our operations."

Michael came back to the podium, "Allow me to tell you a bit about our facilities and actions. First, three days before we activated GoSecure we switched to internal power to assure there would be no power outage. Initially we are driving our gas turbines directly by natural gas being piped from active gas wells. We have a sophisticated backup system. The next step will be to use refined oil stored in secure tanks to drive diesel generators. We also have significant unrefined oil in storage we can run through our small refinery. These can run our steam turbines for at least five years, assuming we cannot access additional crude oil. But there is more. Buried deep within these caves there is a nuclear reactor capable of delivering the power we need for another 15 to 20 years, even once we can leave the caves. I offer this info as just one example of how completely we have planned for what has just happened.

The same has been done to maintain a healthy food supply. As soon as possible, you will have a tour of our hydroponic gardens and our food animal facilities. I think you will be pleasantly surprised with the range and quality of our foods.

You may ask about our water and sewer system. We are located just above a very large aquifer, so water supply is not an issue unless our aquifer is destroyed by something like a nuclear attack. Our sewer system is also state-of-the-art.

To minimize the possibility of becoming a target, we have 'gone quiet'. NewLand is not responding to any communications we receive. This policy is being reviewed on a regular basis.

Next I want to assure you we have an excellent and well-staffed medical system and staff, as well as state-of-the-art medical facilities. The same is true for our library and educational system. Each of us, not just our children, can directly access a large data base. As we move forward in time, our staff will work with each person to accommodate their needs and wants. Extensive opportunities to learn exist and the number will be expanded.

I took this position a couple of years ago. I will continue to be President for only one year after our first election. All of you 18 and older will be first asked to elect a person to be the Assistant President for one year, followed by four years as President after I step down. Second, you citizens will also elect two Representatives to work with me to form our initial government. The Assistant President will only be in an advisory role while learning the role of future President. These actions will be included in our new Constitution.

Next we will develop a Constitution for NewLand with inputs from you, which will be approved on a direct vote by you citizens. I assure you we will do what is possible to be a government as free from red tape, confusion and complexity as humanly possible. It will be up to all of us to assure NewLand continues a free capitalistic community. In the President's third year, a new Assistant President will be elected to continue the cycle of government."

Michael then took a long drink of water and looked around the audience. He continued, "We are open for any questions and comments."

Immediately hands went up around the room. "I guess we are going to have to set up some sort of system to keep some order. How about setting up a category for questions and one for comments? First, how many have questions?"

Over 60 hands went up, then he asked, "How many have comments to make?" and about 20 hands were raised.

"OK, first, who have questions about what has just happened?"

At least ten hands went up with questions ranging from the general, "What happened?" to "How bad is it in New York or Chicago?" to "Did Dallas and Ft. Worth get hit with a nuclear bomb? What about Austin, San Antonio and Houston?" to "What has happened to the people of Kursk who are not here in the caves?" Both Chip and Michael responded for 2 1/2 hours then said they needed a break.

Reassembling a half hour later, questions were asked regarding the conditions inside the cave system making up NewLand, at least until they were able to spend some time on the outside. After another two hours, the questions were still coming. Michael said, "Look, we have been here for over five hours. I am surprised y'all are not exhausted and starving. How about we break for the day? Tomorrow we need to get started on our routine. Many of you know what your role is going to be for the next month. As you will remember from your training sessions, the opportunities for learning are endless. You can dabble from subject-to-subject or you can specialize. We already have people studying teaching, medicine, law, engineering, you name it. The same is true for the wide range of jobs need to be done. One thing we want to do from day one is to prepare for the day we can leave the cave system. At this time, we have no idea how long it will be before we can venture out, much less before we can start re-building a life outside. One thing we are sure of, life will never be the same.

Since it is so late, I recommend you return to your residence and use some of the freeze dried meals which can be prepared quickly. Tomorrow we will start the conversion to a normal diet."

Then the meeting broke up. Many of the people, but not everyone, felt some better than earlier in the day, but they knew a new 'normal' had to be created. They knew life would never be the same. It was obvious to all who just entered NewLand.

CHAPTER 38

THE FIRST MONTH

The first two days had been a state of near chaos, but then the situation started to settle down. On the third morning, Michael and Chip talked to the qualified families in small groups. They were divided into eight groups of about 24 individuals, each with a team leader well trained for the situation. Dr. Dickson, the psychiatrist took the responsibility for the 19 non-quals who were from family units of two or more and his psychologist wife Rebecca took the responsibility for the remaining 8 individuals. Three of the non-qual individuals who were patients in the Kursk hospital were not from the area. They had been injured in a car accident while traveling through the area two days earlier. As expected, they were disturbed, but were happy to have each other with whom to commiserate.

The initial meetings with the qualified family members went quite well. In each case, the team leader already knew the individuals in his/her group. Each leader gave an overview of how to normalize life as much as possible. Employment, education and entertainment options were outlined, as well as how to address each person's religious needs, obviously not an easy process. Many times one or several people would completely break down. Whenever this happened the team leader tried to get the person to see the positive side of being alive, often with other members of the group helping as well they could. Race did not seem to be a problem as Dr. Dickson and his wife were black, as well as two other families and there were a total of 12 Hispanics. There was one military vet and his family who were Asian.

The non-quals presented a much more difficult situation. The people felt like they had been hit by a train from nowhere. The parents in two families admitted some of their friends and family members tried to convince them over the years of the dangers facing civilization, but thought they were being bullied. Like newborn kittens their eyes soon opened to the reality of the situation.

Everybody grieved for lost friends and relatives. Soon they formed a number of new friendships. By the end of the third day, qualified family adults had come to the realization of what happened, having been part of the periodic drills for over a decade. They were faced the dire reality of coping with their world having suddenly very small. Dr. Dickson was aware of the training astronauts went through before leaving for Mars less than a year earlier. By the end of the week, a number of social groups were organized and some immediately began to look for economic and social reasons to cooperate. This pleased Michael and Dr. Dickson to no end.

Most of the children handled the situation better than expected by getting by them involved in a wide range of activities from sports to chess and monopoly. They also made an effort to encourage face-to-face interaction, something which evaporated over the past 20 years due to electronic games, smartphones and similar electronic devices. There were no cell phones. The cave environment made wireless communications almost impossible, but calls were made using a well-planned land-line telephone system which operated like cordless phones, which seemed like a giant step backwards to most.

The staff forced no one into a particular path. They did not want a *The Brave New World, 1984 or Animal Farm* situation and certainly not *Soylent Green.*

One week after the activation of GoSecure, Michael held a senior staff meeting with two actions on the agenda: 1. Review the past week and 2. Initiate the election process.

Dr. Dickson just completed a review of medical activities with the staff. Then Michael said, "Dr. Dickson, thank you. It appears we are right on schedule, if not a bit ahead of where we thought we would be at this point. My biggest concern is we may over-control our citizens. We have no idea of how long we will have to remain here in the caves.

Warren tells me the radiation pattern varies from day-to-day so it is impossible to determine if there is any sign of abatement at this time. His biggest worry is how much the radioactive winds will pollute the environment around us permanently before dissipating to safe level. I know at some point we are going to get antsy and want to get out of confinement. Currently, Warren is projecting a three to six month period until we can venture out for short periods of time, and once we are outside our radiation tags will have to be monitored closely."

Several questions were asked, one of major interest. Dane asked, "Has the drone surveillance program detected any sign of life in the area?"

Warren got up and clicked his remote device. A map of the local area popped up on the wall, "This shows the immediate area out to a radius of 8Km and there has been no sign of any life other than the ubiquitous prairie dog, a half-dozen coyotes and various rodents. Each sighting is documented. This is from the first night after we went GoSecure. Now look at it day by day and you will see the number of sightings is slightly reduced each day. I can't make any conclusions at this time.

Now using drone collected data let us expand the radius to 16Km, which includes Kursk and a number of farms and ranches. There are again no signs of life other than a few animals. I have no explanation of why there are no signs of humans dead or alive. I am completely puzzled at this time.

My only recommendation is we continue our monitoring program. I see no reason to go beyond the 16Km radius, unless you want to do a special drone surveillance of Valley Center."

Michael responded, "No, we have enough problems of our own. It is puzzling we see no sign of any people, dead or alive. I wonder what happened to them."

Next Michael raised the subject of elections. "I make the motion we first do the election of the Assistant President first. Then any losing candidate can then run for one of the two Representative positions. Any comments?"

Rick asked, "Why not get it over in one fell swoop and have both elections at the same time?"

To which Chip entered the conversation, "Look Rick, it is not like we have to rush through this process." Everybody else agreed and the motion passed.

Nominations would be open for the next week and the election would follow 30 days later. They next decided the same procedure would be followed for the Representatives starting a week after the first election, to which Rick added his two cents, "Ockham's razor in real life."

The next day the staff posted the notice of the nomination process online and around the common areas. The first day there were three people who agreed to be nominated, then no one else. First, Dr. Hans Madsen, Dane's son, second Virginia Benson, Liz Houseman's daughter who married Dr. Benson's son, and third a veteran, Kurt Grauman's grandson Jack Barnett Grauman, Jr., who chose to be called JB. He was the son of Jack Barnett Grauman, so named in honor of Jack Barnett, Sr., who had done so much for the German immigrants many years earlier. JB's father had been a Special Forces member who was killed in Afghanistan. JB, as he liked to be called out of deference to his father, studied history at Texas A&M. When his father died, he decided to follow his footsteps in the military after completing college. He also was disillusioned with the government's management of the military, similar to Michael Faraday. He resigned his commission and came home to be close to his mother and eventually married a local woman.

JB immediately became part of Project NewLand and took over military planning efforts for the project. Working with Michael, he made effective use of the system of drones Warren specified and purchased. Being outgoing and well-liked, he soon was the favorite and proved to be the strongest candidate, due to his concern about the long term security of NewLand. He won by a vote of 93 versus a total of 65 for the other two candidates combined.

An interesting turn of events resulted. Both of the losers were nominated for representative and were elected by acclamation without opposition. They then agreed to select who would serve the two-year term and who would serve the four-year term with the flip of a coin. Virginia won. Thus, by the end of the first month, Michael had NewLand's government in place and soon held the new government's first meeting with the Representatives and JB Grauman. Former senior staff members also attended. The first items on the agenda considered allowing non-quals enter into the general population and be given a path to full citizenship. Michael, Dr. Dickson and Rebecca testified it would be a good idea. Thus, NewLand had its first naturalized citizens. They were never considered to be illegal immigrants because they were already citizens of the United States.

At the end of the meeting, Michael gave a status report on the various businesses started. They were satisfied with the progress. Then Warren gave his update on the drone surveillance program. He said the first optimistic signs of radiation reduction began to show, but there were still no sign of humans, either alive or dead. He also noted communications from other parts of the world appeared to end during week three, but transmissions from Mars continued. They continued to be puzzled.

CHAPTER 39

NEWLAND CONSTITUTION

During the fifth week Michael Faraday called the meeting to order and assigned JB, being the Assistant President, the task of recording the details of the meeting with only one item on the agenda: Begin the process of writing and preparing for the approval of the NewLand Constitution.

Michael wanted to be sure the four of them were familiar with the two documents so they could guide the open discussions with the residents. Thus, they were asked to study both documents before the meeting.

Several guidelines were established:

1. The U.S. Declaration of Independence and Constitution would be the guidelines for the NewLand Constitution with an emphasis on maintaining and expanding a capitalistic society.

2. NewLand residents over 18, including the non-quals, could make inputs. Michael later decided younger people should be allowed to make inputs. Many were more knowledgeable of these documents than some of the adults.

3. The President and two Representatives would review inputs, with the meetings open to all residents, including the children who wanted to be involved in the democratic process.

4. Inputs would be summarized in the form of items to be voted on by the citizens of NewLand, age 18 and older.

A notice stating the above went out to all residents. They wanted to have residents informed enough to understand the process. This was particularly true for the younger people. They would be the future leaders. They were amazed at how involved the children were. A series of open meetings to discuss the two important documents were held in the auditorium in cave #11. First they reviewed The Declaration of Independence.

Whereas Thomas Jefferson made the case for separating from the rule of England, the people of NewLand intended to make the case for operating independently until they were able to determine when the United States recovered as a governable country. Then they would rejoin the union. As they reviewed the document Jefferson wrote, they realized the people of the colonies had a definite set of grievances. One by one each of the grievances Jefferson outlined were discussed. They compared the situation in 1776 to the current situation.

Chip thought to himself, "This is basic democracy at its best. Robert Barzinsky and the Barnetts would be pleased."

Although the residents of NewLand were concerned about the direction the country had been taking for years, they were committed to be part of the United States again, if it survived.

A week later they discussed the Constitution article by article, then each amendment, intending to create a stripped down document supporting the U.S. Constitution as much as possible.

They soon realized Article I discussed the makeup and responsibilities of the Congress, but there would be only a House of Representatives, known of as the Legislative Branch until some future date when a Senate would be added. Article II covered the Executive Branch of the government. For well over 100 years the power of Congress had been continuously sapped while the power of the Executive branch expanded over the past 40 to 50 years. They decided this was not the intent of the founders when they escaped the British monarchy. They also did not want to be subjected to any dictatorial form of government.

During the second day of discussions of the Constitution, they first discussed Article III which addressed the Judicial Branch. They examined the evolution of the Supreme Court and the federal judgeship system. They talked about how they wanted to keep this part of the government as uncomplicated as possible. The comments of some of the young people, as young as 14, were pertinent leading Michael to ask for a vote if the inputs of children should be accepted and it was overwhelmingly approved. A couple of the non-quals, who tended to be more liberal than the average citizen, didn't like having young people be part of the process. They believed children should have their minds 'prepared' before being involved in the democratic process.

Michael said, "Ridiculous. I am blown away with how much they how much they knew. Some of these kids know more than you adults." You could hear some grumbling in the audience.

Beth sat with Chip and Sue during the meetings. Sue whispered to Chip, "I am so proud of our young people with their keen interest in the development of the Constitution."

"They are starting out with clean minds and have not been subjected to so much mind pollution. And thanks to the Kursk schools," Beth responded. Little did she realize she would later be asked to be the first Chief Justice of NewLand, a job which she said she would only hold for two years.

Next they considered Article IV which addressed the rights and privileges of the states, except for American territories which would be responsibility of Congress. They realized these issues did not fit their situation.

To finish the second day of meetings on the Constitution, the residents covered Amendment V. They required a 2/3 approval by both houses of Congress or by approval by 2/3 of the states then ratified by

¾ of the Legislatures of the states. They determined it to be of no value to their current status as a small colony.

The discussions of the third day centered on Article VI regarding the Debts, Engagements and Treaties, plus several housekeeping issues. Article VII covers the Ratification process by the various states. Neither of these articles seemed pertinent to their situation.

When they reviewed the list of signers of the Constitution, many were surprised George Washington, the lead signee of the document, headed up the process as President as well as being a representative from the state of Virginia. Some were surprised Thomas Jefferson did not sign the Constitution even though he authored the Declaration of Independence. One of the young people raised his hand and said, "I know why, I know why. He was the ambassador to France at the time." This brought a chuckle of satisfaction throughout the audience.

In the afternoon they dove into the Bill of Rights, the first ten amendments of the Constitution. As expected, they whizzed through all ten. They were understood and agreed to by the majority, especially the first five Amendments.

They worked late so they could complete the Bill of Rights by the end of the day at which time Chip got up and said, "You know, after the first two Amendments, the 10th Amendment has always been my favorite: *"The powers not delegated to the United States by the Constitution, nor prohibited by it to the States, are reserved to the States respectively or the people."* Ironically, in our current situation it does not apply. As far as we know there may not be a federal government at this time and NewLand is a single state. It is blatantly obvious this amendment has been trampled on by the federal government of the United States for many, many years."

It had been a long arduous week and the next meeting was not scheduled until the following Tuesday, but in the interim any inputs from the citizens of NewLand were welcome. They estimated it would take most of another two days to discuss the remaining 17 amendments. When they next met, they decided a number of the amendments had little bearing on their current situation. For example, Amendment

XI applied to other states or foreign entities, which as far they knew, none currently existed. They felt the use of Electors, as called out in Amendment XII, need not be considered until sometime in the distant future.

Discussion of Amendment XIII would be covered by a simple statement there would be no form of slavery or subjugation of any kind. One of the more liberal non-quals said, "I thought you conservatives wanted everybody to be under your control."

Rick could not keep quiet, "You guys have always been so damned closed-minded and never have taken the time to listen to what we believe."

Michael jumped in, "Shut up you guys. We are here to develop the basis for our government going forward, not for you to yell at each other. You must realize why we are here today. We are people who have long been concerned about the direction of world politics and made the preparations for our survival. If you cannot bring yourself to realize this, you are going to have a tough time existing in this environment. Furthermore, it is well established a vast majority of us believe in capitalism with a capital C."

Amendment XIV was considered not to be pertinent at this time, but would be considered at a later date, but Amendment XV pretty much acceptable as stated.

Not surprising, Amendment XVI regarding income tax got soundly booed and rejected. The final Constitution resulted in a basic value-added tax with a deduction based on income level.

To no surprise, they considered Amendment XVII not to be applicable to the current NewLand and Amendment XVIII soundly rejected. They considered Prohibition to be a terrible idea. No voter discrimination would be allowed ala Amendment XIX. Also, Amendment XX was adopted fairly much as written, but XXI deemed unnecessary. Alcohol would not be outlawed in the first place.

They modified Amendment XXII to allow for only one term believing NewLand needed to develop a number of experienced politicians. In addition, numbers XXIII and XXIV were considered inconsequential.

However, Amendment XXV needed to be modified to have the senior Representative become the President if the person holding the office and the Assistant President died or was incapacitated. Language to properly determine what constituted 'incapacitated' needed to be written. The final language stated if two or more Representatives had the same seniority an election would be required within 2 weeks to determine which would become the new President.

Both the right of 18 year-olds to vote, Amendment XXVI, and Amendment XXVII, regarding change in compensation of Representatives, were adopted with slight modification.

Seventeen amendments were thoroughly discussed in one day. At the end of the day, Michael reiterated the NewLand Constitution would be null and void if and when they were able to rejoin the United States of America.

Michael thanked everyone for their efforts. Inputs were documented over the next two weeks, at which time Michael and the two Representatives created a final document for adoption by the residents.

A final version of the Constitution was presented to the residents by the President and two Representatives at the end of the second month. The residents adopted it by an almost unanimous vote, much to the relief of Michael. Chip and Sue, as well as his sisters and their families, were proud of what Michael had accomplished as President in such a short period of time, especially since he had no real interest in politics.

Chip told Sue having Michael wanting to be President no longer than absolutely necessary fit his vision of NewLand perfectly. He felt their family had done enough.

CHAPTER 40

CREATING NORMALCY

In the third month after GoSecure, a certain pattern of life evolved. A total of new six businesses had been established to complement the food growing and processing companies that existed for a number of years. The most successful were a grocery store and a pizza joint because everybody frequented them. A fresh cut sandwich and bakery operation, more or less a combination of several popular contemporary restaurant chains, also proved to be popular. Two young veterans, with Army experience doing equipment repair, began an appliance repair shop. They were waiting for the few electric scooters held in inventory to be bought by residents to add vehicle repair services. In time, they hoped to begin assembling these vehicles. They also planned for additional manufacturing of more complex vehicles in the future after exiting the caves. They were expected to maintain any vehicles found operational when it was again safe to go outside.

A brewery established by the owners of the Kursk Brewery was in its initial stages, but under a new name. The last of the first business group to be opened were a dry cleaners and tailor shop. Both badly needed. Most people came into NewLand with limited clothing, some requiring cleaning and repair. Efforts were made to offer jobs, at first often part time. Having a store providing creative clothing proved to be very popular.

Being idle was not an option. If a person could work, a job was available. This was not really a concern. Virtually all were raised with strong work ethics. Also, no minimum wages were established. Competition for workers was commonplace and getting much worse as the new businesses expanded. The business friendly environment pleased the old-timers and political leaders to no end.

Even with the planning done over the decades and the vast resources existing, the search for a new normality was a constant battle. Just keeping people busy was not a panacea. People needed challenges, but that proved not to be a problem as the economy grew.

Although President, Michael remained highly involved in the management of the education process. He, Warren and several of Warren's people worked hand-in-hand with those involved in presenting an ever expanding array of online courses ranging from K-12 for basic education to a wide range of upper level courses including many areas of professional education. Several students were involved in various medical programs, as well as engineering, law and finance. Two people were already studying law being fully aware some new laws would be needed. While Dane worked part time teaching physics and Beth became Chief Justice.

Progress evolved so rapidly people were amazed at what was happening and what they were able to get done. This did much to improve the mood of 'The 300' as they called themselves. The range of educational opportunities was limitless.

But NewLand continued to have a number of concerns. Two people committed suicide in the first six weeks. This raised a red flag for Dr. Dickson and his wife. They set up a rapid response squad where almost half of the people made themselves available on a moment's notice to help a person in distress. Three groups were of most concern: The young, the very old and the very ill, with counseling available at any hour. Through an active level of interaction, almost everyone found themselves more involved with others than they had been for most of their lives. One child was born and three more women were expecting during the first three months.

One of Steve and Liz (Housman) Benson's sons, James, a recent education graduate and an athlete from TCU, developed a sports program for the colony. With a loan from the NewLand Investment Trust, he soon had an active sports management business and employed a couple of young people. He thought it would be easy to get sports like basketball, baseball, football and soccer established, but he soon realized it was necessary to go slow.

Not only did they have only a limited number of people to be involved in athletics, it also took time to organize teams and recruit coaches and proved difficult to get enough kids of similar age to form teams for many sports, much less a league. James initially concentrated on sports like tennis, racket ball, track and field, and wrestling which were individual participation sports. Basketball turned out to be the first team sport to be organized since only five players on a team were needed at one time. A retired teacher and avid golfer developed a miniature golf course and driving range, which became immediately popular. Both were operated 24 hours a day since there was no difference between day and night inside the caves.

From day one, the police and fire department consisted of one person who managed both with the help of a number of volunteers. Within the first couple of months he added several part time people to provide 24 hour coverage. Unfortunately, more petty crime occurred than they expected and several cases of domestic violence occurred. But the main reason for increasing the fire department was to provide effective EMT services which worked hand-in-hand with the medical staff. Dr. Lansing married a local widow, and then retired from the practice of medicine in order to assist young people interested in medicine while always on call when needed for any medical emergency. A life style he enjoyed very much.

It soon was obvious the recreational and educational programs would not be enough for these people with previously satisfying careers, often even as young children. Still essentially a community of descendants of hard working immigrants, they wanted to be constantly challenged. So, the existing high tech firms formed the 'Council of Challenges' to stimulate the development of new business ventures.

Michael met regularly with Rick and Warren to discuss the status of the world outside of the caves. Warren also reported regularly on the drone surveillance program, which he said had still not found sign of human life out to a radius of almost 100Km. After much discussion, they began communicating to the outside world...and to the colony on Mars. To maintain the secrecy of their location, Warren sent a drone to a remote location to establish a communications relay point. He believed by communicating to this location using a very low frequency carrier, then relaying messages through the traditional bands, they could keep their location undetectable. This idea came from Dane Madsen from his knowledge of low frequency communications used by submarines.

Within two days of establishing the remote station, they communicated with the Mars colony, plus locations on an island in the South Pacific, Western Australia, Northern Canada and Alaska, receiving only grim news. Only the colony on Mars could report they were living a fairly normal environment. The others were desperate. Even though they had sufficient food for the short term, none made preparations to the extent of NewLand. Some thought for the near term it was best to keep the bad news secret, but this troubled Michael. He met with his dad and Rick, both of whom believed it important to always be truthful to the citizens.

Rick said, "Michael, the last thing you want to happen is to have people find out you have been withholding information from them. We have to be upfront."

Chip agreed and said, "But we need to proceed carefully. First, meet with the representatives and Warren. He needs to give his assessment of how bad the situation is at the few reporting stations. Remember how upfront we were with them the morning after coming into the caves. As frightening as it was, we dealt with them truthfully. You must maintain their trust and the same goes for JB and the two reps, as well. An old boss told me many years ago he never lied because his memory was not perfect. Some of the best advice I have ever received."

The next morning Michael asked Chip and Rick to meet with him, JB and the reps. He laid out the gruesome truth. JB handled the news best as a result of his military background, but soon the other two understood the need to be completely truthful to which Rick said, "Bad news is better received than having people find out they had been lied to for a period of time. Once that happens you will never have their trust again."

Once they were in complete agreement, they met with the entire population. Much to Michael's surprise, almost everybody accepted the news as reality relieving Michael but knew the battle to keep positive outlook would be constant. Life in NewLand achieved a new level of normalcy.

CHAPTER 41

NON-PROBLEMS

One day late in the third month Chip and Rick were sitting in the local microbrewery and pub. Funding in the form of a loan was provided for BrauZeit by the NewLand Investment Trust just six weeks before and was owned and operated by the former Kursk Brewery owners. They were doing a tasting of the first newly brewed beer and comparing it to the wide range of beer inventory stored prior to GoSecure.

"You know, Chip, not too bad for a first run. Maybe we have found our New Manning's. All we need now is for someone to start a winery," as he thought back to their days in Minneapolis the 1960s and 1970s.

Chip's mind was wandering somewhere else thinking about how the world had changed. "Rick, do you realize how many of the left's goofy world problems have been solved? The only problem for them is none of them are around to enjoy it."

"What are you talking about?" Rick responded.

"Where is over population! Where is global warming? And look how the use of petroleum products has been curtailed. No need to drill, no need to frack. We don't even have a reason for an energy company anymore until we use up years of inventory." Chip chuckled. "Remember how we used to kid New York City would have 9 feet of horse manure in the streets and an overabundance of flies if the internal combustion engine had not been developed? Hell, now there is no need for New York City."

This got Rick's attention. His friend had been in a purple funk ever since the initiation of GoSecure and he worried about Chip's mental state. Chip felt the conservatives of the world did not do all they could have to stop the madness just taken place. He believed all reason had been lost. Why did the government let the people down? White became black and up became down. Nothing seemed to make sense and no one did anything about it. Falling back to his childhood he began to take some of the blame, just like he did when his father drank too much.

Typical of Rick he broke Chip's somber mood, "Too bad we can't drive down the 405 L.A. or the Eisenhower in Chicago or cruise around downtown Manhattan in a beat-up '49 Hudson Hornet burning oil. Hell, we could probably drive it through downtown Tokyo at 60 miles an hour."

This made Chip laugh, something Rick had always been able to do until they found themselves trapped the caves, even though Chip knew from his initial contact with Jack Barnett what could eventually happen. "Thanks, Rick, I needed that. Let's have another beer."

For the next two hours they amused themselves with the ridiculous things they had seen over the past 2/3 of a century, even going back to their crazy 'disasters and tragedies' sessions.

Chip offered, "You know the comment you made about driving makes me think of a project at the first company I worked back I the late 60s. We tried to figure out a way to control traffic flow using computers. We were trying to figure out how to keep traffic from working like an accordion. You know, bunch up, then spread apart, bunch up, spread apart. It has only gotten worse over the decades, especially in places like L.A. or any fast growing suburban area. You know where many of the liberals drive expensive cars and sit in drive thru lines for 30 minutes burning gas and spewing fumes. Then they bitch about us conservatives and our obsession with the discovery and production of petroleum products.

You have to realize we were working with some fairly primitive computer resources at the time. It was not the worst problem to go after considering the Cold War and other problems that existed. We did not have any of the neat sensing, tracking and communications devices we have today, not even GPS. Well, at least we used to have GPS before the satellites were destroyed. We were not successful. We just took the wrong approach. We should have gotten rid of the cars! Just think, all it took was a bunch of bad politicians to rid the earth of much of its population to eliminate the need for the evil automobile. Simple, they just needed to kill all of the people. You think they would be happy? Naw, they would just find something else to bitch about."

Rick laughed so hard he fell off of his chair. "You ok?" Chip asked in a panic.

"I'm great. I haven't laughed so hard in years. Hey to do you remember the congressman who thought Guam would tip over if we based too many US troops there? I laughed so hard my sweet tea shot out my nose. God was Mary Cate disgusted with me. She said I was still the same hayseed clod she met along the highway years ago."

"And think of some of the crazy global warming claims people from the government have made, like the woman who said global warming caused rape and prostitution. There was prostitution before this round of so-called global warming, probably set up by a couple of cave women that hadn't been raped by a caveman. I'll bet the Vikings would have a big laugh, and I don't mean the Minnesota Vikings. What about the people around the world, like Asia, South America and so forth?" Chip blurted out laughing so hard tears were running down his face. "Then we had the Houston area Congresswoman who was upset because of the names used for hurricanes. Why didn't these jerks concern themselves with real problems facing American people and the world?" he continued gasping for air.

Rick sobered a bit, "We are starting to get ridiculous. Hey, Chip, I have an idea. You want to go for a walk in a really different place?"

Chip thought they had walked virtually every inch of space in the series of caves over the past three months.

"I mean a really different place! You know Michael, Warren and JB are talking about an initial expedition out of the caves sometime in the next few days. Radiation levels are dropping quite a bit at times and the drones indicate there is nothing moving out there. How about us beating them to it?" he came back with his Cheshire cat smile in full bloom.

"What are you talking about? There is no way in hell we can get out of the caves without tripping an alarm."

Rick shook his head, "Not true. I know a way we can go out and enjoy a little sunshine and real fresh air for a few minutes and they will never know we were gone. I would guess we could go for about an hour before someone figured out we are up to something. Let me show you."

They jumped on the tram and headed down the cave system to the stop closest to "The Hull" where they got off. Rick motioned Chip to follow him into one of the small side caves near the secured entrance door.

"See the rectangular rock over there? It is not a rock. Many years ago, while I was checking up on some of the work in this area and I found a small opening to the outside. You know how my mind works. I just figured maybe someday I may need an escape route. I have never told anyone, not even Mary Cate. I didn't even know her at the time and to be honest I forgot about it until we ended up inside here," Rick confessed like a little boy.

"I managed to cover it up before any of the ex-Corps of Engineers guys working around me found it. Then about a month later I came out and built a camouflaged cover for the opening," he said as he walked over to the stone. He flipped it over and a bit of light leaked in."

"I think two old men like us can make it through here to the outside," as he squirmed through the hole.

All of a sudden they found themselves outside. Chip was mortified, but enjoyed the natural light and the breath of fresh air. "What if they find out we have done this?"

"Damn it Chip, we're old, we can claim senility, come on we only have about 45 minutes till sunset. I have been just aching to see a sunset for the past three months. Stick close behind me so the cameras don't catch us. Hell, we have gotten this far, let's not screw up now. Hee, hee, this reminds me of the time we ran away from Scout Camp at Lake Itasca."

Chip said, "Yes and we got caught. We didn't even get to take the canoe ride to the source of the Mississippi, you dork. And we didn't get our badges. My mom said you were always a bad influence on me."

Off they went to the northeast to the edge of the hills so they could watch the sun set in the west. They got to where they could watch the view, totally winded, about 10 minutes before the orange globe settled into the horizon.

As they sat there Rick, in his best imitation of Humphrey Bogart's character Rick Blaine in the movie Casablanca, "Louie, I think this is the beginning of a beautiful friendship."

"You are still such a nut. You may be Rick but I am not Louie. How long have you been waiting to use that line?"

Rick put his head back, as in deep thought, "Let's see it has been a long time. The movie was filmed in the early 40s and we were born in 1946, so I guess it would have been since we were in grade school. Probably over 60 years."

"Next you are going play like you are Scarlet O'Hara from Gone with the Wind and tell me 'tomorrow is another day'".

"Was going to but you beat me to it. What do you think Robert and Jack think about our situation?" as they settled down on a large rock to watch the sun settle in the west.

As the sun made its exit into the horizon, Chip answered, "That is a no brainer. I can just hear Robert saying, 'By Zeus, don't screw it up this time' and Jack adding 'Amen brother. Amen.'"

gary.andersen@aol.com

Jack Barnett, Jr. 1952

CPSIA information can be obtained
at www.ICGtesting.com
Printed in the USA
FSOW01n1451121115
13317FS

9 781514 417386